Digital For

Digital Force

by

Kevin Milne

Digital Force – www.z4ck.org

Copyright © 2006 by Kevin Milne.

All rights reserved. Printed in the United Kingdom. No part of this publication may be reproduced, stored in a retrieval system, or transmitted, in any form or by any means electronic, mechanical, photocopying, recording, or otherwise, without the prior written permission of the author.

ISBN: 0-9552929-0-5

Published by Open-solutions consultancy Ltd.

www.z4ck.org

Digital Force – www.z4ck.org

Foreword

Well here we are again! When I wrote Z4CK I felt that I would only ever write one book. However, due to the overwhelming amount of people who have asked the question 'How about telling us about the 30 year gap that was CyberSecure.' I decided that this second book, which completes the story, might be a good idea.

So sitting before you is another year of work completed on the train, partly on my Zaurus, but mostly this time on my laptop due to the fact that the Scottish rail service finally decided to provide enough seats for its passengers. As with Z4CK, this book could not have been written without the support and help of my family and friends. So I'd like to thank Lynne, for first of all being my wife, and secondly giving her thoughts on the book. I'd like to thank my kids for cheering me up by doing the unexpected and hilarious just when you thought life was getting too serious, and of course the following people who helped with the proofing and constructive criticism: Drew, John, Moray, Michael Hubbard and Kevin Mackie.

I'd also like to say a final hello to the Zaurus user group, Linux and security communities for their support of Z4CK, and for providing me with the confidence and enthusiasm to write Digital Force.

Chapter 1

Meeting at CyberSecure

Duncan pushed aside the net curtain and peered out of his flat on the outskirts of Edinburgh. The dirty window hadn't been cleaned for months. It would've cost too much to have it done professionally and he didn't fancy risking his life by hanging out of the crumbling ledge two stories up. It certainly wasn't worth it now, considering he was leaving for the final time that very day. The car that was due to pick him up at 9:45 am had still not appeared on the quiet narrow street below. He tutted and let the curtain go, before turning back to the living room of the flat. It had been his home for the past couple of years. Unfortunately the memories of this place were not necessary the happiest of his life so far.

It had just gone 10:06am according to the clock on the Zaurus PDA, which Duncan flipped closed and put back into his pocket. The room was barely lit by the light that attempted to make its way through the clouds of a dull February day. His new employers had switched the heating off a couple of days before to ensure that any unexpected bills did not hit them. This left the room cold; but this was the way the government insisted on working.

The flat walls were bare, and boxes packed in a none-to-organised fashion cluttered the room. They represented almost all of his short life so far. He walked over to the kitchenette counter and picked up a cup of coffee from its fake wood worktop. It left a stain where he had spilt some of its contents earlier. He took a casual sip and strolled through into what had been the computer room. The old black desk sat against the wall, its cheap ash finish covered in dust. Almost everything had been removed, and was now in storage - taken away by CyberSecure, his new employers. The absence of dust on areas of the desk showed where his main computer systems had until recently sat.

He made his way across the room that had at one time been a nightmare to navigate and sat down on the old leather swivel chair. There would be no use for it where he was going, or at least that's what he had been told.

Duncan was excited, and yet, at the same time nervous about his new position. He had no idea what lay ahead, whom he would meet, and what the regime would be like. He had no say in the matter. If he didn't go they would throw the book at him, and no matter what, he knew it would be better than spending years in prison, with no prospect of a career on his release.

He closed his eyes and took a deep breath, allowing himself to drift back through the past year. He remembered the completion of Z4CK, the software that had got him into this mess in the first place. A brief smile crossed his unshaven face as he thought about his beautiful ex-girlfriend Lin, a planted government agent cum psychologist. Where she was, he had no idea. Duncan's mood lowered somewhat at the thought of the accident that had killed Al, and his dead enemy Atkins. The corrupt agency for which they had worked, now shamed, had been closed down in great haste by the government with no questions asked. For a second Duncan felt lucky to have survived. In the last year he had had his house ransacked, had been beaten, tortured, and even shot at. He had only just escaped a prison sentence through a deal with the very government who had tried to cause him so much harm. Although Z4CK had got him into the mess, it was still the case that the government knew he was talented and less dangerous on their side...hence the reason for the deal they had perhaps begrudgingly made.

He had been forced to join CyberSecure, the specialist wing of the intelligence services that dealt with computer hackers, Internet fraud, and other such cyber-nasties. Its specific purpose was to protect the interests of the government and its close allies. Beyond this, he knew nothing; he wasn't even sure as to how they dealt with them. Duncan reckoned he would find out soon enough. This would be the first day of 6 months of training, and a ten year contract - one he could not break.

He got up from the chair and strolled out of the computer room, closing the door behind him for the last time. He crossed the beige carpet to the gold rimmed mirror he had left hanging on the wall, avoiding the heavily laden cardboard boxes as he went. He caught his reflection for a second. He had aged significantly in the past year; his hair having greyed, his face more wrinkled. Some scarring from the beating was still noticeable just under his right eye where it had been badly cut. He had also lost weight through stress, although he wasn't sure that this was all bad. Overall he had conquered his physical injuries; it was the mental ones that were taking time to heal.

He continued to study himself in the mirror for a moment, almost falling into a daze, when a sudden hammering at the front door brought him abruptly back to his senses. It was an authoritative, heavy, almost impatient knock - which startled Duncan slightly, even though he had been expecting it.

He straightened his brown leather jacket before walking as casually as he could to the door. He opened it tentatively, always cautious these days. As the door creaked open he stepped back to allow the visitor to enter. A giant of a man peered round the edge, the slightest smile crossing his face, before he strode into the room. At least 6' 5" in height, he was heavily built; his face, which seemed not unkind, was scarred on the left hand side from the top of a steel blue eye to just under his strong square chin. Another scar ran from the left hand side of his nose outwards to the edge of his mouth. His hair, what was left of it, was blonde, and army regulation short. He wore a long black wool coat, which hung to just below his knees. He looked Duncan up and down, taking in his first impression, whilst removing his black leather gloves. After deciding that everything was satisfactory he again smiled and stretched out a large hand for Duncan to shake. "I am Ares and you are Duncan Steele I presume?" His booming voice was surprisingly smooth and lilting; it was not at all what Duncan had expected. He couldn't quite place the accent; up north somewhere, Inverness or Dingwall perhaps?

Duncan responded, trying not to show his nervousness. "Yes Duncan Steele, nice to meet you…Ares." With that Duncan extended his arm upwards towards Ares, being met with a powerful grip as he shook it. Ares took a look at the boxes lying about the floor. "So, is this it then? Is there anything else for us to take?" "No, no, that's it. Everything that is left is here in this room." Ares scanned the rest of the floor-space. "Okay, well, some of our people will be over to get this stuff later. We'll put it in storage for the first few months as you'll be getting to know the other new folk in the team, so you'll be sharing a room during that time. After that, you'll get your posting, and it'll follow you there. Don't worry, we'll provide you with all the clothes and other things you'll need during your training." He paused for a second, looking around to take in more. "To be honest, you won't need much!"

Duncan looked at the boxes. He didn't think he needed anything from them; at least he hoped he didn't. He had expected to take them with him, and had therefore not been careful to ensure he had everything he required. His organisational skills weren't exactly world-renowned, but he was starting to get the feeling they would have to improve. Thankfully, his Zaurus would help out with this side of things.

"Right c'mon then, let's go. We haven't got all day!" Ares snapped Duncan back to reality and began heading to the door. Once outside Duncan closed the chipped blue door to his flat for the last time, pausing for the briefest of moments to ensure it was properly locked. He turned and began to follow Ares down the stairs. It was then that for the first time Duncan noticed the slight limp in Ares' walk, which became more noticeable as he made his way down the stairs to the car on the waiting street below. "So what happened to your leg?" The question echoed around the darkened stone stairwell stopping Ares in his tracks. He turned his head for a second, and raised an eyebrow. "You don't waste any time do you? All in good time my young friend, all in good time."

They continued their walk down the stairwell until they reached the heavy front door that led directly onto the street. Ares again turned to his young companion. "From here on in, the name of the game is stealth. Watch everything and try not to be seen. A single mistake can be fatal. So far none of us have ever been detected, in or out of cyber space. It's important for the sake of our country that it remains that way…get it?" Duncan, slightly taken aback by the sudden lecture, quickly agreed with the giant leaning over him and pointing in his direction. "No worries. I don't intend to do anything too daring, or to muck anything up!" Ares seemed reassured. "Good. Now when we're outside, the first rule…one of many you'll learn, is that you never call out or talk to any one of us using our real names in public. Under no circumstances break this rule. Right, we've got a driver waiting…let's go."

Ares carefully led the way out through the door. It had

started drizzling, which meant the street was fortunately bereft of life, as the young professionals who made up most of the inhabitants, were currently participating in the daily grind of day-to-day business.

The men climbed into a metallic green Audi 80 Quattro, an early 1990's model by the look of it. It was still in good condition, but not conspicuous on this street. Ares gestured to Duncan to get into the back of the car, whilst he clambered in an ungainly manner into the front, positioning his leg as he went.

"Woohoo! Nice tae fucking meet ye!" The car's driver leaned over to the back seat to shake Duncan's hand. "Matt's the name…shit, not supposed to say that am I, or am I? You know, these effing rules are a pain in the arse. Can never remember what the fuck I'm allowed to do and when!" Ares stared at the hyperactive driver. "For Christ's sake, will you shut up and get the hell out of here?" Matt retorted with a jerk of his head, "Just introducing myself you big twat!" This remark met with a stern glare from the tall man. "If you weren't part of this team I'd have battered you silly by now, you little shit!" Matt looked extremely unhealthy. His thin face and hollowed cheeks were covered in pock marked skin. It was obvious that the hyperactivity and fidgeting was part of the reason for his build.

Matt laughed returning to Duncan, "Heh, Heh, we get on like a house on fire …burnt tae fuck! Anyway, ye better call me 'Loki', as in the mischievous one, not Matt. We've all got stupid names." At no stage during the conversation had Loki let go of Duncan's hand, leaving Duncan almost drained. "Err, any chance of getting my hand back?" "Eh, oh yea, ye'll need that for something one day, I mean…there's a real lack of female company where we're off to, and you're going to need Palm and her five sisters for company…if you know what I mean!" Loki winked and bounced back to the driving position, chuckling to himself. "Right my beauty let's move!"

The car took off at great speed, its wheels spinning uncontrollably as Loki put his foot to the floor. An oncoming car was forced to swerve off the narrow street onto the pavement, only missing a lamppost by inches - the female driver visibly shocked. Loki opened his window as he drove past, waving his fist and ranting, "Watch where you're going you stupid women...stick to the sink, or the bed where you're of some fucking use!"

Ares turned to Duncan gesturing that Loki was somewhat insane. The thought was backed up at that moment as Loki began laughing uncontrollably. Duncan leaned forward from the back seat, "I thought stealth was the name of the game?" Ares sighed, "Yeah, but when it comes to this idiot, we get away with it as no-one would ever think he worked for the government, or anyone else for that matter!"

The car continued its journey at break-neck speed. For almost forty minutes, it was driven up back streets, down alleys, and along the most winding roads Duncan had travelled, before getting out into the green, flat countryside. Duncan had never held on as tightly as he swayed from side to side, the seat belt and his ability to close his eyes his only salvation. His clenched jaw ached with the tenseness of several 'near death experiences'. Suddenly, they took an unexpected sharp right turn, which threw Duncan against the window. "For fuck's sake, watch it - do you have to drive like a nutter?" Loki simply chuckled to himself, "Are you some sort of nancy boy? C'mon, where's your sense of adventure?"

They had reached a long dirt track surrounded on either side by large oak trees. February's rainfall had left the track extremely muddy, which explained why Loki had slowed temporarily. The giant trees were lacking any foliage, having shed all of their leaves during a particular cold and wet winter season. Duncan understood well that during the year this track would afford excellent cover. However, the cloudy sky above could be clearly seen at this time. Duncan's heartbeat began to return to normal as the car continued to slow on the approach to a large farm gate. There seemed nothing unusual about the gate, the trees, or the surrounding fence posts that had appeared, but Loki turned to Duncan and winked, indicating something interesting was about to happen. He rolled down his window, and leaned over, apparently talking to the final tree in the row. "Loki, Ares…approve." The red farm gate did not swing open, but instead sank downwards into the soggy February mud. Loki glanced at Duncan, and nodded his head to gauge the reaction, "Nice."

The car continued up another short, narrow road, passing derelict outbuildings, farm machinery, and various abandoned vehicles which had rusted beyond repair through years of neglect. Duncan began to wonder what this place was, and what he would find at the end of the road.

He looked ahead and up the track. Just in front of him he could see a large building, which, to his surprise, looked more like an old country house than the farm he expected to see. Ares turned to Duncan as the car drew up outside the building. "Right, that's us, let's meet and greet, eh?" The mud had given way to a small gravel car park. The stones crunched under the wheels of the car as it came to a sudden halt. Ares and Loki threw open their doors quickly and exited, leaving Duncan trailing behind them as they walked towards the building.

Duncan was surprised by what he saw. He hadn't really expected a secret hideaway. It was, after all, the British government he had joined…wasn't it? He paused for a second to take in his surroundings, turning to consider the view behind him. The house was located on a hilltop with a good view of the countryside and its features below, which were now laid out before him like a giant map. With the exception of the odd barn, there was almost nothing but fields to be seen. He wasn't exactly sure where he was. Even though it had only been a forty minute drive in total, he didn't recognise any of this; but then he had never been so adventurous as to travel very far, except on the odd mainstream package holiday.

A cold, fine drizzle filled the air, leaving Duncan feeling it was best that he moved on into the large house. He swivelled on his heels to face it. Loki had already entered, and Ares stood impatiently at a large heavy door. The blue paint on the doors surface was peeling. It sat beneath a grand, if crumbling pair of Greek columns supporting the porch roof. It seemed out of character with the rest of the building, which looked like an old country house, with the exception of its stone facings. It was a building that a prime minister and his cabinet may have retreated to once upon a time. Now, almost all of the windows had been boarded up, and the grey stone walls had begun to crumble with the passage of time. Definite signs of damp further discoloured the building's lower wall. A ramshackle, splintered green fence had been erected on both sides of the house. Duncan assumed that this surrounded the entire perimeter. How big the garden was he could not tell, shielded as it was behind the main building. Weeds grew three feet tall directly in front of the house, cleared only to provide a means by which to get to the door.

This building, located in the middle of nowhere added to the dark, dank surroundings, filled Duncan with dread. Ares was getting impatient, "Fucking hell, will you move it? We can't stand here all day admiring the view…we're already late!"

Duncan hesitated, "Erm, sure." He walked slowly towards the building. Ares rolled his eyes and shook his head, "Flaming newbie's, I ask you!" He disappeared into the house leaving Duncan to follow him. Finally reaching the doorway, Duncan peered sheepishly into the room. Small streams of light were all that entered through the splinters in the boarded windows. At first Duncan could see little. After a short while his eyes became accustomed to the gloom, allowing him to pick out some of the features of the large main hall. He looked up at the roof, fearing it may collapse at any second, but the high ceiling looked solid enough. The room was bare with the exception of a few wooden chairs stacked up on top of each other in a corner. The concrete floors were dusty in areas, damp in others. Rubble was strewn sporadically across the floor. How could this be a government building, he thought to himself?

As he ventured into the room, beckoned onward by Ares, he could just make out two doors. One to back of the room, the other to its right hand side. Some scaffolding had been erected to the left. Perhaps they had started work on this room, Duncan thought to himself.

"Where's Loki gone?" Duncan asked. Ares replied, "He'll have gone downstairs to the get the rest of the guys; pull up a chair." Duncan walked to the far corner of the room, beginning to feel a little uneasy. Something was wrong...he knew it. But what? He picked up a chair, keeping an eye on Ares who was beginning to limp round the room anxiously.

Duncan placed the seat in front of him and sat down. Within seconds the door behind him flew open with a crash. Four hands grappled with him, throwing him off his chair and on to the concrete floor. The fall winded him. He attempted to get back up but found himself kicked back to the ground. He landed heavily, the filthy concrete dust thrown up into his face, instantly drying out his mouth.

He coughed and spluttered, trying to rub the fine dust from his eyes. They smarted as he attempted to get a glimpse of his assailants, and perhaps find a way to protect himself. Another boot found its way to his chest, making him yelp. Any chance of self defence or getting to his feet was lost in an instant as a polythene bag was tied firmly over his head. He couldn't breathe, and gasped for air in a state of panic. He could see nothing as the bags black plastic removed the last remnants of light from his vision. The nightmare from last year seemed to be repeating itself. "Who the fuck are you?" His muffled cries met with a wall of silence as his hands and feet were tied. His pockets were emptied, his Zaurus and wallet removed. He was helpless; taken by surprise by the efficiency and speed of the attack. Another kick to the back of his leg deadened it, knocking him straight to the ground.

A voice he had not heard before barked out an order. "Haul him up!" Two or more men unceremoniously hauled Duncan to his feet - in the confusion he could not be sure. He felt yet another punch to his stomach, which doubled him over. He groaned with the pain. He gasped for breath; the bag afforded no air, only the taste and smell of plastic. The next order was given, "Get a chair...get him to the scaffold."

It terrified Duncan, "No, no, what the fuck is happening here? Who are you?" Duncan was dragged towards the scaffold kicking and screaming, before being hauled upwards onto one of the wooden chairs. He kicked out, only to be punched in the face - the force jarring his chin. He felt the noose being placed and tightened around his neck. This was it...the end. "What do you want? Tell me what you want!" Duncan screamed. There was a short silence, "The password to Z4CK, that is what we want." Duncan attempted to draw in more breath, but failed. His speech was beginning to suffer. "1ts,a,Zauru5 is the password, let me go...please...take the software...I'll say nothing.

I want nothing to do with this any more." The unknown voice was icy cold, "You heard him men; let him go." The chair was kicked from beneath Duncan plunging him downward to a painful, choking death. He braced himself, ready for the tightening of the noose. It never came. His body stiffened as it fell through a trapdoor, and onto a mattress one floor below. He landed awkwardly, crumpling into a heap.

As his senses began to return to him he could just make out another voice talking in a formal tone. "Oh dear, we've got our work cut out with this one…less than 2 minutes, that just won't do! He didn't check who we were, where he was going, and then to top it all provided the password in…exactly 1 minute 37 seconds. It takes me longer to go to the toilet!"

The bag was removed from Duncan's head, making him wince and strain as his eyes began to focus. A tall man, who resembled what Duncan would have imagined a German nuclear scientist from the 1940's to look like, stood over him, clipboard in his left hand. He was not old, mid to late 30's perhaps. His shaven head reflected the light of a single bulb, as he pushed a pair of rimless spectacles over the bridge of his nose towards his face. He shook his head at Duncan, whose anger was apparent. Duncan spat at the man, but missed. "Yet another mistake Steele…insubordination. This is no place for mistakes. When you have calmed down, we'll have a chat."

He left the small room. Some of the assailants, positioned at the opening of the trap door peered down at the scene below, laughing and patting each other on the back. After a short period they pulled the trap door shut. The light was switched off, leaving Duncan in complete darkness. His hands and feet were still tied, ensuring he could do no more than wriggle about helplessly on the mattress.

"Baaaasssstaaaards!" he screamed at the top of his voice, angry and frustrated at the situation. He didn't fear for his life any more, but these people were supposed to be his comrades, and he was beginning to hate them already.

Duncan lay on the mattress for almost an hour before the door to the small room was opened, and the light was switched on. Ares walked in accompanied by the man with the clipboard he had 'met' earlier. The two men had been chatting, but had quickly fell silent as the door slid open. Ares kneeled down and began to untie Duncan whilst the other man talked. "Steele, you have now completed your first evaluation…welcome to CyberSecure. I know this was quite a baptism of fire, but you must understand we have to estimate your weaknesses and breaking points at every stage. It may all seem like a game, or perhaps not; but one thing is for sure, you will have to become good at playing it if you are to survive any length of time!"

He paused for a second to watch Ares complete the task of removing Duncan's bonds. "I won't tell you my name; you only need to know me as Terminus." Duncan sat up and rubbed his ankles and wrists, which were red and sore from the tightness of the tape. "Terminus…bloody stupid nickname if you ask me!" Ares smiled at Duncan and helped the young man up. "There is a need here for both structure and discipline," Terminus continued. Ares butted in, "However, camaraderie and trust are also important! Come on, lets get something to eat and drink - then we'll give you the tour and set out our rules."

Duncan got up and followed his new comrades through the doorway and down a corridor which directly contrasted the derelict building above. The corridors metallic floor was lined with blue florescent lights which ran down either side. The immaculately plastered walls were painted a strange shade of cream. It was a short, narrow corridor, perhaps twenty yards long, lined with motion detection sensors. The heavy steel entrance at the end of the corridor better resembled a bank vault than a door; secure indeed. Terminus stood in front of a retina scanner whilst swiping his identity card through a reader which was fixed to the wall next to the door. A large bolt in the middle began to unwind, followed by the noise of pressured air seals being broken. The heavy door slowly crept open, allowing the threesome to enter the first of the secret rooms in this underground complex.

The men filed through, Terminus leading the way. As Duncan passed into the room, the heavy door slid closed, sealing the compound to the world outside. Duncan marvelled at the technology on display within.

The room was filled with computer systems of all types. Only a few people worked here, but they all had several systems each, the sound of hard drives, and mouse clicks were the main source of noise in this, all too quiet of rooms. The usual sets of world clocks were mounted on the left hand wall, these were digital however. On the right hand wall hung a picture of the queen. Duncan wasn't the queen's greatest fan, and it began to feel to him like some 'B' rated James Bond movie. "When do I get to meet Miss Moneypenny," asked Duncan? Ares laughed, appreciating the resemblance. "You should be so lucky...this is the real world!" he replied.

Terminus studied Steele as he looked around the room. "Impressive, isn't it?" he said with an obvious sense of pride. "Ares limped on ahead, "Hmm, very pretty indeed, if you like that sort of thing! Come on, let's go...we'll get an early lunch and give you the tour when we're done. We need to get to the canteen first; get some decent food in you...that's more important right now." Terminus laughed, "Food is always more important to Ares, but yes, on you go." He turned his attention to Ares. "Ares, after lunch, get Steele cleaned up; provide him with some clothes and show him to his quarters will you?"   Ares nodded as the two men made their way past various workstations, the people acknowledging Duncan as he walked past.

The food was good, something that surprised Duncan, "I thought the government didn't have any money?" This seems okay!" Ares laughed, "It depends on your priorities doesn't it? Let's just say the government is paying more attention to cyber criminals than they let on. It's a bigger priority now, even since I joined a few years back; and the people are getting more specialized - like yourself for instance."

The canteen was a series of shining metallic surfaces, which had been kept polished and tidy. The cooking area was wide open, with no requirement for a huge amount of kitchen staff. CyberSecure was a small government establishment, meaning the less people who knew about it the better. Duncan wondered if the kitchen staff had any hidden talents like the rest of the people here. An early lunch meant it was quiet, but he got the feeling that it probably never became that noisy, considering there was seating for less than twenty souls, most of whom kept themselves to themselves. The seating was basic, the tables being single units with the seats protruding outward joined by a single bar from the metal chassis. The walls were the same light cream colour as used elsewhere in the building. Duncan felt they must have got a 'cheap batch' from somewhere.

Duncan and Ares took their food from the counter and made their way to one of the tables. Duncan swung his leg over the chair and sat down. Ares took more time, placing his food on the table first before easing his false leg over. "Bloody stupid design, a real pain in the arse this.

Don't know how many times I've lost my balance just trying to sit down!"

They finally settled down to eat, Duncan sipping on a spoonful of soup, whilst breaking apart some bread and dipping it into his large bowl. "So what is your background, your speciality?" Ares winked. "All will be revealed this afternoon when you meet the rest of the crew at your first meet and greet session...it would be a shame to spoil the surprise!" Duncan took another sip, "May I ask what happened to your leg?" Ares replied stone faced, "Oh that, that was a car accident. Wish I could give you a more heroic reason, like saving the world, but that's the fact...anyway I don't really want to talk about that, it's not important. I could sit and be bitter, and go on about the whole thing; to be honest I could have been killed, so I feel lucky I'm still able to work here."

"Do you go out on operations?" asked Duncan. Ares laughed, "Well, not these days. I generally stay here; there's no need for me to go out most of the time anyway, now that you younger guys have joined...no specialist training only. I've got a few tricks you need to know before you go out there and get yourselves into too much hot water!"

The two men chatted for some time, Duncan feeling comfortable in the presence of Ares. The big man, despite being tough, was also very civilised and pleasant to be around. Duncan felt in no way threatened by him, but he somehow knew it wouldn't be too clever to get on his wrong side. He could handle himself; even with one leg missing he would be a formidable opponent. The scars may have been obtained in combat, or again they may have been borne of the car accident. Duncan was interested but felt that he had asked enough questions for the moment; he would find out the rest soon enough.

"That was good, I'm surprised!" remarked Duncan putting his spoon into the bowl. Ares glanced at his watch, "Shit! Is that the time? I didn't realise. Let's get you to your quarters. You can get a quick shower, and change. Then it's all starting!"

They walked through the maze of gleaming corridors, each one the same as the last, before finding their way to Duncan's quarters. Ares handed Duncan a pass card. "Here, you'll need this." Duncan swiped the card through the reader and the door slid open, revealing his temporary inner sanctum. They stepped inside, activating the lighting, which produced a low momentary hum as it powered on. Thankfully the monotonous cream walls had given way to a mild green.

The room had enough space to be comfortable. Two steel beds sat against the right hand wall, a metre separating them. On them sat some regulation blankets and sheets which had been folded neatly. Next to the blankets sat a plain grey set of overalls and some underwear. A small bathroom containing a shower cubicle was situated to the rear of the room. As Duncan scanned the area in an anti-clockwise direction he took in a large desk on the left hand side, and above this, some shelving. The cold metallic flooring had given way to a laminate effect vinyl. Two IBM laptops sat on the desk, their network connections flashing as they transmitted and received random broadcast traffic. Their screen-savers idled, sitting ready to be used. The shelves were filled with books on various subjects. Duncan's attention was drawn to one book in particular. Tao of Jeet Kune Do by Bruce Lee? Is there going to be a requirement for this sort of stuff?" Ares laughed, "It depends which project you're working on!"
"Judging by the two beds I assume I'll be sharing the room?"
Ares smiled. "Aye, we've got another coming in later on…I

believe you know him as Hades!" Before Duncan could reply Ares had moved back towards the door. "I'll leave you to get freshened up. I'll be back in 30 minutes. Please be ready." Duncan held his hand up to ask a question, "One last thing, where is my Zaurus?" "It's with Riddles just now; you will have it returned to you in a wee while." Duncan looked bemused, "Riddles?" he muttered to himself. Ares stooped as he stepped out of the room. The door sliding closed behind him. Duncan took another quick look around the room before heading to the shower. He found this underground complex intriguing and wondered how long he would be here. It was all a great novelty at the moment, but he was sure it would wear off soon enough.

He grabbed a quick shower and dried himself. His earlier traumatic ordeal had left him uncomfortable, dirty, and sweaty. He walked over to the bed and picked up the grey overall, examining it for a brief moment before putting it and the supplied underwear on. A pair of white unbranded leather trainers and socks lay under the bed. They fitted him perfectly. Organised indeed, he thought. Duncan stood up and walked across to the Laptops, hitting the shift key a couple of times to activate the main screen. The hard drive rattled for a second before a white empty box appeared in the middle of the black screen. It sat waiting for a user to log in. Duncan smiled as he caught the text at the bottom of the screen. "Knoppix Security Tools Distribution, good choice!" he said to himself.

The door slid open and Ares walked in. "Right, time for your introduction, and then I'll give you the tour." Duncan nodded, slightly nervous. He was never the best at first meetings, but he was keen to get it over and done with.
The two men walked quietly down several corridors before coming to a halt just outside one of the few wooden doors Duncan had seen thus far. "In you go; Ladies before gentlemen," Ares laughed. Duncan walked through the door

to be met by the sight of several people sitting patiently in neat rows on wooden chairs. Almost all turned round to face Duncan, who paused for a second to see if he could see anyone he recognised.

Terminus got up from his chair and walked over to him. "Glad you're here, all is well I trust?" He glanced past Duncan to Ares who gave an approving nod. "Excellent. Then if you will just take your place at the front next to the white board, you can begin by telling everyone who you are and what your specialty is." Duncan walked forward to the large white-board and stopped rather sheepishly next to a podium.

He looked around the room. "I've nothing much to say really; Duncan Steele is the name, specialty is computer network intrusion and penetration and a bit of programming. I wrote a security tool which got me into some bother, and now here I am…contracted to the government. My interests include fencing, and…"
Loki laughed, "Fencing? Fat lot of good that'll do you here; a game for poofs!" Ares stood up, towering above Loki. "It's a combat sport, isn't it…fast reactions, suppleness and an ability to think on your feet? That's what that means. Just shut your face in future." Terminus interjected, "If you wouldn't mind not arguing please…it sets a bad example. With regard to fencing, yes, Bruce Lee used some of the techniques in Jeet Kune Do, which is something you'll learn. Anyway, thank you Duncan, you may take a seat. From now on you will go by the code name Thor…Z4CK is your hammer."

"How original," Loki remarked.

Terminus walked to the front of the room. "Now to name the others in this elite unit. You have already met Ares. He will be training you in survival techniques, unarmed and armed combat as well as psychological analysis. His S.A.S background and other qualifications have proven to be invaluable to the team over the past few years."

Loki let out a fake cough, "Arse." Terminus turned to Loki. "Loki...believe it or not, is one of our top people. Technically excellent in mechanics, electronics, and communications, his prime objective is to help the project team to enter and exit buildings quickly." Ares now interjected, "And he's a 'class A' nut job!" Terminus continued, "Please, we all have to work together, I'd appreciate it if you would not interrupt."

"I am your team leader. My task is to ensure you have everything you need to do your job safely and within the required time scales. Try to see me as your project manager. Terminus is my code name. I'm here to help you do stay within the boundaries of your assigned missions.

Terminus turned his attention to a small, bespectacled, fair haired man sitting quietly in the back row. He was young, no older than 20, judging by his appearance. "This is Riddles. A real propeller head! He does our research and development work."

Riddles leaned over to shake Duncan's hand. He spoke quickly and quietly, his voice unfortunately high pitched for a male. "It is a pleasure to make your acquaintance. I've been studying your security application and I would like to ask you a few questions regarding the child-like coding of its cryptographic components and control mechanism." Riddles sniffed as he finished his sentence. Loki laughed, "Ho ho, tactless as fuck! We're the only people who would give this socially inept idiot a job!" he continued, pointing directly at Riddles. Duncan was slightly taken aback, "Err, the code works though…isn't that the main point?"

Riddles scowled and sniffed again; cleaning his spectacles on a handkerchief he had produced from his cardigan pocket. "Au contraire, efficient coding is an art form, especially when it concerns the coding of processor intensive encryption algorithms. It really pains me to witness application design of such amateurish standards!"
Duncan was speechless, "Fair enough, we're not all blessed with your obvious brain power!" Riddles agreed, "Indeed…I…I…achoo!" "Luckily, we're not blessed with your allergies either! Now let's get on." Terminus interrupted.

"You'll have noticed that there are only a few people in this building. We have a small amount of technical, military and administration staff. All of us are sworn to the Official Secrets Act. However, it is best that you do not mention current projects to anyone. Everything here is on a need to know basis!" Terminus ended his sentence with a quick glance at his watch. He turned to Ares. "Ares, if you could give Thor the tour and then take him over to the lab, that would be extremely useful. Thank you all, we are finished for the moment." Terminus intimated that the meeting was at an end and quickly exited the room, followed closely by Loki and Riddles.

Ares and Duncan toured the many corridors of the underground establishment, each one similar in design to the last. They walked past the equipment stores, laden with everything from computer parts to military equipment Duncan did not recognise, but would have loved to try out.

There was a single, unimpressive communications room, which housed some networking and server equipment.
Two racks sat in the middle of an otherwise empty floor

containing a single monitor and keyboard, positioned at waist height. These provided console access to a small array of servers, switches, firewalls and communications equipment. Duncan quickly noticed that the racks were identical. Neatly laid blue and red cables plunged directly into a small gap in the floor.

"They're fault tolerant - highly available. We can't afford any downtime…especially during critical operations! We have another identical set of racks off-site in Edinburgh." Duncan was more impressed by this. "So why Edinburgh?" Ares walked across to the rack, and pulled out the keyboard. "Different Internet Service Provider and a different power grid. We don't have an ISP here and with the exception of our honeypot, which is not directly connected, we don't have any inbound links to the Internet either." He hit the shift key, bringing the monitor to life. "You can't even enter a command into these systems without raising a change request!"

"How do we receive mail?" asked Duncan. "It's a secure batch job, pretty convoluted. To be honest, we don't need to communicate outside this small inner circle. Everything inbound and outbound is logged, so tip from the top…no dodgy stuff." Ares put the keyboard back, "You'll land yourself in a big pile of shite! Remember this, the Echelon network, which we are part of, is always watching."

Anyway, the control room and the lab are more interesting; we'll head there next. "You don't get a tour of upstairs just yet. You don't want to know what goes on in the old parts of the building!" "I think I got an indication this morning." Duncan replied. Ares stopped just outside a pair of swing doors. "Now this is a lovely sight, the administration staff - Susan and Angela. Ares walked confidently through the doors. "How are we today ladies?"
Two attractive young females stopped what they were doing

and looked up from their desks. Susan laughed, "Here he comes, the charmer. Who is this you've got with you today Ares?" Ares replied, "Call him Thor." He turned to Duncan, "these ladies will provide you with everything you need from transport to petty cash requirements." Duncan nodded and smiled. "Hi."

"Right then, that's nearly us, we just need to get you over to the lab. Riddles wants to bore you with his theory on how everything works! I've got to meet and greet Hades so let's get going shall we?" Duncan and Ares began their walk down the narrow corridors to the lab. Several locked exits required authorisation before the inner sanctum was reached. Duncan walked in to be met by Riddles. "Ah, Steele, at last…I've been expecting you!"

Ares encouraged Duncan to enter the lab. "As I said, I'm off to meet Hades, he's due now so I'll leave you here…see you soon." Riddles ushered Ares from the lab, "Yes, he'll see you anon, anon…now please leave us…sniff."

Riddles grinned, "Well here it is, the most important room in the entire building, at least as far as I am concerned. Other somewhat deluded individuals have a different opinion but they are obviously missing the big picture! Take a look around. I'm just dismantling this pitiful security tool of yours!"

Duncan ignored the remark. He was already becoming numb to Riddles and his form of banter. Instead he took in his surroundings. Everything in the lab was metallic with the exception of a large wooden bench, which stretched from the left hand wall, intersecting the vinyl floor and stopping two metres short of the right hand wall. It was scratched and burnt, which was unsurprising considering the volume of electronic equipment which must have traversed its surface during the past year. The bench was fully loaded with various on-going projects; electronic gadgetry, computer systems, and what, to Duncan's untrained eye, looked like some weaponry. Riddles worked intensively at the end of the bench, flitting between a powerful computer system, small network hub, and Duncan's Zaurus. He shook his head disapprovingly from time to time; making Duncan slightly nervous of what exactly was happening...after all Z4CK was his baby!

Duncan looked beyond the bench at a back wall filled with shelves. A flat screen plasma television hung squarely in the middle, beneath it, a Dreamcast with several games, a steering wheel and a gun. He strolled casually over to the shelves, studying the books they held, hoping he would get an indication of the type of research Riddles undertook. The books covered a large variety of subjects. Wireless hacking, networking, encryption, computer hacking, physics, mathematics, programming and even cyber weaponry. As far as Duncan was concerned all the useful ones were there, Google Hacking, Hacking Exposed, The Art of Deception, The Art of exploitation. The list was endless. It was obvious that there was no shortage of funds for this research. Duncan continued down the line of shelves, stopping suddenly at a section labelled fiction. "Lord of the Rings? Harry Potter? The Da Vinci Code? Are they relevant?" Riddles raised his head. "As you may have deduced, it is a relatively infrequent occurrence that I venture beyond the laboratory entrance."

Duncan looked further down the shelves, to his surprise seeing a copy of the Bible in the same section. "The Bible?" Riddles again looked up from his workbench, seemingly irked by the continual interruptions. "If it is unproven, and I, after some research have been unable to prove its contents beyond hearsay, then I must label it thus! It is however, an interesting read of an occasion." Duncan raised an eyebrow, "Controversial...logical...but controversial!"

Duncan took a final glance at the far end of the room. A stereo system sat in the corner, not a foot away from a dark brown, heavily stained microwave. He walked over to the stereo picking up a compact disk containing classical music. "Flight of the Valkyries by Wagner, and Carl Orffs - O Fortuna?" He held the CD up to Riddles. "Powerful stuff!" Riddles replied, seemingly appreciating Duncan's knowledge of classical music. "Indeed, it helps motivate me, surprised you are aware of them." Duncan frowned, "Oh c'mon, who could forget the Old Spice adverts with the surfer?"

Duncan finally made his clockwise trip round the lab and found himself not two foot away from Riddles. "So what are you doing with Z4CK?" The short bespectacled man did not bother to look up. "As I mentioned before – first I will disassemble it, then I will improve it!"

"Have you tried it?" asked Duncan. "I'm almost reaching that stage. I prefer to understand the software at a code level first, to ensure it does nothing unexpected. Perhaps another five minutes and you can show me how YOU would use this," came the rather smug reply. Duncan smiled, "It would be my pleasure - which piece of machinery would you like me to destroy first?" Riddles scurried back to his primary system. "How very amusing. So, if you wouldn't mind providing me with a short insight into the software's functionality…sniff." He wiped his nose and put his handkerchief back in his lab coat, whilst taking a step back to allow Duncan a chance to type at the keyboard.

Duncan peered into the small screen, thinking of the commands required to provide Riddles with the show he wanted. After a few seconds of contemplation he was ready. He rubbed his hands before he began to type.

Z4CK --info --target 192.168.0.1

In an instant the PDA's network connection began to flash as data was transferred and received between it and the target system. The small, brightly lit screen was empty with the exception of a flashing cursor sitting like a bomb waiting to go off as Z4CK searched for the best way to retrieve the data it had been asked for.

Suddenly, to the astonishment of Riddles, a stream of information began to fill the screen. At first it was basic; open ports, system banners, connection information. Soon potential vulnerability data began to appear, with recommendations on how to attack. Z4CK sat waiting for Duncan to enter the command to attack. He sighed, "You know Riddles - this is just too easy!" He then entered another command.

> Z4CK --acquire --target 192.168.0.1 --wait

The network connection began to transmit and receive data at an alarming rate. Each individual service on the target was password tested at the same time. Not even 10 seconds later the file transfer (ftp) service had been cracked. Now that Z4CK had found a way in it was a foregone conclusion that the root password would be obtained.

Duncan smiled, looking directly at Riddles, who seemed slightly more concerned than he had only five minutes prior. He shuffled closer to the small screen to take a look.

A final beep from the Zaurus and it was all over. Complete control. "YES!" Duncan shouted. He stood back as the target began to reboot. Riddles looked at him, "What on earth is happening now?" Duncan replied, "You'll see." The system suddenly stopped with a simple prompt - System control complete: please enter password for restore. Riddles was noticeably impressed. "I see, very good…yes very good. You may take your Zaurus now; I have the code…sniff. I can see it will be of some use to us."

Ares walked through the door and over to Duncan, "Having fun?" Duncan stuffed the old Zaurus back into his pocket, "Absolutely!" Ares continued, "Good, your friend Hades has just been welcomed. He's none too happy about his treatment, but he'll calm down in a wee while. In the meantime I think we'll get you out of here." Duncan turned to Riddles, "Thanks again, it has been interesting." Riddles raised his hand, "Err, it would be prudent of you to inform me of the password to my test system…don't you think?" Duncan laughed, "Sorry, can't do that…you see only Z4CK holds the password. Perhaps tomorrow I can plug it back in. In the meantime you're on your own." Riddles jaw dropped, "Of course…err shouldn't be too difficult." With that, Duncan and Ares walked out through the doors to meet up with Hades.

Chapter 2

Training begins

Ares and Duncan walked the long metallic corridors back to Duncan's quarters. As they drew closer the sound of Hades cursing and swearing behind the door could be clearly heard. Duncan swiped his pass card, and the door slid open, stopping Hades in mid rant. Cam, who was known as Hades to the hacker community stood upright in his grey overalls. His shock of blonde hair was wet from the shower he had just taken.

He began to rant again whilst continuing to walk toward Duncan, hand outstretched. "Duncan! Did these bastards tie you up and pretend to hang you as well? I've a good mind to tell them to shove their fucking job up their arse! As for that little bastard bloke - what's his name…Loki, he's just an annoying, crude, hyperactive midget! I've a good mind to give him a kicking!" Ares stepped forward. "I wouldn't do that for two reasons: One, you'd end up in the slammer, and two, and more importantly - Loki would batter you, and you'd end up in the slammer. Let's all just calm down eh?"

Duncan walked over to meet Hades, "Yeah, calm down and tell me how it's going? It's been a couple of months." Hades shook Duncan's hand and began to relax whilst continuing to scowl at Ares, "Well, I was looking forward to this until I had a fucking plastic bag forced over my head and found my neck in a noose! That Terminus bloke, there's another officious idiot; and where's the gorgeous agent Shaw? I haven't seen her yet - and she was one of the main reasons I joined!"

Duncan remembered, "Yeah, where is agent Shaw?" he asked, turning to Ares. Ares towered over both of the men. "She's on a mission at the moment. Everything here is on a need to know basis and that's something you don't need to know! If there is anything for us to do with regards to it we'll find out soon enough!"

From there the day ended swiftly. Both Hades and Duncan ate dinner with the rest of the team before retiring early to chat about their own experiences over the past couple of months. They traded thoughts on the characters they had met so far, laughing one second, becoming annoyed the next, all the time wondering what on earth tomorrow would bring. What would they learn? They were still unsure - the syllabus had not exactly been laid out for them. By the end of the evening Duncan found himself lying awake, staring up at the ceiling. The light from the laptop's screen-saver casting the occasional shadow that danced across the smooth grey plaster. He couldn't help thinking, as he listened to Hades snore, that this wasn't going to be the easy life of hacking computer systems that he had been expecting. On the contrary, he had the feeling danger was just around the corner. The next day would provide some of the answers. This he knew.

"Where the fuck are our clothes? I didn't expect to be wearing a stupid grey sack all the time," Hades mumbled as he climbed out of bed. "The clothes will get to us soon enough," came Duncan's dazed reply. An alarm had gone off, waking both of the new recruits from a deep and mostly peaceful sleep. "Bloody hell, it's only half past five. I didn't think it was the army I was signing up for!" Hades was less than impressed, but he continued slowly with the task of dressing himself. Duncan struggled out of bed and dragged his naked figure to the shower. Fresh towels hung on the polished steel radiator, warm to the touch. Everything was spotless; meticulously cleaned by a tiny army of two dedicated, security-cleared cleaners. At least most of the mundane tasks were taken care of whilst they were here - Duncan thought to himself. He couldn't help wondering if letting cleaners into each room was a security risk. But hey, these places had to function, he supposed.

He stepped into the shower, forgetting to let it warm up first. He inhaled, not by his own choice, as the freezing water hit him. It woke him up with a jolt, which was just what he needed. Soon enough the warm water began to flow, making him feel better, allowing him to finally exhale and relax.

Ten minutes later, feeling refreshed and ready to take on any task, he opened the shower cubicle and stepped back on to the slate floor. At 5.55am Loki rattled on the door before entering. "C'mon ye pair o' poofs - breakfast!" Hades and Duncan followed Loki out and down the corridors to the canteen, Hades taking every opportunity to pull faces, and indicate his general dislike for the small man.

Suddenly, with no warning, Loki turned and grabbed Hades by the throat, his rage and aggression apparent yet perfectly controlled and harnessed. The combination of Loki's unexpected speed and strength sent Hades reeling into the metal wall. "Look, you little fuck," Loki began with a slow deliberate whisper, pushing his thumb into Hades windpipe. "I don't like you. You haven't earned MY respect yet, so don't disrespect me...or I'll beat you into next Wednesday!" Hades threw his hands into the air as his eyes began to bulge from the pressure around his neck. "Okay, okay...point taken!" he managed to gasp.

In an instant Loki let him go. Hades fell to his knees clenching his bruised neck, struggling to take in air. Loki stood over him for a second before throwing a final glance at

Duncan. It was a simple but efficient warning. Duncan felt warned. He was a hacker...not a fighter.

Breakfast passed without further problems - the new recruits having learnt an early lesson. "Right," said Ares, "time to see the control room!" The two men were led to a room not seen the previous day. On making their way through the sealed, bullet-proof doors, they were shown an extraordinary circular room. Port holes had been cut at shoulder height, evenly spaced around the wall and filled with tinted glass, allowing a small glimpse of the corridors outside, whilst maintaining the privacy required within. Racks of expensive computer machinery filled any space that may have existed around the walls. High bandwidth communications links, expensive networking equipment, and an array of other hardware were packed in from floor to ceiling. A myriad of colours winked in the semi-gloom as L.E.D's flashed, hard drives strained and systems listened. Each system, each connection, each scheduled command, working individually, processing for the greater good of the country.

A couple of technicians conversing at a rack turned to weigh up the newbies, returning to their task only seconds later. Duncan looked up at Ares' towering figure. "I thought we saw the servers in the comms room yesterday?" "Those are the Intrusion Detection Systems, such as OSSIM. We've got a few probes on the outside. They report back the happenings of the big old Internet. We've also got the probes reporting from some other less friendly networks," he winked and continued, "but that's another need to know for the moment!"

Hades walked over to the control console located at the centre of the room. The console's jet-black marble worktop was built in two layers. On the first layer sat four keyboards and their corresponding mice, with the base-units neatly hidden from view in the cupboards below. The upper layer, sitting a foot above, held four large flat screen monitors. Retina scanners were attached to the right hand side of them. Hades sat in one of the four comfortable black leather chairs. "Christ, were these leftovers from Star Trek?" Ares laughed, "Yep, they are pretty cool - and comfortable." Duncan had by now joined Hades at the control console. "So what are these systems for?" Ares sat down in another of the chairs. "These, my young friend, are the attack systems. Remember, our primary objective is to take people out, not monitor them. That's why you guys are here...supposedly the best we've got. The systems all run Knoppix-STD, the Security Tools Distribution. You can't write to them, they are firewall protected, have all the tools we require...and we have an instant standard image. We've made a couple of additions, such as the biometrics and retina scanning, as well as a couple of our own tasty tools. The web browser gives us secure access to the other systems. Again, everything you do is logged to a central database, so no mucking about! You're not in college now," Ares continued, looking directly at Duncan.

It was becoming obvious to Duncan that his new team knew more about him than he had previously thought. Hades laughed, "Us muck about? As if! We already know all of these systems and the associated tools; what training do we need?" Ares nodded, "Yes, we know you know this, but out there it can be dangerous, so I'll be training you in armed and unarmed combat, a bit of psychology, and we'll need to get your fitness levels improved. I'll also teach you the correct way to drive a car! Hades, I've heard you'll be posted to Australia. Duncan is likely to go somewhere in Europe temporarily...how's your French?" Duncan looked slightly alarmed, "Pretty crap, learned the basics at school!" "Well, we'll teach you a bit of French and German...you'll need some to get by!"

With that, Hades indicated that the two newcomers should start by logging into the system, "Feel free to take a look around." The two men logged into the system, quickly familiarising themselves with the slight differences. "I thought we'd be using Z4CK?" said Duncan. "Once it's ready we'll integrate it, and it'll be installed on a couple of the new toys we're developing for you...don't worry, your work has not been wasted! We'll see to that," replied Ares.

Timeline: June 2005 - 5 Months of training completed

Like a schoolmaster, Chaos paced pensively back and forth across the room. Judging by his watch Terminus was almost two minutes late, and he was not impressed. He walked up to one of the many photographs on his wall and smiled. His children, who he had not seen for several weeks, smiled back from behind the glass. He brushed a spec of dust from his pinstriped suit and patted down some of his thick grey hair, which had had the audacity to stray out of place. After another minute of strolling around, he sat down, tapping his fingers impatiently on the oak desk.

Another five minutes ground by before a knock at the door was met with an impatient "Enter!" Terminus hurried in. Apologies for the late arrival Sir, been a bit of activity from the Eastern European sector. We were alerted by MI5 of an attempt to intrude on one of our military installations. We've got Duncan and Hades working on it. "Duncan? Does he not have a code name yet?" "Yes. Thor." replied Terminus. "Then why isn't he being referred to as such? You are aware of our policy aren't you? How are we to hit the ground running with these new recruits if we can't even follow simple policies regarding code names?" Terminus nodded, "Of course, I will indicate to the men that we must refer to each other using code names at all time."

Terminus laid the folder carefully on the desk.

Chaos glanced at the folder Terminus had been carrying, "Are those the reports you promised?" "Correct, these detail the progress of both Duncan, sorry...Thor, and Hades over the last sixteen weeks. I've got to say they are as ready as they will ever be." Terminus picked up the folder containing the reports and handed them to Chaos.

Chaos opened the folder, carefully flicking through each of the individual sheets. He cleared his throat and looked up at Terminus. "They are indeed excellent hackers, but a few things here are slightly concerning. Hades seems rather insolent to me...a real wild card. Can he handle himself, more importantly...can we trust him?" Terminus replied, "I understand what you mean, but in both the physical and psychological tests he has come through with flying colours. I feel he is trustworthy. Most of the men here have their quirks...their own eccentricities. They are all intellectuals."

Chaos continued to study the document. "And regarding Thor? This seems to indicate he is physically unfit." Terminus stood up, "Yes, I would agree with that. It is something we are concentrating on. A couple more weeks and his fitness levels should be satisfactory...he has been leading a far too sedentary lifestyle. However, Ares has stated that Thor has remarkable reactions, due to his training as a fencer. He is quick thinking, has taken to the martial arts and we've found that psychologically he is stronger than Hades. His linguistic skills are also coming along well...and he has less arrogance about him...in fact I would say even a quiet demeanour."

Chaos tapped on a laptop sitting in front of him. "I'm glad to hear this is the case, as only this morning I received a secure communication stating that they are to be sent out to the field as of next week."

Terminus grimaced, "Next week? Standard training is usually six months...is there a problem?" Chaos replied, "You could say that. We'll need to take this one off line for the moment, but let me just say there has been a paradigm shift in thinking amongst the upper echelons."

Chaos leaned back in his chair. "Hades will take up his position in Australia, diverting temporarily to Hong Kong to deal with the Chinese and Korean threat. Their government-backed hackers have been giving us a severe headache over the past few months, and it's now time to run them to ground. It'll be tough, but armed with some of the new weaponry Riddles has cooked up, he should manage."

Terminus leaned over the table, "What about Thor?" Chaos replied, "We have a major project starting in Brussels, problems with neo-Nazis. We're posting him, Loki and Ares." Terminus looked confused, "Ares? He hasn't been out since the accident. Do you think that is wise?" Chaos got up from his chair. "I think it would be best all round. Anyway, you had better get back and see what's going on with this European sector issue." With that Chaos adjourned the meeting. As Terminus reached for the door Chaos called to him, "Keep me informed, I'll chat to the troops tomorrow." Terminus closed the door mumbling under his breath, "Interaction - now that would be a first!"

All four screens in the control room tracked the hackers as they attempted to gain entry to the naval research base at Faslane. Terminus swiped his pass card providing him with entry to the sealed room. Hades spun back and forth on his chair between the screens, whilst Duncan stared into a test laptop that had just been provided to him by Riddles. "How is it going," asked Terminus, rushing across the room. "Are we any closer to getting a lock on them?"

Hades answered with great excitement, still wheeling his chair between the screens. "They're sneaky bastards that's for sure. They're hiding their trail through multiple systems. The problem is finding which system is the source. They must have been busy boys over the last while to have taken control of so many. Don't worry we'll get them though." Terminus walked over to Duncan. "Any idea how close they are to breaching the target?" Duncan did not look up, "They seem to be getting pretty close to getting in, God knows what will happen if they do. Faslane is pretty keen to shut the connection down, but I've asked for another ten minutes to do the trace. It's pretty tight though; I can't tell if we'll make it in time. As soon as the connections closed, they'll run."

Hades typed furiously at his keyboard, his pupils widening with the increasing excitement. Suddenly he jumped up, "Yes! Toasted! Found the swine. I've done a netstat on what seems to be their first hop, and I've seen the same pattern of open ports on every other one leading back to the last. However, look at the one behind it! It's completely firewalled off, but there is a hell of a lot of data being transmitted from it!" Just checking it with the Hackback tool that Rome Labs developed for us. He paused for a minute to type several commands into the system. "Yep, that's confirmed, it's them all right!"

Terminus rushed over, "So where are they?" Hades beamed with glee, "As we suspected, according to Visual Route, it's somewhere in Moscow!" "Fire over the address then!" shouted Duncan, sounding slightly agitated, "we've no time to waste!" Hades shouted out the IP address. "Duncan quickly loaded the new version of Z4CK which had been converted by Riddles to run on their Knoppix security workstations. Duncan took a deep breath, "Okay, here goes nowt!"

His fingers rattled over the keyboard, a bead of sweat appearing on his brow as his heart rate increased, pumping blood to the extremities of his body.

> Z4CK --target 212.11.140.9 --scan --info

He pressed the 'Enter' key and sat impatiently. Almost instantly the screen began to fill as Z4CK attempted to obtain the information they required. A single port - 10000 appeared to be open, and through this Z4CK provided the information it had been asked for. Duncan remarked, "They've shifted the SSH port! According to Z4CK it's vulnerable. I'll ask it to fire an overflow attack against them and hope for the best!" he stated, turning to his waiting colleagues. At that second the phone rang, "Terminus picked it up. "No, don't switch off your connection; we've got them...yes OK another five minutes!" Terminus looked straight at Duncan, "Get the jist?" Duncan turned back to the laptop and typed another command.

> Z4CK --target 212.11.140.9 --overflow --attack --replicate

His finger hovered over the enter key for a fraction of a second, before he finally gathered the nerve to push it. The green cursor at the bottom of the console began to flash, thinking - like a chess master sizing up his opponent. Then, as if the brakes of a Formula One car had suddenly been released, green text began to flood the laptop's small black screen with data being shovelled up and down the network connection at a phenomenal rate. All there was to do now was wait and watch. The three figures gathered round in the semi-gloom, the green text from the screen providing riveting viewing. The counter attack had begun.

A cold, dark room in Moscow city centre was filled with the hum of computer fans and the frantic clicking of keys. The rooms only light emanated from the laptops and computer monitors stuck in the corner. Log files scrolled up the screens as the men ran their Nmap and Nessus scans, reporting their target's findings to their masters.

A red neon sign from a bar across the road flashed intermittently through the misted window, adding to the atmosphere within the room. The wooden floorboards, strewn with coffee cups, beer bottles and cigarette ends, creaked as the youngest man traversed them, pacing up and down, anxiously waiting. Against one wall, a haze of smoke from cheap cigarettes hung over the two young men who sat back down at their laptops. Their concentration was intense, their goal almost within reach. They had been working hard on their target, and having found a weakness they began to convert an old exploit to suit their purposes. Soon they would be in. They were sure success was theirs for the taking.

The door bolted from the inside ensured they would not be disturbed. The two men were scruffy in appearance. One in his late teens, the other in his early twenties, sat typing in bursts at their keyboards. They would stop occasionally to scratch their beards or light yet another cigarette. They spoke to each other in Russian, their native tongue. Their excitement grew as they drew closer to the crucial information their Mafia bosses sought. They would be paid well for this work. Information on nuclear weapons systems was big money on the black market. The older of the two men drew on a cigarette and made a joke, which made the younger snigger as he swigged from his bottle of beer. They had not yet been traced; their intrusion detection systems showing no more than usual Internet noise associated with a modem connection. The firewall had a single port open to allow secure remote access to a laptop.

It, they believed, was not vulnerable.

A new alert flashed from the intrusion detection system. The young man looked perplexed, never having seen the signature before. He quickly got up to take a closer look at the monitor, but after a few seconds, turned to his colleague and shrugged his shoulders, "False alarm?"

He sat back down, turning back to his laptop, making a smart comment about their invulnerability. The laughter and jokes ended abruptly as a high-pitched screeching noise filled the room. A look of disbelief crossed the face of the younger man as the screeching quickly spread to the other systems. The older of the two men shot up from his seat and lunged across the desk to save his precious laptops. Already the systems were dying. The scrolling text stopped as system after system froze.

Within a minute they had pulled the plug, breathless and sweating. Finally, after a short while, they switched the systems on again. They both breathed a sigh of relief as the systems powered on and performed their test routines. The men began to relax as the systems booted, all they could do was wait to be prompted to log in. Finally all of the systems beeped, seemingly in unison, leaving each and every one with a prompt at the bottom - Hacked by Z4CK.

The younger of the men banged his fist on the table in front of him whilst the older man, more aware of the consequences of failure, ran around from keyboard to keyboard in a state of panic. Their systems were unusable - the keyboards had been locked. Even if the password was known, there was no way to enter it. He glanced at his watch. They must escape and hide quickly before their masters arrived for their next visit. He grabbed the younger man out of his seat and pulled him towards the door. He unbolted and opened it, only to find two large men standing before them. It was too late.

The two hackers backed into the room, obviously fearful. The two larger men looked at each other before following them in. The door was closed and bolted.

"You have the information?" the larger of the two men asked, taking a sip of beer from a bottle which stood on the table. "No, erm...we were stopped at the last minute," stuttered the older hacker. One of the large men wandered casually over to the row of computer systems and read aloud, "Hacked by Z4CK - Please enter the password for recovery." He looked over to the second man who was shorter and wider in stature. His short black hair and thick eyebrows added to his menacing looks. "How polite!"

He laughed, "Well, you are hackers; can't you figure out the password?" The two hackers had moved backwards, the older pushing the younger, unsure of the larger men's intentions. "The older hacker spoke. "It will take time to get the systems back, and now they have been alerted to our presence. We will have to try another time." The larger man shook his head and sighed, leaning over the table. "That is a shame, a waste of time, machinery and talent. Uri will be less than pleased. Unfortunately as you are aware there is no other time." The younger man stepped forward, "We can do it; it was bad luck, pure and simple." The older hacker intimated to the youngster that this was not the best time to talk.

The larger man stepped forward and pointed to his associate. "Do you know why he is named Zaitsev?" The younger man shook his head, "No...err no." The larger man laughed, "He never misses!" As he finished his sentence Zaitsev produced a gun that glinted in the light projected by the neon sign from across the street. Slowly he screwed a silencer on to the end of the barrel, removed the safety, and aimed it straight at the youngster. Both of the hackers backed themselves up against the wall. With nowhere to go their muscles tensed. They prayed this was a scare tactic. In a low course voice the shorter man stated, "Let this be your lesson." In an instant he re-aimed the gun at the older hacker and pulled the trigger. The bullet hit him between the eyes - a small entry wound became a large exit wound as the bullet exploded out of his head, spraying blood, brain and skull fragments in all directions, before embedding itself in the concrete wall behind. His eyes rolled upwards and he dropped to the floor – dead.

Blood continued to gush onto the floor as his heart pumped it up and out of the gaping wound. Soon it had ebbed to a trickle, the victims face almost unrecognisable as it lay in a bloody pool on the floor. The younger man screamed, "Ivan!" as he looked down upon his lifeless friend, mentor, and most importantly brother. The mafia killers laughed. The larger man walked up to the younger hacker who took cover, curling himself into a ball in the corner. "As I said, you will not forget this in a hurry. Do not fail us again. We will be in touch...oh and I would get someone new to play computer games with." He pointed at Ivan, "your brother has logged off for good!"

He and Zaitsev could be heard laughing as they walked down the dark, squalid corridor of the tenement block. The silencer had done its job. No-one had heard the fatal gunshot. The young hacker, known only as Vasily, remained curled up. At first he sobbed - afraid and shocked; grief stricken by the loss of his brother; his hero. Soon the fear turned to anger. Vengeance would be his at any cost. The 17 year old got up and grabbed his duffel coat from the back of a chair. He took one last look at his lifeless brother, wiped a wet salty tear from his cheek, and took one of the laptops, before disappearing off into the Moscow night.

"Well done, well done. The attack has been halted. Z4CK is indeed an excellent piece of kit," Terminus exclaimed, as relieved as he was happy. Duncan nodded to Hades who returned his gesture with a simple thumbs up. "Let's get something to eat," said Duncan, closing the laptop. He leaned back in his chair momentarily. "Seems I could get used to this!" Terminus approached them both. "Tomorrow Chaos will have some news for you. Your time here is almost over and your first mission has been scheduled. Come, let's eat."

The men walked off to the canteen, feeling good about themselves, unaware of the fate that had befallen their adversaries.

The next day was unusually bright and sunny. Breakfast was taken at the now regular time of 6.30am, and the men were enjoying the sunshine within the confines of the grounds that had been their base since early January. It was now June, and as far as they knew, the final day of training. They were unsure of what was to happen over the next while; where they would be posted, for how long, and with whom - if anyone.

"What time did Chaos call the meeting for?" asked Hades. He was seated in a relaxed manner on a log near the back wall of the building. He sipped an orange juice whilst enjoying the morning sunrise. "9.a.m as far as I can remember. It's amazing isn't? All this time we've been here...in such a small so called elite team, and yet we've never clapped eyes on him!" mused Duncan. "Yep, typical mushroom management, keep us in the dark and feed us shit...or nothing at all in this case!" replied Hades. Duncan had decided a while ago that is was not his place to ask questions.

It was easy to just follow orders and let others sort out the political problems. "It's not for us to question why, but to do or die...or something like that!"

Hades was as cynical as ever. Four months locked away in an underground bunker hadn't done him any favours. He was at last starting to feel that there was light at the end of the tunnel and that Australia was beginning to beckon. He had been promised a posting there; how long it would take to get there he wasn't sure, but he knew he would get there. "I feel almost institutionalised, do you know that?" stated Duncan, as he finished the last of his coffee. Hades agreed, "It's great to even get out in the fresh air. I didn't think it would be like this. A little bit of hacking, time to learn new techniques, meet new people as interested and good at the same thing, not to mention a chance to legitimately beat the baddies". But no, what do we get?" Hades stood up and walked along the old buildings wall. He stopped suddenly, raising his voice, obviously agitated. "First tortured...beaten up several times in the name of martial arts training, the chance to learn foreign languages that are of no bloody interest and so far...no new toys.

"Still, it could be worse, thank Christ that twat Loki has been out for the last month or so. I was really starting to hate him!" Duncan nodded, "Yeah, he is a bit unstable. Ares makes up for it though. One leg down or not, ex-SAS or not, he's someone you would want on your side if the going got tough." Hades agreed unwillingly. Where Duncan preferred and relied on team work, Hades was more of a loner. He trusted no-one but himself to get the job done. Why shouldn't he? It had always worked for him in the past.

Duncan joined Hades at the wall looking down onto the endless fields that rolled out like a patchwork quilt before them. It was a perfectly lit, clear day, with the sun sitting in the distance before them.

It was never that warm in Scotland, but on this day it was comfortable. Comfortable to these Scots was good enough. The countryside looked lovely in this weather, no mountains here unlike the west coast. Scotland was a small country carved out by the ice age, providing several changes of scene in the space of a single journey. To Duncan, it was all he knew...and he always looked for the best in it.

"You know, I probably wouldn't have been doing this if the weather in Scotland had been any better. I would have done something outdoors. The rain is a great reason to stay in and tap away at a computer. Soon you are looking for more challenges than the latest game!" Hades gave Duncan a bemused look, "Nah, not me. Looking at this countryside is nice, but I'd get bored. At the minute it's peaceful and quiet, but I need the adrenalin rush. Breaking into stuff gives me that! No, an outdoors life, sounds like hard work to me!"

Edinburgh was a distant speck on the horizon some forty miles away. The men had only been permitted out a few times over the last month, and the mist of the Scottish lowlands had obscured the city during the early morning. For the first time the weather had been clear enough to allow a glimpse. Hades pointed in its direction, "A night out on the piss and some female company, that's what I really need. Fat chance of that by the looks of things; Yep, one thing about this lifestyle...it can be bloody lonely!"

The troops as they were termed by Chaos were called to the meeting room at precisely 9am. Duncan wandered in behind a casual, almost arrogant Hades. Agent Shaw, code-name Athena had been recalled from her last mission. She sat in the front row next to the large frame of Ares, who was busy fidgeting in an attempt to get his false leg into a comfortable position. Duncan and Hades eventually took seats in the second row next to Terminus. Some two minutes later Riddles walked in, sniffing and blowing his nose, unused to being outside the confines of his lab. He carried a black plastic container no bigger than a shoebox under his arm, which intrigued Hades and Duncan.

Duncan turned to him, "What's in the box...any new toys?" "Patience, patience, and please, it would be preferable if you did not refer to my creations as toys! I find the term somewhat derogatory!" Riddles gestured that all would soon be revealed. It was easy to tell he was excited about it.

Chaos flew into the room almost ten minutes late, slamming the door behind him. He was not in the least bit nervous and showed no embarrassment at the fact that after four months, on their final day, he would meet and greet the new recruits for the first time. In fact, he seemed oblivious to anyone's feelings towards him. Duncan felt this inability or unwillingness to communicate with the lower ranks was dangerous, especially considering that at times their undercover work may put their lives at risk. Everyone had to be trusted and trustworthy. This, Duncan felt, only came with an understanding of all the people in and associated with the team. If he ever got to that level he would know everyone and everything, without having to have it reported to him by subordinates.

Chaos positioned himself behind the large table in front of a projector. He took the stance of a college professor about to give a lecture he had given a thousand times before. It was well rehearsed. He paused for a second to look straight at Hades and Duncan.

"Thor, Hades, congratulations on the completion of your training. According to Ares and Terminus you have coped well with the syllabus. He brandished a red folder in the air. "In this folder I have your first assignments.

Let's make them a quick win for CyberSecure and the British Government. The assignments were read out in due course, with some surprise being mooted at the fact that Ares was to be sent out on assignment for the first time in several years. As expected, Hades was to be sent to Australia with a few weeks in Hong Kong, where he would, as it was termed by Chaos, 'touch base' with the local agent currently on secondment to the Asian sector. He seemed please and somewhat relieved, having had his concerns about the potential of being double-crossed.

Ares and Thor were to be sent to Brussels where they would meet up with Loki, who was currently in Amsterdam. Ares laughed, "Meet Loki in Brussels? How do you plan to drag him away from Amsterdam? That's paradise for him!" The group laughed - although it was a concern. It would not be the first time Loki had gone AWOL, never too keen to follow orders, especially when things were going his way.

The speech dragged on for another unnecessary fifteen minutes, mostly populated with management doublespeak, Chaos making a vain attempt to inspire the new recruits and praise everyone else. The audience knew it wasn't meant sincerely. He didn't know them; all of his knowledge had been gleaned from reports submitted by Terminus. Chaos summed up his speech by handing the folders to the respective agents in an almost ceremonial fashion. "All of the details are there as well as new passports and some local currency. You have been booked places in hotels reasonably close to your targets. This is more than just a little bit of digital insurgence. In order to achieve our goal in this instance, one of you will need to penetrate both the buildings and the group in question. The people we are about to bring to book have caused a couple of high tech crime units a real headache. Let's just see if we can 'Aspirinise' the situation for them!

Hades whispered to Duncan, "What the fuck does Aspirinise mean?" "Don't know; I guess it must be something to do with removing a headache, but I'm going to use it for a laugh," came the jovial reply.

Chaos finally handed over to an excited Riddles, who walked to the front and carefully laid the container down on the table. Removing the lid, he produced four customised Zaurus SLC-3000 PDAs. Hades leaned out of his seat to have a closer look. "Wow, beats your SL-5500 into the ground," he said turning to Duncan. Riddles beamed with pride. "Let me inform you of the modifications I have made to these Zaurus portable computing devices."

The lights dimmed to allow Riddles to begin the presentation. It was obvious that he was pleased with the improvements, and at every juncture stopped to gauge the reaction from the agents around the room. The SLC-3000s had been significantly modified having been given inbuilt wireless connectivity, a camera, and a GSM phone. It had become slightly more bulky, but the modifications were obviously worthwhile. The system had been made more rugged with the outer casing swapped for strong titanium. The tiny internal hard drive redesigned to encrypt all files.

Riddles smiled. "Of course, in the event of an agent being caught, the system has a remote controlled self-destruct mechanism. This is based on a small electro-magnetic pulse, which will fire, instantly destroying the electronic circuits within the unit. I have been working on an Ion Cannon, but unfortunately, due to power issues, targeting, and shielding problems, this has not as yet been possible to achieve in a controllable manner. However, what you see before you is a by-product. Simply use the infrared port, or this additional button, and the system will be incapacitated…permanently. Finally, I have also, after many months of reprogramming, installed optimised versions of Z4CK and OpenZaurus."

Riddles looked over to Duncan and gave a smug grin. "I've also implemented Biometric thumbprint recognition to increase device security."

Ares laughed, "And what about the stylus? Can it kill a man at 50 yards?" Riddles, who was generally devoid of humour, was unimpressed by the sarcasm. "It is made of Titanium...I'm sure someone of your nature and background would find an opportunity to stab or gouge some hapless individual with it, if you must!"

Chaos interrupted, keen to move on to his next meeting or scuttle back to his office. "Anyway, there is a time for joviality...and this is not it. If we grasp the low hanging fruit on this one, I'm sure it will lead to greater recognition for this team. Good luck; I'm sure you won't need it!" With that Chaos left the room, leaving to Riddles to hand out the new toys.

"Well, I guess this is it then? Farewell for a short while," said Hades turning to Duncan as they looked over the new SLC-3000s. "S'pose so. Keep in touch eh?" Hades nodded, "will try, but I get the feeling we're going to get a bit busy over the next while." Ares towered over the two men, patting Duncan on the back. "Right, let's get ourselves ready...it's been a while since I've been out there, but I'm raring to go!"

Chapter 3

The Belgian Job.

The Ryanair Boeing 737 touched down in Brussels Charleroi airport at the expected time. Ares and Duncan had been sitting at separate ends of the plane. Duncan sat quietly and comfortably toward the rear; in contrast Ares sat snoring at the front. It had taken him a while to manoeuvre his large frame and false leg into the less than ample seating space. Not being too keen on flying he had done his best to sleep through the short trip from Edinburgh to Brussels. To the dismay of those directly next to him he had succeeded, with the accompanying noise difficult to bear, even for the hard of hearing. He awoke with a start as the plane hit the runway, the sudden jolt and deceleration enough to bring him back from his slumber. He rubbed his eyes and smiled at the small woman sitting next to him. Aware that she was less than impressed, he cleared his throat and decided that it was best to focus on the wall ahead until he could exit the plane and meet up with Duncan.

Duncan attempted to relieve the pressure on his ears, holding his nose, whilst trying to swallow. The change in cabin pressure always seemed to leave him with a sick, light headed feeling that took a good thirty minutes to clear, one of the main reasons he didn't fly too often. He began to put his jacket on as the airtight doors opened, having decided earlier that there was no point in trying to rush out of his seat. Instead he watched with interest as everyone else jostled for the chance to get off first; people watching was of interest to him. He could never see the point of the mad rush; what was an extra two minutes in this situation? He pondered for a minute on the inefficiencies of public transport. His last job had involved train travel. A lack of seating had always brought out the selfish animal in people, even to the detriment of the old or infirm. Getting a seat on the train had become a case of survival of the fittest.

Ares had already exited, having been given special dispensation and the seat at the front on account of his disability.

When Duncan eventually managed to exit, he made his way through customs with little problem, his British passport affording him a reasonably smooth entry into the heart of Europe. Duncan's only worry was getting in and out of Europe with his new Zaurus; luckily it's resemblance to a standard PDA meant that, in Charleroi at least, it raised no suspicions. He remembered the difficulties of getting into America on his last trip in 2003, and pondered on the differences in the security set up.

Duncan and Ares had been ordered not to communicate until they reached their destination, and once there, to refer to each other without mentioning their names. Duncan had a vague idea of what the operation was to involve but Ares understood the project in detail, having transferred the relevant contact and project information on to his Zaurus, which had automatically encrypted the files.

Following a one hour bus journey across the flat green Belgian countryside, and a underground trip from the centre of Brussels, they reached the rather ugly Crowne Plaza hotel, striking up a seemingly innocent conversation in the pristine marble reception area, whilst they waited to check in. Their hotel rooms had been booked and paid for them by independent companies, both of which were simply names owned by the British government. Ares would be leaving a day after Duncan, in two weeks time. This was the amount of time designated by Terminus as being sufficient to deal with the Brussels problem. They settled in to their respective rooms, agreeing to meet up for a meal later on.

Now all they had to do was sit, wait, and hope that Loki would show up as arranged.

Duncan showered and made himself a cup of tea, before lying back on the crisp, clean bed sheets. The room had both telephone and broadband connections, but he didn't feel it necessary to plug himself in and pay an extortionate rate for his Internet access. He took his Zaurus from a small black bag he had been carrying with him, and opened its Titanium case, carefully switching it on. Riddles had done an excellent customisation job he thought, admiring the new toy. He quickly logged in, placing his thumb on the small touch screen, allowing the biometrics reader to confirm his identity. He started scanning for wireless access points, picking up quite a few in the direct vicinity. He quickly noted the ones he thought would be most useful to him, but knew that if he was going to get the most chance, indeed, any real chance of finding a relevant access point, he would need a more powerful antenna. They had not brought one with them from Britain, as it would have raised suspicion at border control. He felt a visit to the corner shop, or at least the Belgian equivalent, would be required.

He was sure he could buy the raw materials needed to make his own antenna there. However, this was neither the time, nor the place to start hacking around, potentially drawing attention to his presence. He put the Zaurus down on the pine bedside table and picked up the remote control, switching on the large television, which sat in the corner of the room. It wasn't long before he became bored with BBC World wide and the selection of European television stations, most of which were in Dutch or French. His French was better than it had been a few months ago, but it was not at a conversational level yet. He decided to get up and dress, before venturing a look out of his window.

Laid out before him was the Rue de la Loi, a wide street busy with cars at this time of day. Across the road sat two buildings used by the European Union in Brussels. The first, positioned diagonally across from the hotel was the Berlaymont building. Duncan had seen the structure before on the television, but hadn't taken any notice as to what it was. It had one of the strangest designs Duncan had seen, each side of the building curving outwards, almost like a banana. He liked it, getting in looked like a challenge. In front of him, beyond the Crowne Plaza car park, sat the predominantly glass Justus Lipsius building. A few flags and a small fountain adorned its frontage. The glass building looked as though it was held together by giant blocks of pink marble. At first glance there seemed to be only one way in. It would be difficult to wander round the area unnoticed as the whole street lay in an open configuration. No alleys or tall buildings to hide in here.

He glanced at his watch and sighed. He had been unable to take any rest, and was looking forward to getting out for a bite to eat; hunger starting to get the better of him. There had been no word from Loki, who had been due an hour ago. Duncan paced the room, "Christ, this is boring!" he murmured to himself. After another ten minutes or so, he decided to take the bold step of heading to Ares' room. He took his Zaurus, wallet, and passport with him, ensuring he had left nothing of use or value, before carefully locking his room door and strolling the short distance down to room 247 to call on Ares.

His knock was met by a confused grunt as Ares awoke from his second short slumber of the day. He called out, "Loki, is that you?" Duncan replied quietly, "No it's me, Thor." The door handle rattled as Ares struggled with the lock. "Come in young man. No sign of Loki then? What a surprise!"

Duncan wandered into the room. "Do you want to get something to eat? There's not much point waiting here, he could be ages!" Ares agreed, and the two men decided to head out to find some food. It was a lovely warm June evening - the weather in Belgium on the whole better than back in Scotland. They walked along Rue Archimedes until they reached a small restaurant called Balthazar. Ares turned to Duncan as he walked through the door, "Remember let's not talk too loud, and try not to use our names...light chit chat at this stage is good. I've heard the food is good in here, which is the most important thing.

They entered the restaurant and found themselves looking at an old fashioned, well-established eating area. Ornate cornices complimented the light yellow interior and high ceiling. The tables and floor were mahogany. Gleaming silver cutlery and crystal wine glasses sat, neatly positioned, next to the white cotton napkins. Most of the tables were taken at this time in the evening and they hoped that something was free. It was spotlessly clean. Duncan looked up at Ares, "Is this not a bit posh for us?" Ares reassured his younger colleague, "Not at all, the posher the better. These people won't want to bother us."

They were shown to some seats in a corner towards the rear of the restaurant, and before long were tucking into some pasta, a nice wine, and plenty of bread, which went down well. The two men got on well, chatting and laughing about the usual things men do - Football, politics, favourite films, favourite women, and the rest. Duncan was keen to find out more about the time Ares spent in the SAS, although he realised that in public was not the best place to talk about these things. They did mention the army, but specifics were not touched on for the moment. Ares did however mention he had stories to tell, later perhaps. Ares was wise beyond his years; his life had been rich in experience, and at quieter times, in private, he was willing to share it.

He was by nature a friendly if slightly cautious man, having spent years undertaking one covert operation after another. Ares was the mentor, and Duncan was determined to learn all he could from him.

The two finally made it back to Ares room at 8:45pm, but it wasn't until just after 9pm when a knock at the door interrupted their conversation. Loki leaned against the door, whispering as quietly as was possible for him, "It's me ye pair o bastards, let me in." Ares opened it. "Finally, where the fuck have you been?" Loki beamed, "What a fucking time I've just had...Amsterdam...the ladies, the beer...magic!" "Getting to the point, what about the project? Was it a success?" asked Ares. Loki smiled, then jumped into the nearest chair, "Heeeyyyy, this is me, always getting the job done first time!"

Ares limped back to the nearest available chair, shaking his head. Loki had taken his seat and was currently relaxing. "How's it going bufty boy?" Loki said, turning his attention to Duncan. Duncan frowned, "Yeah, things *were* good, cheers for asking." Loki frowned, "cheeky bastard," before he continued, putting his leg over the chair, "Come on then Ares, spill the beans...what's the fucking deal with Belgyland? I'm raring to get this over and done with. I'll tell you this; Loki proceeded to put on a fake, rather poor Dutch accent, "once this is finished, I'm off back to Amsterdam to see the ladies; the sooner the better!"

Ares produced the file from his holdall and opened it. He was irked by what he felt was Loki's unnecessary boisterousness. "I'll tell you what it's all about if you bloody shut up for a second!" He began to read, trying to contain his frustration at Loki, who lit up a cigarette, and got out of his chair to make a cup of tea. "I'll wait until the kettles finished boiling will I?" Ares remarked, trying to make himself heard over its whistling. Loki laughed, flicking his cigarette ash onto the pine dressing table, "naw, just get on with it. I never listen to your crap anyway!"

The project, as it was termed by Ares, was to focus on the closing down of a rapidly growing neo-Nazi group named The Fourth Reich. The group, which had been operating out of Brussels, was believed to be controlled by the son of an ex Waffen SS major who had served as part of the 'SS-Fleiwilligen-Flandern' division during the war. Peter van der Krueger, the father, believed in Flemish independence. He felt, like many other Flemish, that this independence could be achieved through German victory. Like many Flemish within Belgium at this time, he joined the SS.

Captured by the allies at the end of the war and sent back to Belgium, he faced the consequences of his actions. Like many other traitors he dealt with the humiliation of a forced march through the streets of Brussels, where, having been beaten by baying crowds, only narrowly escaped death. Having fought against the allies and therefore the Belgian state, he was automatically denied state benefits, such as a pension, which in his later years left him penniless and desolate.

His pride stopped him from seeking help, and in his sixties, suffering from depression, he had committed suicide. DeWitt, his son, had grown to hate the European nations for the treatment of his father, who had indoctrinated him with his Nazi beliefs and a sense of pride in his Arian origins. The young boy had grown into a man filled with a hatred for his own country, as he watched his once proud father deteriorate, before ending his life with his Lugar. DeWitt still believed in his Arian superiority and in a free state for the Flemish people. Now, in his mind, he had been given a real reason to seek it.

Ares leaned back in his chair, the folder lying open on his lap. "So far the group has undertaken various digital attacks and distributed Nazi propaganda via email, using the domains of government departments, which has caused obvious embarrassment. Their latest denial of service attacks on European Union websites caused havoc. Most recently they have successfully hacked several government and military systems." Loki sat down with his cup of tea. "Can't the locals just pick the fucker up?" asked Loki. Ares continued, "That is one of the problems. Van Der Krueger is the leader, but we don't know who is doing the hacking on his behalf. He is not particularly technical, just the business brain. However, we need to get to him first to find his hackers. We're also concerned about the increasing violence the group is using. There has been an increase in the physical attacks, and there is a real fear that if this group is not stopped, it will escalate into a force not unlike the IRA was in Northern Ireland, looking once again for an independent Flemish state. There have been no deaths as far as we know, but we've been informed that the chances are increasing as the group attracts more unsavoury characters.

Duncan seemed confused, "If his father was part of the SS during the war, how did DeWitt manage to get a civil service position?" Ares replied, "Good question, perhaps he has contacts further up the chain? Remember, that is one of the reasons we are here…to find out how far this goes. We're going to have to be careful." Loki finished his cup of tea, dumping his cup onto the floor. "So when are we going to meet our local contact?" "That will be tomorrow. In the meantime, I think we should all get some sleep. I get the feeling we're going to be doing a lot of watching and waiting over the next few days."

Duncan rolled over in the bed and reached for his Zaurus. He checked the time. It had only gone 11pm. He decided to get up, completely unable to take any rest, unsure of what the next day would bring. He left the room and took a stroll down the corridor, passing room 247 as he went. Just as he passed the door, Ares opened it, "How's it goin? Can't sleep either eh? D'you fancy coming in for a night cap? There's a mini-bar here." Duncan was only too happy to have the company for a short while. Ares walked over to the mini-bar and bent over awkwardly, to reach in and pluck out a small whisky. "What do you fancy?" Duncan replied, "Oh, a whisky would be good too, not too fussed." Ares poured the drinks and added some ice, before limping over to hand the cool drink to Duncan.

"So, tell me about the SAS, what's it like?" Ares talked for a while about several of the missions he had been involved in. His time in Northern Ireland, the Gulf War in Kuwait, and other missions in some countries Duncan had never heard of. "Ireland was the worst. You never knew who was who. The whole thing was at complete odds with our training." Ares said, shaking his head. "In most combat situations you know your enemy and could deal with it accordingly. There were several of our guys who acted either in haste or too late, and paid the price." He paused, thinking of the friends he had lost. "The bastards were scared of us though. They'd avoid the SAS at all costs; we had to be brutal in dealing with them.

I never found it easy…we got the sympathetic farmers to dig ditches at the edge of their fields, near woods usually. I'll tell you this, there's nothing more sure to turn a hard bastard into a whimpering child, than taking him to a ditch with a gun pointed at his head. They'd be all cocky for a while, until they realised their time was up. Listening to them beg for mercy, telling you how many kids they had, their names and ages. It made finishing them off tough…but it had to be done. It was them or us - or some other poor bastard." Ares took a sip of his whisky, "Anyway, those days are gone, thank God...hope they never need to be repeated; sometimes you've got to do what's necessary, but it's a dirty business." Duncan ventured another question, "So was it the car accident that ended your time in the Special Forces?" Ares sighed, "The car accident finished it. Even if I had come out unscathed it was time for me." Duncan was intrigued, "If you don't mind, may I ask what happened?"

Ares took another sip of the whisky, leaned forward, and hung his head. His voice began to quiver. "I had just come back from a short term in Oman. Everything was great. Jill, my wife, was 8 months pregnant, and it was likely that I would have the chance to see the birth of my wee girl. We knew our wee one was going to be a girl, and we were looking forward to a magical time together.

I'd been thinking of leaving the SAS...it's no place for a dad to be." He sniffed, and tried desperately to pull himself together. "Anyway, we were heading down a country lane, probably a bit too fast...Jill was driving...I told her to slow down. We hadn't seen each other for a couple of months and I remember we were busy laughing with each other. I must have cracked a joke or something. It was dark and we just weren't used to the roads." Ares inhaled, finding it difficult to finish the story. "A deer seemed to appear from nowhere you see, they do that on some of the highland roads, and, well, Jill panicked. She swerved and hit a tree. I don't remember much else, but my world ended on that day. Everything I loved was gone. Ares did not lift his head, "Maybe if I'd driven, or bought a better car with an air bag...maybe I'd have my family now. The doctors told me I was lucky." His voice trailed off to whisper, "They told me I was lucky."

Duncan was unsure how to react, "I am so sorry, I didn't realise." Ares wiped his face with a large hand, "Its fine; don't worry about it. I think I need a bit of time to myself, if you don't mind." Duncan smiled, "Sure, I'll see you in the morning." Duncan closed the door carefully behind him. Walking down the corridor he could hear the faint sound of Ares crying. He felt awful.

A dark haired man of medium height stood impatiently in the resplendent surroundings of the hotel lobby. He was dressed in a black suit, not overly smart, ensuring he did not stand out too much. He had unbuttoned his jacket, a plain blue tie falling just short of his trouser belt. His shoes, although clean, were not highly polished. He held on tightly to a black leather briefcase looking slightly nervous.

The receptionist approached him and asked him a question in French, to which the answer was "non merci, pas de probleme!" He looked around and decided it would be best to grab a seat at a table. At a shade before 9am Ares descended carefully down the large, carpeted stairway, clinging with one hand to the polished mahogany banister.

The Belgian had been told to look for a tall man with a limp, making Ares instantly recognizable as he walked across to greet him. They moved back to the table, which had been claimed by the placement of the man's briefcase, and sat down, comfortable on the finely upholstered Georgian chairs. The Belgian looked around, before finally asking a waiter standing nearby to bring them a coffee. Exchanging credentials and engaging in idle chit-chat for a short while, both men took the time to scan their surroundings intermittently, ever careful of someone taking too much interest.

The lobby was relatively empty for this time in the morning. An older couple sat near the window at the opposite side of the room, drinking coffee, occasionally tearing a strip from a large croissant they were sharing. A businessman rustled his morning papers, a plume of smoke rising from his cigarette which sat smouldering in a glass ashtray. Two business colleagues sat in the opposite corner, preparing a presentation on their stylish high-spec laptop; their voices were occasionally raised, drawing some attention from the other hotel guests.

Very little time passed before the waiter returned with two black coffees and a piece of paper for one of the men to sign. The Belgian reached out for it, and taking the pen from the waiter, drew the necessary funds from his wallet, whilst retaining the receipt. The waiter nodded to the men, before withdrawing, pleased with the small tip he had received.

Both men raised their cups to each other before taking a sip of the hot liquid. The Belgian spoke with an almost perfect English accent, a French lilt only slightly detectable. "First of all, I would like to thank you for coming here. As you are aware from our initial communication, the problem of the Fourth Reich is becoming more serious by the day." Ares nodded, "We're here to help, it is important these groups are stopped, and our team are experienced in this type of operation."

Over the next half hour the Belgian, known as Hercule, provided a full background on the Fourth Reich, which included information on the building just across from them, and why it was important that the Belgian and European authorities obtain the help of CyberSecure. He handed Ares plans the relevant areas of the building. "We have tried to obtain his communications, but they are being very clever. We can never tell what they are planning next.

If your team can find out that information, this would be a great help. DeWitt is a well-respected man with many friends, which means we have to be careful how we deal with this one. This is one of the main reasons we have asked for your help. Your group has no ties and is not known to anyone here. You can move around without raising suspicion or being recognized."

Ares glanced at the plans to the building for just enough time to get a feel for what they were dealing with, before folding up the sheet of paper and placing it next to him on the table. "So, I have been informed by my superiors back home that you have been assigned to work with us?" Hercule nodded, "Our government does not wish to place any future burden on you. We are keen to learn and help…covertly of course, in any way we can. If we could learn some of your techniques, this may help us to deal with similar problems in the future." Ares was nervous about this arrangement, having been used to working on his own for years. He had however found out that this was the reason for his deployment on this mission. "When do you intend to join us?"

The Belgian seemed bemused, "I thought I was reporting to you from today!" Ares smiled and finished his coffee, placing it down carefully on the saucer. "Well, we better get going then, hadn't we?" The two men collected their things, and got up from the table, before ascending the stairs to begin phase one of the mission.

The men were to congregate in Duncan's room at 9.30a.m which it now was. Ares and Hercule stood outside. "The guys are not aware you will be joining us today. Let me talk to them, to allay any concerns they may have. If you don't mind, I'd like you to stay here for a second." Ares knocked on the door three times, before turning the handle, mindful not to knock off the *Do not disturb* sign that hung from it.

Duncan and Loki sat at a small table they had positioned near the window. The window faced the Justus Lipsius building across the road. Duncan was busy converting a Pringles can into an antenna, allowing them to get a better signal from the multiple wireless networks that were available in the business district. Loki looked on in interest, "A fucking Pringles can? How on earth do you think up this shite? Why can't you go out and buy an antenna?" Duncan frowned, "Yeah, great idea, if you want to trail about Brussels looking for one, on you go...this will do the job just as well for what we need!"

Ares walked the short distance across the room. "Glad you could join us," said Loki in one of his sarcastic moods. Ares held his hand up, and spoke in a whisper, "We have been allocated a Belgian agent. We're supposed to show him how it's done, but I don't think we should show him everything. I suggest that we don't use Z4CK, for today at least. Traditional insurgency methods only, we don't want to tell every Tom, Dick and Harry about our cyber weaponry."

Duncan nodded in agreement. Loki was not pleased, "What the fuck are we doing with hangers-on? We're not here to bloody baby-sit anyone, never mind someone we don't even know. I'm saying nothing to him." Ares sighed, "Christ, I don't know why he's been assigned. Blame Terminus, it was his idea! If that's the way you're going to be then so be it. At some stage he's going to go home for the day, and that's when we can do the bulk of our work...fair enough?"

Loki seemed slightly happier with this. "Fine, ye better get the Belgy in then!" Ares went back to the door and opened it to find Hercule sitting on a chair across the landing, his briefcase sat next to him on the floor, his jacket on his lap. "Is everysing okay?" Ares ushered him into the room. "These are our two agents from CyberSecure, Loki, and Thor."

Duncan began to get up from his seat to go across and shake hands with Hercule but was nudged back down by Loki. "Nice to meet you...now don't get in our way!" said Loki, returning to the Zaurus. Hercule retracted his hand, looking slightly confused.   Ares was more pleasant, "Never mind him, he's like that with everyone. We'll let them get on with what they're doing, and if you join me I can talk you through the tasks that will be undertaken.   Hercule protested, "I'd really like to see it first hand if you don't mind."   Ares became more forceful, "Sorry, but we shouldn't get in their way." He pointed to more seats in the other corner of the room.   Hercule hesitated, but Ares' insistence ensured that the recommendation was followed.

Over the next hour Ares provided Hercule with some standard information. Hercule would occasionally strain to hear what was going on in the opposite corner of the room. Loki and Duncan whispered so as not to be heard too readily, all the while hoping their unwelcome guest would give up and leave them to get on with the job in hand.

A short while into the test Duncan pointed excitedly at the screen. "This seems to be the link we're looking for. I've used Kismet to scan for wireless networks. Not using Z4CK is making it slightly more difficult, but seeing as it's only using WEP encryption, we should be able to crack the stream. There's a hell of a lot of traffic coming from that link, so getting enough Initialisation Vectors to funnel in shouldn't take too long."   Loki, although working for CyberSecure, wasn't particularly interested in computer hacking of this sort, he was more hands on.   Driving, physical combat and forcing entry to buildings was what he enjoyed and excelled at. Most people thought he had serious adrenalin problems. If he weren't on a mission, he would be taking part in extreme sports, or at worst, looking for a fight.

Another hour passed, Duncan used Wellenreiter to decrypt the stream, which had not been particularly difficult due to the huge amount of data traversing the wireless link. Loki had become bored, choosing instead to study the security surrounding the building across the road. His binoculars glinted in the sun as he scanned the building, looking for the best time to get in. He walked over to Ares and Hercule, "Any chance of getting a look at the map of that building?" Ares took it from under a pile of literature that was now strewn across the small table. Hercule sat up, hoping perhaps that he would be asked for some help. Loki ignored him completely, taking the plans and strolling back to the other side of the room, where he settled down next to Duncan. He sat back in the chair, putting his feet up on the bed next to them, before unfolding the plans and scrutinising them at arms length.

One after another Duncan gained access to each of the individual wireless links. He was becoming more exasperated, unable to find a connection to the right network. His makeshift antenna had picked up more than he had bargained for, and what he felt initially would be a relevantly simple task, was taking longer than expected.

He came to the penultimate access point on his list. "One of these has got to give me access," he said under his breath, slightly embarrassed at not having gained a foothold yet. Ares was beginning to struggle to keep Hercule entertained. He offered the team a coffee and took the chance to look over Duncan's shoulder. "How are you getting on?" Duncan studied the small screen in front of him. "This is the second last on my list. I'm getting there. It's taken a bit longer than I had expected." He continued tapping at the tiny keyboard. "This is not likely to be linked to the building, it's not even encrypted. It won't give me an IP address, so maybe it is restricted. I'll set the Zaurus to listen to the traffic. Duncan typed in a couple of commands and a graphical interface began throwing out information, most of which was useless. Duncan left the software running until he spotted a couple of addresses that seemed to be consistently transmitting and receiving data. Duncan looked back over his shoulder at Ares. "I'll change my mac address to mirror this one. Perhaps then the access point will allow me to join," he said, pointing at an address scrolling by on the screen. Duncan quickly changed the network cards physical address to mimic that of the transmitting system. He then used another piece of software to send a de-authentication packet to all the attached systems. The information being received by the Zaurus began to increase; he had obtained a connection. Duncan whispered in triumph, "Yes...got you!" Ares exhaled, slightly relieved, before patting Duncan on the back and carrying on with the task of making drinks for the team.

Loki was more pleased, "Ya fucker...at bloody last, maybe now something interesting will happen?" Duncan continued his attack on the rogue access point, attempting to gain control of it, before probing deeper into the attached network.

Only ten minutes later, Duncan had full control of the access point. He moved on into the network, searching for a mail server, scanning for email systems, eventually finding one; but was it the right one? Hercule was becoming extremely interested in the goings on at the other side of the room and could no longer be contained. He walked over to where Duncan and Loki sat. "Perhaps I can be of some assistance here?" Loki looked up, "How would that be? Do you have an IP address of a mail system we might be able to use for example?" He laughed sarcastically. Hercule was less than happy about his treatment, but continued his conversation, mainly focusing on Duncan. Duncan smiled at Hercule. "What can you tell us about their internal network infrastructure?

Digital Force – www.z4ck.org

I can't keep scanning it; I'll trip every intrusion detection system for miles!" Hercule walked behind Duncan and Loki, making Loki slightly nervous. Peering over Duncan's shoulder he stated very slowly and deliberately the network address required.

Loki was incredulous, "Why didn't you give us that information in the first place?" Hercule now had the opportunity to be smug. "You would not let me! We tested the systems previously by sending a mail into the system that was sure to bounce. The mail headers gave us the information we needed." Duncan began testing to see if the system would respond to a connection on the mail port. Again he typed at the keyboard:

    netcat -v 192.168.1.14 25

It was the mail server, or at least one of the mail servers. The system allowed the connection and sat waiting for input. "Great, all we need to do now is gain access to the thing. The Sendmail system was running an old version of the software and had been left unpatched. Duncan used some exploit code he had just previously compiled to try to gain access to the system. Ares had now joined the men, and stood towering above them, waiting patiently. They had no idea if the exploit would work. What if the system had been configured to give out wrong information? It may not even have been Sendmail. A system banner could be easily changed to hide its identity. A nervous wait ensued, with Duncan beginning to sweat, aware that all eyes were on him and the Zaurus. "That's it! The exploit has worked; it has dropped me into the system. There it was - a shell prompt.

Quickly Duncan traversed the mail directories, finding the relevant mail file, which he quickly copied to his Zaurus, before shutting it down. Hopefully they had got out before they had been traced.

Duncan and Loki spent the next while trawling through Van Der Krueger's mail file, but to no avail. "Fucks sake, what a waste of time," stated a frustrated Loki. He put his Zaurus down on the table, got up, and walked across the room, kicking the dressing table at the other side, before finally sitting down on the bed dejected. Duncan gave a sigh, sitting back in his chair. "There is no mention of any Fourth Reich, or anything else to do with Nazi's. He hasn't even sent a prolific amount of mail to any one account that we might target. We'll have to get at his PC if we're to take this any further. There is no way of knowing where it is located." Loki agreed, "Having looked at the building I've figured out a way of getting someone in, but it's where to go from there!"

Hercule stepped forward, tentatively lifting his hand in the air, like a schoolboy who knew the answer but didn't want to show off. "I have the exact location of his computer. We have been watching him for a while." Loki sat up, "Well, well, the Belgy gets more useful by the minute. Ya beauty, how could I have ever doubted you? Give us the info and we'll get you your Nazi."

The tables were pulled together from each side of the room, finally signalling full co-operation between the two nations. For the next hour plans were made, checked and double checked. It was decided they would execute the plan tomorrow, the sooner the better. It had almost reached 5pm by the time the men finalised their plan for the following day. Ares summarised, "Okay, so it's agreed. Loki, as the buildings security is tight, we'll need a diversion to get us in. If you set off the fire alarm, Thor will use the opportunity to mingle with the staff whilst they are outside. When they go back in, you will walk back in. The mass influx will hopefully allow you to slip past security without a pass. I will detain Van Der Krueger long enough to give Thor enough time to get in and install a key logger on the target machine, or a direct tap on his phone. With a bit of luck, we'll have our information within a couple of days. Then it's show time."

All men agreed in unison. Tomorrow would be a crucial and potentially dangerous day. Duncan was about to have his first taste of physical insurgence, and he prayed to God he was up to it.

Chapter 4

Taking risks

The next morning began with breakfast at 8:30 am. Duncan had not slept at all well, seeing as today would be the first time he would attempt to get into a building with reasonably strict security. The men had taken their breakfast at separate times so as to draw minimal attention. Loki walked in just as Duncan finished his second cup of coffee. He had missed his English breakfast, but had to admit the croissants and strawberry jam had almost made up for it. Loki sat down, picked up a paper, and began to read it. He threw a quick glance of acknowledgement to Duncan, but nothing more. The waiter arrived, and Loki ordered his breakfast in Dutch, which impressed Duncan.

Finishing his coffee a couple of minutes later, he placed the china cup back onto its saucer and slid it across the white tablecloth. He gathered the crumbs of croissant up, before carefully depositing them onto the plate, rubbing his hands to get rid of the last of them. He got up from his comfortable, high backed chair, and left for his room, thanking the waiter as he left. The lift to the second floor was empty, allowing him to step in and check his hair in the mirror for the short time it took to ascend. Once back in his room, Duncan settled down at his Zaurus. He had hacked his way into an open access point prior to breakfast and was now taking advantage of his work, by happily checking his e-mail, whilst catching up with the latest news on Slashdot.

By 10:15AM Ares, Loki and Hercule had arrived. "Right," said Ares, "are we ready to go? Loki - is the information provided by Hercule enough to give you an idea of how to set off the fire alarm?" Loki answered quickly, "Of course, it's not the first time I've done this, is it?" Ares smiled and turned his attention to Duncan, ever mindful of using his codename when amongst outsiders. "Thor, do you have all the info you need?" Duncan was as sure as he could be. He had slight concerns about the amount of time he had to undertake the incursion, and worried that, once inside, his legendary sense of direction would get him lost. Not only did he have to get in, deploy a phone tap and a key logger, but he also had to somehow get out as well. "Right, let's go over the plan one more time. Loki will set off the fire alarm by means best known to him…just don't get caught!" Loki sat relaxing in his chair. "No problems big man, you'll see. The info provided by the Belgy over there will get me in…as long as it's not total shite!"

Ares continued, "Once the alarm goes off, Thor will enter the building whilst everyone else decants. Finding Van Der Krueger's desk, he will apply the adaptor to the phone socket, and install the key logger. I'll try to ensure that he has enough time to complete the task by keeping an eye on DeWitt, only intervening if necessary. After that, all we need to do is get out, come back here, and get the info we need."

Everyone nodded in agreement, showing they fully understood what was required. "Okay Loki, let's go." Loki smiled, casually got up from his chair, and left the room. "Caio, see you in a few mins." The men watched him through the window as he walked across the car park, then the road, and disappeared behind the Justus Lipsius building.

No more than five minutes passed before Duncan's Zaurus rang. He picked it up, "Okay, I'm ready," he said, his heart rate beginning to increase slightly. He carefully closed the clamshell lid, and along with Ares, started the walk down the stairs and out to the hotel car park. Across the road, as expected, the fire alarm had just gone off. Through the mass of windows at the front of the building, the three men could see people getting up in an orderly manner and heading to the doors. Duncan needed to move, and quickly.

Striding across the road, he headed for one of the fire exits to the rear of the building. At the very moment he reached the heavy door, it swung outwards and several people in expensive suits decanted, chatting and laughing with each other. Duncan tried to quickly squeeze past them, drawing some looks of disbelief. A man holding a newly lit cigarette stopped Duncan as he tried to enter. Duncan attempted to act as normally as possible. The man asked him in French where he was going. Duncan put on his best French accent and replied, "I have left something extremely expensive inside. I really need to get it. I will be quick!" The man shook his head before letting Duncan pass. Duncan quickly moved into the building, struggling up the stairs, moving as he was, against the mass of descending office workers. Although he seemed to be drawing some attention, no one else questioned him, all too busy leaving the building to ponder too much on his movements. Some two minutes later he had struggled to the third floor, to begin the task of searching for DeWitt's desk.

Ares scanned the front of the building. According to Hercule it would be likely that DeWitt would exit from the main door. As it was almost impossible for Ares to pick DeWitt out from his position in the car park, he too decided to cross the road. Carefully he limped across, neither too close to draw attention, nor too far away to watch his target. Still there was no sign of the tall, blonde, blue-eyed man in the reconnaissance photos.

Within minutes the red Mercedes fire engines of the Brussels regional fire brigade had appeared, and as he watched, Ares finally spotted the figure of DeWitt near the front door of the building. His consternation grew as the tall Arian put on a fire marshals hat and moved inside with some of the fire fighters. He realised he would have to warn Duncan to get out as quickly as possible. Dialling the touch screen on his Zaurus he got through to a slightly panicked Duncan on the other end. "Duncan, how's it going?" Duncan replied with a stutter, his nerves starting to get the better of him. Perspiration from his increased heart rate was becoming a problem, dripping into his eyes and blurring his vision slightly. He attempted to answer the call, whilst fumbling with the phone line connection located under Dewitt's desk.

"I'm okay. Why? Is there a problem?" Ares limped up and down nervously on the other side of the road. "You don't have much time. Get the kit in, and get the hell out. Try to use the back stairway that you came up. DeWitt has just entered through the front door." Duncan finally managed to plug the phone line into the telephone transmitter. "Right, that's that, thanks for the info. I've just got the key logger to fix into the back of the PC, won't be a second." Toward the end of the corridor Duncan could just hear the faint sound of footsteps. Listening carefully, he could just make out two, maybe three people, conversing in French. His heart began to pound harder as his sweating palms allowed the key logger to slip out of his grip and on to the floor. It landed on the thin, hardwearing carpet and bounced under the desk. "Damn," Duncan muttered under his breath. He looked round. The footsteps became louder - the voices closer and now very clear. A sudden surge of adrenaline gave him a sick feeling.

He made a snap decision to hide under the desk, scrambling for the key logger as he went. The voices and footsteps suddenly stopped. He held his breath as the men began to whisper to each other, the footsteps drawing slowly closer. Duncan knew he would have to get out before the staff spilled back into the building. He gulped, thinking of his next move. Would he make a run for it, or sit still and hope for the best?

For what seemed an age, Duncan crouched quietly under DeWitt's desk, not daring to breathe, as the men wandered almost aimlessly around the office. Cramp was beginning to set in, his thigh and calf muscles burning. He wished he had chosen a more comfortable squatting position - if there was such a thing. Eventually the voices grew more distant, the footsteps fading again. Duncan let out a quiet gasp, and drew in some fresh air, before peeking out cautiously from under the desk. He quickly plugged the key logger into the keyboard port on the PC, before finally crawling out from his hiding place. The coast was clear. He quickly got up, and headed along several corridors, mindful of not slamming the interconnecting doors. After what seemed an age he entered the stairwell. The grey carpets and warm surroundings of the office gave way to the echo of its cold empty stone walls and dark stairs. The acoustics were not designed for the nervous. The exit through which he had entered was still open, and through it he could see the shadows of several workers inbound.

He never thought playing hide and seek would stand him in good stead for anything; he was wrong. He exited the building as the office staff began to stream back in. He had made it - walking through the on-coming crowd, the same man who had stopped him earlier waved to him, asking in French, "Did you get it?" Duncan smiled, "Yes thanks," and with that he moved on up the street, keeping to the same side of the road, not crossing for the moment. Once he felt he had walked far enough down the Rue de la Loi, he quickly crossed. Doubling back, he headed to the Crowne Plaza. He was calm now, relief sweeping over him in torrents, as he realised that, for the moment at least, he was out of danger. He was glad to have made it out without raising any suspicions, or so he thought.

Through the glass frontage of the Justus Lipsius building, a shadowy figure could be made out, hovering almost ghost like next to one of the windows at the far end of the building. He had not decanted during the fire alarm; neither had he any intention of it. What's more, he had watched with great interest everything that had gone on over the past thirty minutes. He now studied Duncan as he walked in through the front entrance of the Crowne Plaza hotel. He smiled to himself, before walking down the corridor to one of the large glass offices where he closed the door and sat down to relax in his executive chair.

DeWitt walked back to his desk, chatting and laughing with one of his fellow workers, when suddenly he stopped and stared. He was sure he had pushed his chair in when he had left. He always did. So why was it three feet away? He shrugged his shoulders, slightly confused, but decided not to waste too many brain cycles on it. He pulled it back to the desk, sat down, and logged into his machine, little knowing that his every keystroke was now being monitored.

There was great excitement in Duncan's room as the men congratulated each other on successfully planting the required surveillance equipment. The telephone receiver had been tuned to a frequency of 80 MHz, allowing the men to listen to DeWitt's telephone conversations. Ares had also set up his Zaurus to act as a secure Internet server. The advanced keylogger had already started transmitting encrypted data back to it, traversing the European Community firewall infrastructure, on its way to the tiny but powerful computer. All they needed to do was sit and wait. They were sure that it would be a matter of days, maybe, if they were lucky hours before they had all the information they needed.

So they waited, hours turning into a day, and then another. By the third day the men were becoming irritable. "Does this bastard do any work?" asked Loki, bored and frustrated. "He has been on his phone almost all day, and it has all been complete crap! It's the gravy train alright." Duncan sat in front of Ares' Zaurus, watching the log file increase in size, as website after website was surfed, laborious EU policy documents were typed, and internal e-mails were sent. But there was nothing of interest - nothing at all. He sat back in the chair. "Fuck this for a game of soldiers; let's get out of here before our brains turn to mush." Ares stood patiently at the window watching both the Berlaymont and the Justus Lipsius. Occasionally an attractive female would pass by, catching his attention, giving a welcome break to the monotony. "Yeah, let's take a break, if there are any interesting calls the system will record them…same with the logs. Let's get out of here, this is going nowhere."

Loki jumped up, "Hallefuckinlujah big man! Come on Duncan Donuts…get yer lardy arse out of that chair and we'll go and get a drink. I could murder a pint or five!"

The men gathered their important belongings, before locking the door and heading down the stairs. "I hear Kitty O'Sheas is good. Let's head there. Terminus surely can't grudge us an afternoon off," said Ares.

The men walked down the busy side streets of Brussels, eventually reaching Boulevard Charlemagne, the location of the well known Kitty O'Sheas. They walked in, Duncan following a more than eager Loki, but entering before Ares, who, always cautious, made a final check of the surrounding area. The Irish theme pub was one of a group, but seemed more genuine than many other run-of-the-mill theme pubs that had sprung up in competition. The Irish music playing in the background added to the lively atmosphere; its heavy drum beat immediately lifting Duncan's mood.

For a short moment he felt he was on holiday; able to forget the pressure of the task he was undertaking. The dark oak roof beams matched both the flooring and seating, much of which was arranged in small booths, able to accommodate between four and six people each. Intimate tables for two were located against the walls, providing an ample space for drunken revelry around the bar. The centre of the room was dominated by a large square bar area, its dark polished oak, gleaming in the sunlight which radiated through the window on this summers day. Irish memorabilia amongst other objects of interest were hung on walls around the room, and from hooks on the bar. To complete the authenticity, there was a smattering of red-haired Irish bar maids mingling amongst the odd Australian or local.

Duncan was surprised at how busy it was considering it was Thursday afternoon. There must have been almost a hundred patrons there. The men moved toward the bar area, Loki stating boisterously that he would get the first drinks in. He smiled at the attractive red haired barmaid, before ordering for the three men. Ares and Duncan sat down in a booth and began to study the menu. "Here ye go, get that down you," stated Loki, slamming two pints of Stella, and a pint of Guinness on the table. Ares picked up the pint of Guinness, and saluted his two colleagues. "All the best!" The scar at the side of his mouth contracted as he smiled. Loki was as hyperactive as ever, gulping down his drink, finishing half of it in a single breath, almost before he had even finished sitting down.

Duncan didn't feel he had much in common with Loki. He knew he was efficient and seemingly devoid of adrenaline. His highly aggressive nature, quick temper, and crude demeanour made Duncan feel that he was someone to be avoided, rather than befriended. The short, wiry man had no problem in finding trouble, or conversely, looking after himself. The more Duncan got to know Loki, the more he was reminded of Begby, the character from the film Trainspotting. Duncan knew it was best not to get on his wrong side. Ares, on the other hand, was an entirely different matter. He had spent quite a lot of time with the giant of a man. A trained killer, almost ten years his senior, had been an excellent mentor and Duncan hoped, at some stage a good friend. If there was anyone Duncan felt he could rely on it was Ares. His stories were legendary - always funny or relevant depending on the mood. Talk on any subject and Ares could recount a relevant, interesting, or funny story. In contrast, Loki talked of car chases, or which 'big bastard' he had battered at some stage or another.

Ares tolerated Loki to a certain extent. They often argued, but Ares was almost the only person Loki had any respect for. Duncan wasn't exactly sure why this was the case, but he was thankful, as it at least meant that Ares could exert a modicum of control on an otherwise dangerous wild card.

Duncan on the whole kept himself to himself. The hacking was important to him. He had a thirst for knowledge and new techniques, but had not really learned anything since joining CyberSecure and the Echelon network. He found it incredible that he had access to almost all of the world's secrets at his fingertips. The technology was good too; kit that money couldn't buy, and if even if it could, he couldn't afford. That said - the money was not at all bad.

He stared into his beer, tired from the continuous, less than glamorous monitoring he had been doing over the last couple of days. He hadn't slept particularly well; log files and IP addresses rattling around his head had disturbed his already troubled sleep.

"Hey Donut ye fucker…it's your round. A man could die of thirst in this place!" These words, blurted out by Loki, brought Duncan back to reality. Being called Duncan Donut was also beginning to get on his nerves. But what could he do? "If you don't mind, I'd appreciate it if you wouldn't call me that. It's starting to piss me off!" Loki laughed, "Ooh, it's starting to piss me off!" he repeated in a sarcastic tone. Duncan ignored the remark, squeezing past Loki. He turned to him and Ares. "Are we going to order some food? I'm starving." Both Ares and Loki agreed that this was a good idea, and subsequently chose items from the menu. "Right I'll be back in a second." The bar was becoming steadily busier, and accordingly, it was taking longer to get to there. Squeezing through a couple of groups, and reaching it, Duncan eventually managed to attract the attention of the barmaid by waving his money in the air. In less than a minute she had taken both his order, and his money.

The men sat and chatted. Loki becoming louder as the evening went on and his small frame filled up with alcohol. The hands of the clock hanging on the wall directly opposite from their booth, seemed to travel round the face more quickly the later it got. It was getting late, past 11 P.M, and Loki showed no signs of lowering the volume. He had however, lowered the tone.

"Wooahh, they're fucking gorgeous!" he roared, pointing at a couple of girls standing in the centre of the floor. The bar was packed, and luckily the noise levels were high enough for him not to be noticed by too many other people. Duncan was glad about this. The last thing he and Ares wanted was to attract any attention. Loki didn't seem to care anymore. The testosterone and alcohol were taking control. "I told you not to drink too much," Ares shouted across the table. Loki rolled his eyes, "Who the fuck are you, my mother?" Duncan was becoming uneasy. "Let's just calm down eh, we're here to enjoy ourselves." Loki threw his arm round Duncan. "I am mate, just be a good little donut and get me another pint!"

With that he slapped Duncan on the back of the head.

Duncan bought more drinks from the bar. Laying them down, he addressed both Ares and Loki, "I think this should be our last one, don't you?" Loki gave him a derisory look, "Aw, c'mon," his words were slurred, as he began to sway back and forth across the table, pointing at Duncan, "Are you trying to spoil my fun, ye wee bass?" This was the most threatening tone that Loki had used yet. Ares raised his hand, "Loki, Thor is right, we should drink up…it's been a long day!" Loki laughed, "Thor, that's a fucking stupid name, it should've been donuts." He gulped his pint down, slamming the glass on the table. He was now starting to attract the attention of the other customers in the pub. "Ah, fuck ye. I'm off."

Loki got up from the table and began the journey out of the crowded pub. Swaying from side to side, he bumped and bungled his way into several people. So many in fact that Duncan couldn't tell if it was deliberate. Surely he wasn't looking to start trouble was he? Ares indicated that they should follow him, and both he and Duncan left the booth. Their fears were not unfounded.

At the other end of the pub Loki had become an unwelcome interruption in a group get together. He had already thrown crude remarks at the females of the party, and was squaring up to two of the young men. They towered above his tiny, slim figure, pushing him backwards, towards the door. Ares shouted to Duncan, "Quick run up there, and break it up, we don't have much time!" It was too late. Loki sprung like a cat, butting the nearest man in the face. He dropped like a sack of potatoes as blood sprayed from the ridge of his broken nose. The women in the party screamed as others turned to see what the commotion was. The man had not even hit the ground when a well aimed kicked to the head knocked him unconscious.

Ares had now got close enough to intervene, whilst the other males in the group attempted to grab Loki. Duncan headed for the door just a few metres away, holding it open to allow the overspill he expected in the next few minutes.

Ares grabbed Loki and pulled him outside. His fore-head and white T-Shirt stained with the blood of his hapless victim. Duncan and Ares hauled him down the street as fast as they could, Ares shouting at him, "You arsehole. I'm definitely reporting you, you're a fucking liability...let's just hope that group doesn't follow us. The group were following; four men, all in their early twenties had decided that the little bastard who had led the unprovoked attack would pay.

Having careered up the Boulevard Charlemagne, they soon caught up with the small group; the first man lunging towards Loki was stopped instantly by a lightning punch from Ares; well timed, and heavier than Duncan had ever seen. The man's jaw cracked, he staggered, and then dropped to the ground, out cold. The second grabbed at Loki, who swivelled on his heels and delivered a roundhouse kick to the throat. He too fell to the floor, clenching his throat and gasping for breath. Loki attempted to follow through with a kick, but was knocked off balance by Ares, who grabbed his arm. Ares held his arm out, warning the other men to stay back, stopping them in their tracks. They hesitated, deciding it was better not to end up on the floor in the same manner as their colleagues. Ares grabbed Loki by the neck and hauled him, kicking and screaming down the road, whilst Duncan led the way - glad he had not had to get involved.

Loki had calmed down by the time the men had staggered back to the hotel at nearly 11:45PM, but the blood on his T-Shirt still raised a few disapproving glares from the reception staff. Eventually getting up the stairs, they entered Loki's room to ensure he got to bed safely. True to form, he started to protest, demanding he had another drink from the mini bar. Duncan was an easy target, and soon Loki began squaring up to him, whilst Duncan attempted to calm him down.

Ares had had enough. He tapped Loki on the shoulder, and as he turned to face him, a heavy fist thundered into the middle of his face, causing him to stumble onto the bed - unconscious. Ares bent over him to check his breathing, before getting up and dusting some dried blood off his shirt. "There, that should shut the little arse up till tomorrow!" Duncan was stunned, "He'll go berserk in the morning." Ares laughed, "What, Loki? He won't remember a thing. If his face hurts, we just need to remind him about the fight he started. No, it'll be fine; this is not the first time the stupid little twat has got himself into bother." He shook his now aching fist, "Boy…that was enjoyable, he's needed that for a while! Anyway, let's get some sleep; this has been too eventful; let's hope there are no repercussions from this."

Duncan awoke next morning to a small glint of sunshine slicing through the space in the middle of the heavy velvet curtains. It found its way to his face, causing him to turnover and bury his head in the pillow. He had a headache, which thumped like a drummer going into battle. He groaned, and thought about getting out of the bed; but lifting his head made it all the worse. Duncan lifted his arm to look at his wristwatch, finding it difficult to focus on the small silver hands. The realisation that it was almost 9:30 A.M made him jump out of the bed, causing a dull jarring in his skull. "Christ, that's the last time I drink for a while!" He limped slowly to the bathroom, and filled a glass with water, which he drank greedily.

It tasted awful, but he finished it, and filling it again, drank some more. He reeked of stale beer and cigarettes. It was time for a shower.

Following a quick shower, and even quicker continental breakfast, Duncan headed back to his room to be met by Ares, waiting on the small seat in the corridor. Loki could be heard grumbling at the end of the lobby as he made his way down to meet them. "How is he?" Duncan asked Ares. "Ares smiled, "You'll see!"

Loki had two black eyes. The powerful punch from Ares had radiated outward, causing bruising across the ridge of the nose and round both of his eyes. A myriad of colours, from deep reds near the tear ducts, to light green on the outer rim of his eyes covered Loki's small, battle hardened face. "Who the fuck did this to me?" he said, pointing to his eyes. Ares laughed, "You did it to yourself you stupid fool. Don't you remember the fight we bailed you out of? You were getting a real kicking?" Loki looked flummoxed, "Err...nope...don't remember that one." Ares shook his head, "Drink, it's got a lot to answer for. Anyway let's get on, we're late already."

Duncan could see Loki desperately trying to remember what had gone on the night before. He couldn't. He just had to accept Ares' account, and ensure he didn't aggravate his painful nose.

"So, what exciting bits of information are we going to pick up today?" Loki said, rather sarcastically. "This has all been a complete waste of time...chasing some stupid, supposed Belgian Nazi group. I mean...these Belgies are a bit boring to be getting into anything as exciting as that. The Fourth Reich...even the name is stupid!"

By this time Duncan had sat down at the Zaurus, and was peering into the tiny screen, scrolling carefully through the log files. Ares donned the headphones, playing back through the previous evenings wiretaps. Loki simply put his feet up, and opened his complimentary copy of the local paper, turning to the sport, even though foreign news was of little interest to him.

A short while had passed in which time Ares moved forwards and backwards through the digital recordings. He was surprised by their clarity. He was able to distinguish every piece of spoken French, the main language within the European Union. Suddenly he cocked his head to one side, screwing up his face, concentrating. A call had grabbed his attention. It was in Dutch, or Flemish, he wasn't sure, but it was obvious that it had made Van Der Krueger agitated. "Loki, come here a minute, I think I've got something, but I'm not sure what is being said." Loki jumped up, dumped his paper on the bed, and bounded the short distance across the room, almost wrenching the earphones from Ares' head. He put them on, "Well, play the fuckin tape then," he said, motioning to Ares.

He listened for a second, "Yep, this is in Dutch. The caller is simply saying he picked up the email that DeWitt had deposited, and that Saturday at the arranged time is good for them. He then starts on about something to do with troops or soldiers." Loki became more excited as he listened on, "He's now getting a bollocking from DeWitt for calling him on this line, being told not to be so stupid in future. He then tells him to get off." Loki looked up, "The call is then terminated."

Ares was pleased with the information. "Thank Christ for that. I was starting to think this was a waste of bloody time!" Duncan stood up. "You're not going to believe this. I think he's actually typed the email from his workstation -

not so clever after all! I've got a mail server address, an account and password. It seems that they use this account as a deposit box. They never send anything from it, only creating draft messages. That way, messages can't get picked up as they travel through various networks; sneaky." Loki and Ares moved across to the Zaurus. "Well, let's have a look before he deletes it!"

Duncan quickly brought up a browser window, inserted the website URL, and logged into the mail system. "Jesus, check this out! Everything you could want is here. Website hit lists, attack types, targets, and internal memos." He suddenly stopped, the colour draining from his face; a shadow cast across his face as he drew his gaze away from the screen to the keyboard. "What the fuck is the matter?" shouted Loki, bemused by Duncan's behaviour. Duncan simply pointed to the screen, "Read that!" he said, in what could only be described as a low pitched whisper.

Loki picked the small computer system up, adjusting its screen to allow him to read it better in the glare of the summer sun, which forced its way into the room. "It's in English!" he said with some surprise. "The plan to obtain agent 'H', who is close to our discovery, is go." read Loki. "Yeah, but read the end of the mail." Duncan said, not raising his head. Loki continued, "Saturday, at the arranged time, will be the termination point. The first but not last. It will serve as a warning to those who would attempt to stop the greater good of both the Flemish and Arian peoples. "Why is that in English?" Duncan asked. "All other communication is Dutch, French, or Flemish."

Ares ventured a guess, "I think this is maybe bigger than we thought. Most of the communication is between certain parts of the group. Maybe it is in English for those components within the group coming from further away? Most people in Europe speak English...how many Brits speak any other languages? No matter what, we've got to warn Hercule, just in case he is agent 'H' in the messages. We've definitely got to gatecrash this party; looks like this one is a goer after all!" Loki smiled, "Magic, something interesting to do at last!"

Chapter 5

Rallying Point

Ares put down the Zaurus, having left a warning for Hercule. He looked concerned, glancing at his watch as he sat down on his chair. He had a habit of limping around when speaking on his mobile phone; something that annoyed the hell out of Loki. "Thank God you've sat down. You would've worn a hole in the bloody carpet with all that pacing around! Up and down, up and down...bloody arse!" He paused to take breath, "Well, what's happening then?" Ares scratched his head. "No answer, so I left a message. Hope we're not too late!" Duncan walked over to the window. Shielding his eyes from the glaring sun, he peered across to the Justus Lipsius building, squinting in an attempt to focus on the people wandering its corridors. "Do you ever get the feeling you're being watched?" Loki laughed, "Don't be fucking stupid...see these newbie's, either gung-ho or paranoid!" He had gone back to reading his paper with his feet up on the desk. "The Belgy will be alright; he's due here in the next half hour anyway isn't he? Christ you guys worry about nothing. Now, more importantly, will someone put the kettle on, the drinking last night has left me as dry as a nuns chuff!"

Ares joined Duncan at the window. "I know what you mean. We just need to keep an eye out and be careful not to be too obvious. Tomorrow is going to be risky, believe me. We'll just scout around the area first...if we find anyone in danger, then it'll be time to act. It's unlikely we'll be able to finish this tomorrow. It'll be just too risky.

Duncan was slightly relieved by this. He hadn't fancied walking into a hall full of hostile Nazis, even if he was accompanied by Loki and Ares.

Another hour had passed, and with no sign of Hercule the group were now becoming concerned. Ares had attempted to reach him twice more, with no luck. "It just keeps ringing out. There's something not right here. We're going to have to hope they haven't already got to him."

Duncan continued to monitor the key logger, watching DeWitt compose a large proposal detailing cross border co-operation between Russia and Finland. Ares had begun pacing awkwardly around the room again, to the great annoyance of Loki. Finally, after the second barrage of verbal abuse from Loki, he decided to sit down in the chair next to Duncan. "Found anything interesting?" Duncan replied, "Not really, just a document proposing that Russians from border towns should be able to use Finnish hospitals. It's strange that someone who sets up these things can, on the other hand, have such a racist streak in him. Ares was used to seeing such contradiction. "It's the way of the world, lad, it's the way of the world."

The men continued to chat until Duncan suddenly raised his hand, "Wait a minute, he's logging in to their secure mail server." Loki, who had been slouching on one of the comfortable chairs, sat up and took notice. "Shit, they've got him!" Duncan blurted out. Loki pulled himself out of his chair. "Go on, read it then!" Duncan drew his finger back across the text. "It simply say's Agent H obtained. Meeting is YES, as arranged from earlier communication."

Duncan picked the Zaurus up from the desk. "Shouldn't we try to find him now, before this meeting? I don't think it's a good idea to go rushing into this tonight. Besides, what if we turn up too late, or Hercule is being tortured. He could give the game away!" Loki smiled, "You're right, we should find him, and kill him before he says too much!" Ares was not amused by Loki's quip. "It's not really a laughing matter. We're going to have to get him back somehow, but we've no idea where he is. I don't think they know anything about us, and are less than likely to ask him about it. No, we'll get to this meeting tomorrow, early, and then we'll sort it out."

The clock had just struggled its way past 4:30pm on the evening of Saturday 16th. Duncan was becoming more nervous as the clocks hands edged its way to the deadline of 6pm. He knew at any moment there would be a knock at the door and they would be ready to go. He dreaded it. Although he had been trained, this was the first time where he felt he could be in mortal danger; a thought he did not relish.

His heart pounded faster as Ares knocked on the door and beckoned him to join them. He quickly picked up his black leather jacket, which had been draped over one of the chairs. He was never one for hanging clothes up. He spotted the SLC-3000 in the corner, but decided to leave it, fearing it may get broken, or worse, fall into the hands of others; the installation of Z4CK was still active, although hidden. If some other hacking group, which The Fourth Reich was, got their hands on it, there was the potential for great damage. No, he would stuff it in a drawer, and leave it there for safety.

Finally, he looked around the room, checking his pockets to ensure he had everything he needed. For a change, he had. He exited the room, where both Loki and Ares stood waiting, and locked the door behind him. Loki smiled, "This is where the fun begins." His eyes sparkled with adrenaline. It was obvious he was looking forward to taking someone out, and he was thriving on the possibility. Ares was more subdued. It had been a while since he had been out in the field, but his military training ensured that he was as best prepared for this as possible. To the astonishment of Duncan, both men produced guns. "Where the fuck did you get those?" asked Duncan in disbelief. Loki replied, "You don't need to know hacker boy. You do your job, and leave the important stuff to the men!"

"So am I not to be armed?" Ares produced a six-inch knife encased in a leather sheath. "I've taught you how to use this, hopefully you won't need to! Now come on, we've no time to lose." All three men left the Crowne Plaza, heading into the car park, where they all piled into a car that had been organized the day before. "You know where you're going Loki, do you?" Loki fastened his seat belt, "Just get your fucking seat belt on, and leave this to me. We'll be there faster than you can hack a Windows server." Duncan smiled, "Didn't know you knew what a Windows server was!" Loki retorted quickly, "I wouldn't laugh mate; right now it's more secure than you!" Duncan quickly sunk back into his seat. He had been feeling slightly better about the situation. Loki took off at breakneck speed - the wheels spinning violently, threw up a cloud of smoke, screeching like an eagle attacking its prey.

It was easy to notice the Renault Megane leaving the Crowne Plaza car park. Two individuals had a particularly good view of it from their common vantage point on the third floor of the Justus Lipsius building. One of the men refocused his binoculars on the window of Duncan's room. They waited five minutes, before synchronising their watches. Walking to the older man's office, they completed their preparations; putting on light brown trench coats made of thin material, ideal for the summer weather, but still official looking. Each man stuffed a pair of light gloves into his pockets. Finally they picked up their ID badges, and loaded their weapons.

"Tu es pret?" asked the older man. The younger man nodded, "Oui. Je suis pret!" The older man smiled, and walked calmly towards to the glass door, followed by the younger man. They stepped calmly out of the lift, and exited the building, whereupon the older man got into a waiting car. The driver simply nodded as he was ordered to drive. The younger man looked over at the rather ugly Crowne Plaza hotel, scanning the area for any sign of someone watching or returning. His walk took on an official manner as he entered the building, and headed to the reception desk. He held up a badge, which the receptionist studied for a second; a look of surprise crossed her face. He delved into his inside pocket, from which he produced a search warrant, placing it on the reception desk. The duty manager had walked over, interested in the proceedings. He pulled the paper towards him, whilst looking up to study the Belgian's badge. The young man spoke; his voice stern, and curt. "I required the key to room 247. This is official business."

With slight hesitation, the key was placed in the man's outstretched hand. Hercule Riboud, or Hercule, as Loki, Duncan and Ares knew him, began the walk up the stairs. His goal of obtaining a customised Zaurus SLC-3000, and the hacking tool known to them as Z4CK, was now in sight.

Loki drove through the streets at a ridiculous pace, considering it was nearing rush hour in the Belgian capital. The almost maniacal driving of the Belgians did not please him one little bit. He shouted, cursed, and shook his fist at almost every motorist, whether they sat in front or behind him. Ares asked him to calm down and concentrate on the road, which drew a frustrated look. At around 5:20pm, they drove in to one of the newly developed suburbs of Brussels, where Loki slowed to a pace that pleased Duncan. On most occasions he would have sat back in relief, but nervous tension prevented him from relaxing at this time. As they drove around looking for a place to stop, Ares tapped the dashboard, and pointed to a large house which was being renovated. "Here it is, on our left. Thank God, it seems to be nearly finished. I certainly wasn't looking forward to making my way through mud, cement or sand.

They drove on, travelling another hundred yards down the road, before parking the black Megane in a side street. They sat for a few seconds, checking the plan. "Right," Ares began, "Two objectives; get Hercule back, and deal with Van Der Krueger as quickly, and quietly as possible. Loki, from your reconnaissance yesterday, you found there is a back entrance that we can enter?" Loki undid his seatbelt, "That's right. So if you follow me, we can get in there, and get a good position before it all kicks off."

All three men got out of the car, attempting not to attract too much attention. Luckily, most people living in this area were at work, and had not yet returned, making the task easier than it might have been. They hurried along the street, Ares' limp holding him up somewhat.

On turning the corner they only had a short walk to the building. Standing three stories tall, it had once been a remarkable piece of architecture, but had fallen into disrepair. Following the death of the owners it had sat empty for almost twenty years, until a Belgian developer had decided to purchase it; splitting it into what looked like three luxury flats, one on each floor. Most of the buildings red brick walls and slate roof had been vandalised at some stage, or suffered rain damage. Weeds grew thick in the front garden, something which wasn't, as yet, a priority for the developers.   Ares studied its frontage.   There was no obvious way in. "You said there was a way in round the back...are you sure?" Loki smiled, "of course I am, come on."

All three men made their way over a two foot wall, and crossed to the left hand side of the house as quickly as possible. Duncan was tempted to look through one of the large bay windows, but was quickly ushered on by Ares. A new wooden gate, six foot high, and three foot wide, as yet unpainted, linked a tall boundary wall to the building. Loki quietly lifted the latch, and followed by the other two men, crept down the small unfinished path, grass protruding through the cracks in its paving stones.

Suddenly he stopped and held his hand up, indicating that he had heard a noise coming from the back garden. Ares gestured to Loki to produce his gun; something which Ares had already done. He moved in front of Duncan, pushing him back, and against the wall. The men carried on down the last few yards of the path, clinging as tightly to the wall as they could. Loki peeked round the corner, and into the considerably sized garden. There was no-one there. At least, they could see no-one. It would have been possible for someone to hide in the large clumps of weeds scattered around the area, or behind the cement mixers and other building machinery. The tall wall at the back provided no easy exit for escape Ares noticed. Loki continued scanning the area for movement.

A rustling, then a crash, made the men jump. Instinctively Loki aimed his gun in the general direction of the disturbance, only to see a small black cat scarper across the garden, and knock over a loosely assembled pile of building tools. From there it lunged onto the top of the garden wall. Having reached its goal, the cat glanced round at the figure of Loki, arms stretched out before him, gun aimed in its direction. Loki shook his head, "You lucky bastard, you nearly got it there!" The cat stood motionless, watching Loki; before deciding that it was best to leave it's foraging for another time. In a flash it had disappeared into next doors garden. Ares and Duncan joined Loki at the end of the path. "It would be handy to be able to move like that right now," Duncan said, loosening the tense grip on his knife. "Cats - fucking rodents if you ask me," Loki stated, shoving the gun back in his short denim jacket.

Ares took control, moving up to the back door. "Right, let's not forget what we're here for, open this door then, its nearly time." Loki produced a slim, white piece of hardened plastic, not unlike a credit card. He quickly studied the door, carefully turning the brass door handle and pushing forward. The door did not budge. Loki turned his attention to a small Yale lock positioned just below head height. Slotting the plastic between the doorframe and the door, he gave it a quick nudge. With a click the door unlocked, allowing him to carefully open it and step inside. He crept cautiously through the ground floor rooms, before quietly returning to the front door and beckoning the other two men into the house.

Duncan was nervous. He had never broken into a house before, except in training. The last time he had been anywhere he shouldn't have, with the exception of someone else's computer system, had been in his childhood; playing on the building site that had been his local estate in the early days, before the buildings had been completed. In those days it was only the watchman he had run from, and he never carried a gun.

Ares and Duncan stepped inside, aware that time was now ticking; 5:45 - the group would meet in 15 minutes. They would be here; how many, they didn't know. Loki had crept carefully up the stairs, and could be heard walking around, the refurbished floorboards creaking as he moved. After a few more minutes he rushed back down. "All clear, should we move up?" Ares shook his head. "No, we may have a better vantage point up there, but it's best to stay here, better access if we need to make an escape. We wouldn't want to be trapped on the first floor with no way out, would we?" The others agreed.

The ground floor was an empty shell. White washed walls, some complete, some midway through plastering work, reached upward fourteen feet to the decorative cornices. Bare light cables dangled from the centre of the ceiling, surrounded by an ornate centrepiece; an original feature. The old floorboards had not yet been polished, lying under a covering of concrete dust, dried mud, and the odd splash of white paint. Builders' tools lay on upturned boxes, next to yards of coiled black, grey, and red cables. The living room, as it was, extended from the front to the back, a clear view straight to the garden was provided by a large window, next to the door through which they had so tentatively entered. Ares looked for hiding places, beckoning everyone else to join him in one of the bedrooms off to the left. The time was near. All three men fell silent as they waited for their targets and their Belgian colleague to arrive. Duncan felt it was already too late for Hercule.

Two floors up, watching from their control room, behind a false panel in the wall, three members of the Fourth Reich watched the crouching British agents with great amusement. The house, although incomplete, had many features several intelligence agencies would have been proud of. The darkened control room housed computer systems and other equipment useful for digital attacks. Monitors displaying the current Internet virus trends sat next to those showing the immediate vicinity; the back garden, and street out front.

The British agents had been watched every step of the way. A tall man dressed in black put a mobile phone to his ear. He conversed in Flemish. "Yes, as expected they are here. No they didn't find us. They are crouching in the bedroom as we speak!" He smiled, listening to the man on the other end of the phone burst into laughter. "Yes, we will see you soon." He flipped the lid closed on the phone and put it down on the table, before quietly folding his arms to wait the others to arrive. A look of satisfaction filled his young face as he looked at the table in front of him. The telephone transmitter and key logger sat there, a trophy of the day.

They had seen and used technology like this before. How easy it had been to trap the British he thought to himself. Another man with a pale complexion, slightly shorter, walked up behind him and peered into the monitor, shaking his head. "Soon, we will see what they are made of; judging by their performance so far, not much I think!"

Hercule stood in front of a dark heavy door. The polished brass numbers 247 reflected and skewed his image as he gazed at them. This is the room in which he had stood with the British agents - leading them into the trap, just as the Fourth Reich had asked. It had gone surprisingly smoothly, he felt; something which was obviously aided by the far-reaching power and government positions held by members of the group. He had liked Ares and Duncan. They were polite, helpful, and willing to listen. He felt slightly saddened that their time was up; but the needs of The Fourth Reich were greater than those of a couple of British agents. One day, a Flemish country, independent of Belgium would stand proud within a Europe where Arian and Nordic races, the original rulers, once more held power. As for Loki, misfits like him would find themselves locked away; disappearing amongst his own kind, the violent and disturbed. Like the Nazis before them, the highly powerful members of the Fourth Reich had answers to many of what they perceived to be Europe's problems.

Hercule took one final look around, before quietly unlocking the door, and pushing it open. He had been tasked with obtaining as many new technologies as possible, to help the group in their digital insurgence and information gathering. With the exception of the Zaurus SLC-3000 used by the men, he had seen nothing new or startling. Whilst snooping around various secure networks, the group had come to hear of Z4CK, and it was this he wished to obtain. The British agents had been careful to keep Z4CK from his prying eyes, using only defined hacking techniques to obtain information when he was around. He was sure however, that getting his hands on a Zaurus would afford access to the software.

He walked up to the window, checking to ensure the Megane had not returned to the car park. Of course it had not. He smiled, and continued his search round the room, initially checking the worktops, before going through the various drawers and cupboards. Finally, he came to a mahogany bedside cabinet, on which a half finished cup of coffee sat, next to the Gideon's bible. He opened the drawer, and pulled out Duncan's Zaurus SLC-3000, which he held for a second, examining the outer case, the infra-red port, and the other wireless accessories. He flipped open the dull grey, Titanium lid; the TFT display burst into life. On a white background of shimmering pixels sat a Bio-metrics fingerprint screen, which waited silently for his imprint. Surely nothing would happen if he tried it just once? His curiosity was great. A PDA with Biometric finger print recognition was something special, and he simply had to try it, just to see what happened. He carefully positioned his thumb on the screen, and waited. The unit switched itself off, the screen going dark. He removed his thumb, and gave the machine a bemused look.

Hercule closed and reopened the lid, but nothing. He pushed frantically at the on button - again nothing. On providing an incorrect print, the Zaurus had fired the ultimate security mechanism. An electro magnetic pulse, a side effect of Riddle's research into Ion Cannons, which had completely crippled the electronics. The Zaurus was now no more than a thin lump of Titanium, crystal, and plastic.

Hercule was angry. How could he have been so stupid? The Fourth Reich would not be pleased at this loss. His rage and frustration grew almost instantly, kicking over a table, which stood in his path. On reaching the door, he turned and threw the Zaurus hard against the wall, before storming out of the room. He slammed the door, which bounced back open with the force, before composing himself, walking calmly down the stairs, and out of the Crowne Plaza. Perhaps the others would obtain a Zaurus and the means by which to use it? The Zaurus lay on the floor of room 247, just beyond the bed, near the window. The titanium shell was unscathed, but the device was now useless; the pulse of energy that had seared through its circuits, bringing instant shutdown.

A black car drew up at the front of the arranged meeting place. A tall, grey haired man, in his early fifties, got out of the car followed closely by the driver. The grey haired man exuded an air of confidence. He fastened his long coat, and put on the leather gloves he had removed during the short journey. Finally, he pulled the jacket taut, before nodding to the driver who stood next to him. They knew they would not be ambushed. They knew exactly where the British agents were located, and in due course, they had a good idea of how they would deal with them. They moved on through the overgrown front garden, down the side lane, and into the back garden. A Fourth Reich officer communicated the British agents' position at all times through an earpiece worn by the older man. The driver took the lead as they entered the house, carefully closing the door behind them. Walking to the centre of the unfinished room, they produced small handguns, which they pointed directly at the door to the bedroom. The three British agents finally began to sense there was a problem. What had happened to this supposed rally? Where were the Fourth Reich members? Who were these two men?

Loki, Ares and Duncan crouched behind the door of the bedroom, little knowing their location and every move was known. Duncan was feeling a combination of emotions. He was relieved that a large group of neo-Nazis had not appeared, but this was paralleled by the confusion of what was actually going on. Loki was itching to confront the two men, and Ares seemed to agree; after all, they were all armed, and they had the element of surprise…

"Let's get this over and done with. We came to terminate them, let's do it!" said Loki. Ares whispered to Loki, reminding him that Van Der Krueger was the target, and that anything else had not been sanctioned. "Fuck sanctions!" Loki got up from behind the door, and prepared to charge, to be met by two guns pointed in his direction not ten foot away. In an instant he pulled the trigger, the gun emitting a loud bang, but nothing else. For once Loki's adrenaline levels soared as he realised they had been duped. The gun was firing blanks. Duncan and Ares quickly followed, but they too were halted. Loki turned to Ares, hands in the air. "We've been set up; the Belgy fuck gave us blanks…the whole thing was a trap."

The grey haired man and his driver stood before them, occupying the centre of the room. Three more men walked calmly down the stairs to their right, outnumbering and trapping the British. Ares noticed that Van Der Krueger led them. On descending the stairs, two of the men took positions behind the British, whilst Van Der Krueger joined the grey haired man and his driver. Duncan's blood ran cold, this was it...he was sure it was the end. The man with the grey hair began, his English almost perfect. "Let me explain exactly who we are, and what has happened to you, before you leave us."

Van Der Krueger threw the key-logger and the wiretap back to Duncan. He smiled, and shook his head, "Your knife..." Duncan threw the knife to the corner of the room, where it landed near a broom, which had been used by workman to clear up some dust.

The grey haired man began to pace around the room. "If you wouldn't mind throwing down those useless lumps of metal, I would appreciate it. Guns, even ones that are useless, still make me feel rather uneasy. I like to think of myself as someone who is slightly more sophisticated than all of this." He paused, leaning on an ornate, white fireplace. He waited for Loki and Ares to drop their guns. They did; they were useless anyway. He continued his lecture. "You know, I really don't bear any real grudges against the British or Americans as a people. Your group...CyberSecure...which is part of the Echelon network is where my problems begin. We feel we have a genuine cause; the Flemish people have a right to self-government, as do the Nordic and true Arians.

It is plainly obvious to us that it would be a better all round if the country was given back to their rightful owners. Immigrants are the last thing we need, putting a strain on our resources, taking up hospital beds, and degrading the quality of life for us. Immigrants are no better than rats feeding off the rubbish we leave. Trouble is, as I see it, they've infested the house, and are eating away at its foundations."

The grey haired man brushed some dust from the sleeve of his long jacket, and rejoined the group. "We are peaceful, we have our own views, and yes, they may be strong views; but for some reason people see us as racists! His tone changed, his voice booming, "Why is it, that if Africans, Asians, or other so called minority races speak out against us, they are simply defending their rights?"

He took a deep breath, continuing in a slow, monotonous tone, "Now where was I? Oh yes, CyberSecure. As you may have noticed, we have been undertaking, in the course of our protests, certain digital attacks against governments and groups who would try to suppress us. If any nation decided to defend themselves against such attacks, then that is fair. All nations have a right to defend themselves. However, when it is decided, that one, or indeed, our entire group are to be removed through physical action, we feel we must resort to the same. We know your agency is good at what it does; we have been aware of you, and watching you now for some time through official channels. To be honest, we are as well connected as you are; hence the reason you find yourselves here."

"You have been fooled. Do you honestly think it would have been so easy to get access to us? No. Hercule has been extremely helpful to us, and once the taps and key-logger were in place, it was simply time to reel you in. It is amazing what someone will do for one hundred thousand euros don't you think! So, now you know, there is only one thing left to do. The new Zaurus technology you have is by all accounts impressive. I would appreciate it if you would hand them over." Ares and Loki looked at each other, and drew their Zaurus's from their pockets. The grey haired man nodded to Van Der Krueger who stepped forward ready to collect them.

In unison, Ares and Loki pushed the small red button on the back of the units, instantly sending an electro magnetic pulse through them – destroying the circuitry. They were then thrown on the ground at the feet of Van Der Krueger, and the grey haired man.

He looked down at the dull grey titanium case, before pointing his gun at the agents. "That was a BIG mistake!" Ares and Loki dived to the floor just as the bullet left the gun barrel; the force blowing a large exit hole in the plaster of the lounge wall, before ricocheting into the bedroom, and embedding itself in the oak floorboards. Suddenly, where there had been reasonable calm, there was confusion, as Van Der Krueger, the driver, and the older man, found themselves staring at the two Fourth Reich thugs, whilst the British agents scrambled around on the ground, looking for anything they could use as a weapon. The grey haired man prepared to fire another round.

Duncan ran to the left, cart wheeling along the ground as he reached the opposite corner of the room. He gathered the knife, discarded earlier, which he threw with as much force, and precision as he could muster. Its tempered steel blade embedded itself in the driver's arm. He squealed - dropping his gun. He grasped his arm and limped off towards the door. The others began to round on Duncan. Now unarmed, he picked up a nearby broom, which he snapped three quarters down the shaft. It left a shard of pointed splinter, an ideal weapon for a man with his combat experience.

Yards of coiled black and red cable lay on the floor. Loki jumped up; throwing the box that had shielded him; knocking the grey haired man to the ground. Grasping the cable, Loki used it as a whip, hitting Van Der Krueger across the face. He managed to keep hold of his gun, letting off a round, which just missed Ares, who was still at this moment scrambling to get up. Finally he grabbed the gun, discarded by the driver. The driver began making his way to the exit; realising things were not going to plan. Van Der

Krueger regained his composure to find Ares taking aim. He did not miss. The bullet penetrated Van Der Krueger's chest, ripping through his heart, and stealing what life he had left. He crashed backwards onto the ornate fireplace, before finally coming to rest on the polished marble in front.

Duncan continued to tackle the two thugs, who had rounded on him. The first wielded his baseball bat, taking a swipe that, had it connected, could have removed Duncan's head. Duncan ducked under the bat, which thrashed by, only inches above him. Lunging forward, he drew the sharpened wooden shaft back, before stabbing forward and upward. It hit his opponents groin at full force, piercing his pelvic cavity. A shrill cry rang out, before he fell to the floor - his death inevitable and agonising. The grey haired man had recovered his poise, firing at Ares. The bullet hit his hand, knocking the gun from it, before ricocheting off the metal and shattering his thumb. He fell to his knees, lucky that another desperate shot from his enemy only removed part of his ear. He slumped to the floor. "Ares!" Loki screamed; his rage growing like a volcano. He jumped on the grey haired mans back, coiling the cable round his neck, applying a devastating pressure. An almighty struggle ensued, the taller man firing wildly; each shot missing the thin, wily figure of Loki.

The driver had made it out into the garden. Duncan turned to give chase, but was beaten down by a baseball bat, which, aimed for his head, had only just missed, crashing down on his left shoulder. It was enough to send him hurtling forwards into a pile of slates. The thug continued his pursuit, bearing down on a dazed Duncan. In most circumstances the pain would have been too much, but the situation ensured that it was ignored for the moment. Duncan had no time to lose; another swipe of the baseball bat missed him, as he threw himself forward, desperately reaching for one of the slates on the pile. He hurled it, hitting his aggressor on the side of the face. The man reeled backwards, blood spraying from a fresh wound just beneath his left eye. Duncan limped to the pile of building equipment, and picked up a shovel that lay on top. Now at least, it was even. The thug breathed heavily and clenched his teeth. He wiped the blood from his face, and charged. Duncan swung the shovel at full force, but the aggressor ducked under the swing, grabbing Duncan's waist. Duncan felt his stomach muscles collapse under the power of the hit.

Winded, he fell backwards onto the ground, his head falling short of some bricks that lay discarded on the grass. He was powerless. Every second played out in slow motion as his energy began to disappear. He had almost nothing left as the man on top of him drew his knife, pushing it down, towards his throat. He strained as the man pushed harder, an evil grin of victory showing prominently through his gritted, blood stained teeth. Duncan's strength continued to fail as the blade drew closer, piercing the fine layer of skin on his throat. The thug prepared for one final, murderous push, when a sudden, horrendous thud saw his head lurch forward, and his body go limp.

The knife fell from his hand, and Duncan closed his eyes, relief washing over him. Ares stood above him; blood dripping from his shattered hand and torn ear, holding the shovel Duncan had dropped. He shook his head. "Aye, every now and again, you've got to shovel a little shit!" In the background Loki ran out through the door and up the path. "Where the fuck are you going?" Ares cried. "I've got a driver to chase. I'll come and get you when I'm done." He disappeared from sight, leaving Duncan and Ares with the task of cleaning up an almighty mess.

Ares helped Duncan up with his good hand. "Right, let's see what the damage is, clean it up, and get out of here. This has been the biggest balls up I've ever been involved in - a

fucking mess from start to finish. Let's see if we can at least get out of this God forsaken country without embarrassing ourselves any further!" Duncan hung his head, "How were they able to dupe us all like that?"
"God knows, but there will be hell to pay when we get back, that's for sure! Come on; let's get this mess sorted out, and quick.

Duncan and Ares limped back into the house. It was a scene reminiscent of a medieval slaughter. The bodies lay strewn across the floor; their death masks contorted from the obvious pain they had suffered during their last few moments of life. Duncan felt sick. He had seen dead bodies before, but these were more gruesome than he could have imagined. It was one thing to see this in a gangster movie, or even on television, but real life was a different matter altogether.

Van Der Krueger lay in a pool of blood against the ornate fireplace. He had died the instant the bullet had passed through his heart. Blood spattered on the walls and ceiling, dripped onto the floor, or seeped into the woodwork…something that could not be cleaned up. The grey haired man sat in a strange upright position, his head sitting against the wall. His eyes bulged, and mouth sat open in a silent scream. Eerily, he still clung to the electrical cable wrapped tightly round his neck; his lips a deathly shade of blue, the bruising round his throat now evident. Duncan walked over to the thug lying near the door, and began the task of removing the sharpened broom shaft. A vacuum had formed, making it difficult to remove. He stood on his victim's groin, to afford him enough leverage to remove the wood. The blood had not congealed, and sprayed from the pelvic cavity on removal. Duncan ran outside and vomited.

Ares limped upstairs, amazed to find the hidden control room. This was an ideal place to hide the bodies. He returned downstairs, the pain from his torn ear, and the wound in his hand, causing him obvious discomfort. "Let's get them upstairs, you'll need to see this anyway!"

Duncan and Ares began moving the bodies upstairs. Luckily for the British agents the house had just been freshly decorated. Plastic sheeting was found upstairs, ideal for wrapping the bodies. It was not easy to lift them up to the first floor - the dead weight hampering their attempts to traverse the relatively narrow stairway. Finally, when the last of the Fourth Reich antagonists had been unceremoniously dumped in the control room, they were able to take stock, and look around. It was obvious how they had been spotted. Tiny CCTV cameras were everywhere.

Some of the latest technology was also owned by the group, some of which was almost as impressive as that owned by CyberSecure itself. Duncan and Ares took a last look round before finding the locking mechanism, and sealing the door. They headed downstairs and picked up the titanium shelled Zaurus's that sat in the middle of the floor. "They may not work, but we can't leave them here," Duncan sighed as he stooped to pick the second one up. "Let's just hope we can get back to the hotel in time to get the other. If I get my hands on Hercule he's mince meat!" Ares agreed, "Aye, hard to believe it, but Loki was right about him all along. Never mind, he'll get caught in the end, they always do!"

They took one last look at the blood stained room, before quickly leaving. They had no means of contacting Loki. Badly injured, Ares had ripped part of his shirt to create bandaging for his hand. For once they were lucky. They had not walked far when Loki came roaring down the road, almost crossing over, instead of going around a small roundabout. The breaks screeched as the Megane came to a sudden stop by the injured men. "Get in ye pair o' fuckers. I couldn't get the bass; he was too far away. We've got to get out of the country and fast!"

Ares and Duncan got into the front and back seats respectively, before Loki took off at an incredible speed. "We've got to get to the airport, there's a special flight being scheduled to get us back to Edinburgh before too much shit kicks off!" Duncan tried to lean forward in the back seat, but was thrown backwards by another short burst of acceleration. "What about the Zaurus, it's in the room?" Loki replied, "Its gubbed. I spoke to Terminus, and he said the tracking mechanism on it stopped transmitting a good hour ago; a short while before the other ones did. That's what prompted Terminus to start the back-out procedure."

The car sped out of Brussels and down the motorway to Charleroi Airport. Within half an hour they had parked in the airport car park, where two men in pilot uniforms met them at the front door. "Come this way, and don't ever say the British government doesn't look after you!" They limped through the small but busy airport. Their state drew some attention from onlookers - a small girl pointing at Ares, having noticed his torn ear.

A small plane was waiting on the tarmac, fuelled and ready to go. The men clambered in, collapsing into the comfortable leather chairs of the private Lear-jet. Loki breathed a sigh of relief as the doors closed and the plane prepared for take off. "Thank fuck we're out of that disaster. God knows what they'll say when we get back!" Duncan hung his head, "My first assignment and this happens." Ares was beginning to doze, the loss of blood taking its toll on his giant frame. "There were mistakes made higher up than us…unfortunately shit flows downhill; we'll know soon enough, but I've got the feeling this will be my last time in the field." He closed his eyes and tried to get some sleep, as did the usually hyperactive Loki. Duncan was left to look out of the window at the view, and worry about how this failure would be dealt with.

Two days later, the three men stood in the office of the highest authority in CyberSecure. Chaos had called Terminus, Ares, Loki, and Duncan to his office. "Loki looked around the room, "Wow, not bad; so this is where you hide out - comfortable." He had little respect for someone who was so detached from the team. It was only due to the fact that the team was so small that Chaos could put any names to faces.

"So," Chaos began, "please brief me on how this mission failed. Terminus?" Terminus was not his usual confident self. "Quite simply, we were conned. If I remember correctly, the order to help the Belgians on this one came from further up. We were following orders and basically trusted our contacts." It was obvious that Chaos felt threatened and was searching for a scapegoat. "The powers that be are looking to launch a full investigation into this one. People are dead. Technology extremely important to the British government has been destroyed, and our relationship with a foreign national has been strained." He paced back and forth across the room. "I've kicked this around for the last couple of days and have drawn my conclusions. Partly it may be my fault for not being plugged in to this one. Terminus, as far as I am concerned you were in charge of this mission. You failed to do the necessary background work, and therefore there is no other option open to me, than to demote you. I am removing your team leader status." He sat back down behind his desk. "Ares, you will no longer be asked to undertake field work. You are more valuable as a trainer. Duncan, Loki, you will receive formal warnings, and it will end there. Let us hope the Belgian government do not wish to take this any further."

Ares spoke up, "And what about you Sir?" Chaos stared at Ares, "What about me?" "You gave the initial order to go out to Belgium." Chaos was furious. "I will ignore your insolence on this occasion. Now leave!"
They closed the door behind them, Ares shaking his head, "As you say, shit flows downhill."

Chapter 6

Meeting with Vasily

Timeline: November 2014 - 10 years later.

The bells echoed out across a square in Moscow on a cold February day. A man in his late twenties leaned back in his comfortable chair watching the people struggle to make their way to work in the snow and slush. Even in the dim light of the city's grey sky, Moscow looked beautiful to him. Life was good. He leaned over the table and picked up the steaming hot cup of black coffee he had poured not two minutes before. Almost everything he had set out to achieve since losing his brother ten years before had been completed. This final transaction extracted the remaining funds from almost every bank account known to be held by the mafia bosses who had ordered the killing. He had duped each of the families into thinking the funds had been stolen by the other, causing the largest mafia war the Russians had seen. His joy grew as member killed member, their desperation and paranoia growing. In time, he had removed one of the biggest single threats to Russian society since the beginning of democracy.

He thought no one knew his identity, having held down a menial position within a manufacturing firm for the duration of his activities. People weren't quite sure how he managed to afford some of the luxuries he had on the salary he had been taking home, but whenever the tax authorities investigated, they found nothing untoward. He was very careful in his cash dealings, and was always good at hiding funds around the world. As computer hackers went, he was the best. It became easier to hide his activities with the increase in wireless networks, and people who had no idea how to secure them. Cyber café's were also a favourite haunt, but never the same one too often. He trusted no one, never worked for anyone else and always worked alone. He had learned a lot from his brother in the early days, but had now honed his skills beyond anything he could have achieved. There wasn't a system he didn't believe he could get into, with the exception of one. The Echelon core network had eluded him. He hadn't tried too often in the past, as the need to remain anonymous and focus on the destruction of his mafia enemies was far more important to him. Echelon and its inner workings intrigued him however, and he felt that this was the time to find out more.

He gulped the last of the Colombian coffee; one of the luxuries he had decided he should have, and put the cup back down on the table. He spotted some children in the square throwing snowballs at each other and smiled, thinking of their innocence and naivety of the world around them. He remembered those days; times had been harder then, but his family were close, and they brought fond memories.

He glanced back to the laptop. The wireless network he had been using for the last half hour was still active; his oversized antenna picking up anything within a two mile radius. In this day and age that was plenty. He had written software to crack various encryption protocols, but unlike many hackers who had sought respect, he never mentioned his achievements to others. It was still believed that the latest iteration of the World Wireless Encryption Standard was secure; allowing him to use the complacency surrounding it to his benefit. He logged back into the Linux laptop, and looked at the on-line booking system of Aeroflot. He began thinking that it was time to cash in his chips, and move abroad. He hadn't been caught, but one day his luck may change. He would now be able to put his English lessons to good use, and get closer to the ultimate network - Echelon. Little did he know that whilst he looked for them, they would come to him.

At CyberSecure, the aggressive wing of the Echelon network, final preparations were being made for the retirement of a very dear friend and mentor to Duncan Steele. Ares had now reached his fifty eighth year, and was to retire; to do what, he was unsure - but he knew it was time to make an exit. He had met his second wife three years prior - four years after Duncan had tied the knot with his wife Andrea back in 2007. Ares was the most settled he had ever been.

"It's definitely time for me to go. I'm sure I'm making the right decision; besides, they have a new trainer now. CyberSecure has changed. There is no real need to learn unarmed combat or advanced driving skills. Cyber warfare is for the young, or should I say, younger. I can think of no-one better to teach them than you Duncan." Despite his age Ares still stood tall and proud. The battle scars on his face, his torn ear, and his missing finger, less noticeable than they had once been. Duncan and the remaining team posted at Echelons Scottish headquarters looked on, knowing it was the end of an era. Chaos, Terminus, Riddles, Loki, and Duncan patted Ares on the back and wished him well.

Hades had remained in the Australasian sector, but had sent on a video message. He too had occasionally worked and trained with Ares when recalled to Europe. Duncan had not been in the presence of Hades since the day they had completed their training, but he had communicated as often as possible over Echelons secure network.

Ares would need to be replaced, but with who? In a sense, Ares leaving was bad timing for Duncan. His time a CyberSecure was also due to end. His ten year contract, now complete, meant that he had also began looking to leave in the very near future, to spend more time with his family. His son Tom was growing fast, and as far as he was concerned, he was missing it. Andrea had never understood why he had to travel so much. He hated keeping her in the dark as to his movements. He was bound by the official secrets act, but was worried that he was losing the trust of his wife. Next week would be Tom's sixth birthday. Already Duncan had missed his first day at school, as well as other events important in a young boy's life. If that was not bad enough, he could not remember the last time he had managed to do something special for his anniversary, or even take his wife out for that matter.

Duncan did enjoy what social life he had. He had few friends with the exception of his fellow workers, but he enjoyed their company, especially that of Ares. He wondered how it would be without him there. Riddles was still his same old self; arrogant and socially inept; having spent the last ten years living in his lab. Loki had been forced to retrain; his brand of skills less required since the 'debacle of Brussels' as it had been termed. Any really dangerous dealings with criminals, where a gun may be essential, was dealt with by the British special forces. CyberSecure agents still went out to meet contacts, but were never expected to do anything life threatening any more. This was not to say that death threats had not been levied at the team.

As Duncan said farewell to Ares, he made the decision that there were more important things in life. He believed it was time to move on, and armed with a reference he would be able to do just that. The problem might be getting one. CyberSecure and the British secret services didn't exactly hand them out. Andrea had been giving him grief for almost a year now about cutting down his working hours. She was completely unaware of who he worked for. An IT consultancy she thought. "Why can't you just leave?" she would often ask. "What is more important; that bloody job, or us?" Duncan had no answer to these questions, but now that his ten year contract was up, a chance to leave had finally presented itself. He had done well at CyberSecure, having taken over the training and team leadership positions in the last few months. This had meant an increase in salary, which was more than he would probably be paid by a private firm.

It was nearing the end of the day, and time to talk to Chaos was running short. Duncan felt that whilst he was feeling this way, he should talk to him. Leave it till tomorrow and he may have changed his mind. He walked over to Chaos, who was busy shaking Ares by the hand; thanking him for the years of service he had given. Ares smiled whilst Chaos talked, but knowing him as well as Duncan did, the smile was just for show. In anything other than the most extreme circumstances Ares had never said much about his superiors. His respect for superiority and rank had ensured this. Even now, when he could have said anything he wanted, he kept his thoughts from Chaos. Ares turned to Duncan as he reached him. He patted him on the shoulder, their friendship as strong as ever. Chaos began to look rather uncomfortable. It became obvious that he was looking for an exit. "I was actually hoping to talk to you, if that would be possible Sir; can we arrange a meeting?" asked Duncan in a forthright manner. Chaos was surprised by Duncan's approach. Even after all of these years, he was not used to chatting to, or being directly addressed by the troops.

He had backed away slightly, but now moved towards Duncan. "I see. Nothing serious I hope?" Chaos was a tall man; over six foot, whose close proximity made Duncan feel uncomfortable. He hated the way everyone sucked up to him, never really telling him what they thought. What was worse, Chaos never really listened to any of the teams' opinions anyway. He was totally unapproachable. Duncan continued, "It is important to me. My ten years are almost up…next month in fact - and I'd just like to ensure that you were aware of this." Chaos became slightly flustered, feeling that he was being put on the spot. Ares and Duncan did not help by simply standing and waiting for an answer. "Yes, I had heard. But I don't think this is really the time or the place. Let's take this one off-line." He began to walk towards the door, hoping to escape having to give firm timescales. "When Sir?" asked Duncan. Chaos paused for a moment, annoyed that Duncan had not backed down. "Tomorrow...tomorrow first thing." replied Chaos. "That will give us the best chance of hitting the ground running. I need to talk to you about on-boarding a new recruit anyway. Yes, 09:00 hours sharp. That would be best for me." With that, Chaos made his escape.

Ares smiled, "That's one arsehole I won't miss! There...that feels better. I never had much respect for him to be honest...but he is the boss. God knows who appointed him!" He turned to Duncan. "So are you honestly looking to leave too?" Duncan replied, "My time's up, and if I don't get out of here, I'm not sure how long my marriage will last." After a few final drinks, Duncan bade a fond farewell to his good friend. Although they would no longer work together, he didn't feel it was the last time they would get together, Ares having indicated as much. It was just a matter of when he would have time for anything except work, considering how busy they were at the moment. The years from 2010 onwards had seen a phenomenal boom in cyber crime, with almost the entirety of earth's population now on-line.

Duncan had aged quite considerably in the past ten years. Although he enjoyed his work, it was stressful. He had gained a couple of stone in weight; a side effect of both age, and a more sedentary life-style. In fact, he did almost no exercise, and his fitness levels had plummeted. His healthy eating plan and exercise regime were always due to start the following week. It had been like this for years. His face had also aged; the worry lines on his forehead prominent, his hair almost white. Over the last couple of years his eyesight had began to suffer, forcing him to wear spectacles. He could have worn contact lenses, but they irritated him, and comfort was more important than looks.

The headquarters of CyberSecure had not changed since Duncan had started there. The remote country house had been repaired several times, but it wasn't noticeable. He still wasn't sure if this was a plan to maintain the buildings decrepit appearance, or if it was down to lack of funds to do the job right. He walked out through the back door, and into the courtyard where his car was parked. The importance of the building as an Echelon station had grown over the last couple of years; but as technology had moved on, the need for the huge golf ball shaped satellite dish had diminished. A much smaller satellite, only 4 metres wide, sat at the far end of the courtyard. Despite being twelve feet high, it was hidden from public view by the courtyard walls.

Duncan stepped further into the courtyard; the intense beam from the security light suddenly switched on, almost blinding him as he neared his car. He paused for a moment to take in the rest of the courtyard. It was quiet; eerily quiet. He studied the old buildings brickwork, and then scanned its blackened windows. They glared back at him, leaving him with an uneasy feeling. Someone could be watching; you never could tell. His inner circle had diminished over the past few years, and he trusted no-one outside of it. He stood in a daze for almost two minutes, before the security light automatically switched itself off. He shook his head, pulling himself back to reality.

He hadn't even noticed the time, 8:15pm - late again. He should've phoned Andrea, but he had simply been too busy. He had left before Tom had got up this morning, and his son would be in bed by the time he got back; yet another day in his life lost. There were other, more important things in life now. Chasing cyber criminals around the world, and breaking into computer systems for such a long period of time had drained him. Travelling no longer held any excitement. One hotel room was much the same as another. His determination to resign had become stronger than ever. He started the engine of his shining silver Mercedes E Class and pulled on his seatbelt, stopping for a second to contemplate his time at CyberSecure, wondering what tomorrows meeting with Chaos would bring. He put his foot to the floor, and began the forty minute drive back to his house, hoping that Andrea would not be too annoyed by his late arrival.

Just over forty minutes later Duncan pulled into a street full of new-builds. It was dark as he made his way through the neatly mono-blocked roads to his own driveway. The unremarkable box shaped houses were standard fare all around the country, with developers putting profit before individuality. If you wanted to be a home owner, short of paying a fortune for an old property, this is what you bought. Although they were built in close proximity, with space a premium, this did not make the street a community. Duncan had lived there for several years with hardly a word exchanged with the neighbours. He didn't care; he wasn't interested in their shallow lives anyway. These days the majority of people were forced to work to pay their mortgage, and other trappings of wealth they had to have right now. The problem was compounded by easy access to credit; and if you couldn't pay that, you could get a loan to pay your loans. The year 2010 had seen a huge government drive to getting everyone, including women, into work. More workers meant more taxes.

Where once it had been normal for men to work, and for women to take care of the children and the home; women now faced the embarrassment of having to admit that they were housewives - being frowned upon by others for not pulling their weight. Childcare was now more prominent than ever, with couples stretching themselves to the limit to buy their property, and in turn leaving their children with companies whose prime goal was not the welfare of the child, but profit. It seemed that everyone and everything had become shallow and materialistic. You would often see the children in the street dressed in designer labels, unable to play for fear of tearing their latest CK T-shirt. Mercedes Benz and BMW cars adorned almost every driveway, with even the youngest children aware of how much they cost.

Duncan had, to some extent, got caught up in it all, having bought his own Mercedes a year before. It attracted some interest from his neighbours, who for the first time approached him, interested in where he had got it, and at what price. He could afford some luxuries, but didn't believe in living beyond his means, unlike some of his neighbours.

Andrea was one of the few housewives in the area. They had made the choice to bring up Tom themselves, not happy about farming him out to anyone else. It was for this reason that it was so difficult for Duncan to be absent to such an extent. The longer he was absent, the guiltier he felt; having missed almost every important phase in his young son's life so far. It was not what he or Andrea had expected, or planned for. He hoped a new job, when he took one, would change the situation for the better.

He pulled into the dark driveway, switched off the headlights, and slammed the car door. It sounded solid, making him marvel at the build quality of the German engineering. He locked it, before heading to his front door. He took a deep breath before venturing inside, hoping his wife would not be in a bad mood.

"Daddy, Daddy!" shouted Tom as he came running down the

stairs to meet his father. Duncan dropped his briefcase to lift him up. "How are you Tiger?" he said, pleased that he had come to see him. Andrea walked through from the lounge, and switched on the hall light. "You know it's past your bedtime; you can see Dad for a couple of minutes, and then it's off to bed with you!" Duncan hugged his son, spending the next couple of minutes asking the excited boy about his day. "Dad, I've been picked for the school play. It's next week, will you come, will you, please?"
Duncan smiled, "That's great, of course I will, wouldn't miss it for the world!" Tom beamed at his mother, "Mum, Dad's coming to see me in the play next week!"
"That's really good; tell your dad what you're doing in the play."
"I'm going to be a wood chopper, and I kill the big bad wolf." He flexed his muscles, which made both of the parents laugh.

Finally it was time for Tom to go back to bed, "Can you read me a story?" Duncan looked at Andrea, "Now Tom," she said, "its past nine o'clock. Off you go...you'll see dad in the morning!" Toms face filled with a look of disappointment. This is how it had been for a while now. He longed to spend more time with his father. "I'll pop in and see you tomorrow morning before I go to work, I promise, okay?" Tom smiled, "Okay, as long as you promise." With that Tom slowly clambered upstairs.

Duncan smiled at Andrea, "How was your day?" Andrea walked past him, and headed into the kitchen. "I've cooked you some fishcakes and potatoes for your tea. You'll need to heat them up. I'll put the kettle on." Duncan followed her into the kitchen, "And your day?" She leaned back against the fridge and exhaled. She looked tired as she brushed her long dark hair out of her eyes. "Same as usual, got up; cooked, looked after Tom, and explained to him you wouldn't be home in time to read him a bedtime story again." Duncan sat down on one of the hard wooden kitchen chairs. "I'm sorry. I know it's tough just now, but we're really busy. I plan to sort it out. I've arranged something with my boss." Andrea took the food out of the microwave and put it down in front of Duncan, but said nothing. She knew he would tell her what he had arranged.

"You know you were saying I should look for something else?" Andrea looked up, taking more interest as she removed a soggy tea bag from the freshly made cup of tea. "Yes."
"Well, my contract is up, and I've got a meeting tomorrow. I'm going to see if they'll give me a reference. I plan to get a job that will give me more time with you and Tom…it will mean less money probably."

Andrea smiled, "You know money isn't the most important thing to me. I'm happy as long as there is a roof over our heads and food on the table. It's Tom I worry about. He really misses you; he needs a father, and at the moment he barely has one." Duncan took a sip from his tea, "And you? Do you want to see me more?"
"That goes without saying. I wouldn't have married you if I didn't want to spend time with you! What time is your meeting tomorrow?"
"First thing."
"Why wouldn't they give you a reference?" asked Andrea, frowning. "Your contract is up, it's only fair!"
"It's a bit of a funny set up. They can get a bit huffy if you want to leave. They see it as disloyalty." Andrea shook her head, "Shouldn't have joined that company in the first place." Duncan nodded in agreement, "I know, but there wasn't many other choices at the time…we'll just have to see how it goes tomorrow."

Duncan finished his tea, and got up from his seat. "Are you coming through then?" he asked, putting his arm round her.

Andrea smiled, "Yeah, there's a good film just starting; let's go."
The two parents walked through to the lounge, switching off the hall lights, and closing the door behind them.

At 9a.m sharp, Duncan knocked on Chaos's door. Having been asked to enter, he walked in and took a seat, smiling. He had decided that the best plan of action was to be as nice as possible, and hope that Chaos would be reasonable. In general, even the worst bosses would understand family commitments. Duncan thought this may be the case for Chaos; after all, he had a wife and kids too. Chaos had been typing at his keyboard, but momentarily stopped, apologising that he just had to finish this quick email before beginning the meeting. Chaos often kept his staff waiting. Everything he or his superiors did was of more importance and always took priority, no matter what. Finally he finished rattling on the keyboard, and turned his swivel chair slightly to the left, to face Duncan.

"Now Thor," he said, rubbing his hands together, "what seems to be the issue?"
Duncan felt slightly nervous, unused to talking to Chaos. "Well, as I mentioned yesterday evening, my contract is up. It's been ten years now, and I'd really appreciate the opportunity to move on." Chaos nodded his head. "I see. What has brought this on?"
"I really need to spend more time with my family. I'm missing my son growing up, and I am slightly worried about my relationship with Andrea." Chaos leaned back in his chair, "Andrea, she's your wife…partner?" This annoyed Duncan, "My wife!" Chaos thought for a moment. "Well, you know I can't stop you leaving. I would be disappointed to see you go, and we are short of people. If you wish to hand in your notice however, I will accept."

Duncan felt relieved. He couldn't believe it had been that easy. "Thank you Sir. I know it is busy right now, and we're slightly short staffed, but this is important to me." Chaos smiled, "No problem. Always happy to help a member of staff in any way I can." Duncan felt confident enough to move on to his next point. "Who should I obtain a reference from? Would that be yourself?" Chaos shook his head, and smiled again. "A reference; are you serious? That's a no-can-do regarding the reference. It would compromise the security of CyberSecure...you know that!" Duncan felt his heart sink, "So there is nothing you can do? Without a reference, I'll have real problems getting another IT job, especially at my age!" Chaos replied, devoid of emotion, "Yes, that is a shame. But rules are rules. Now, if you wish to leave, it's up to you, but beyond that I can't help you."

Duncan was becoming angry with the blasé attitude displayed by Chaos. He tried desperately to stop himself shouting at him, as he sat smugly in his leather chair. Chaos sat up, and leaned across the table. "You know, it is unfortunate; if you had only asked last month we might have been able to do something; your timing is poor, what with Ares leaving." Duncan prepared to get up. "Okay, you've given me my options. If you won't provide me with a reference, I'll have to think about my position. I will have an answer for you tomorrow." Duncan headed to the door, only to be stopped by Chaos. "Wait a minute. I'll cut you a deal." Duncan turned to listen, intrigued by what his boss was about to say. "Please sit down. We are currently searching for a new member of the team. We have our eye on a young Russian cracker who has made contact with us." He got up from his chair and paced round the room. "We need someone to go and meet him next week in Moscow, and bring him back." He paused, looking directly at Duncan, "If you do this, I'll see about getting you a reference."

This option seemed reasonable to Duncan. He was about to agree, when he suddenly remembered that he had promised Tom he would watch him in the school play. "I can't make it next week. I've already got other family commitments. It would break my wee boy's heart if I didn't go to his school play. I don't want to let him down. Would it be possible to go the following week?"
"I'm afraid not. We have only a small window of opportunity on this one. We have to act with great velocity if we are to reduce the threat surface currently facing us." Duncan protested, "Surely, one week won't make a difference?" Chaos shook his head, "Sorry, next week is our target date. Are you in or not?" Duncan took a deep breath, and thought about the options open to him. Chaos turned back to his computer system, "Short term pain for long term gain. There will be other school plays."

Duncan gave in. "Okay, I'll do it, and I'll get a reference when I come back." Chaos smiled, "Good man, you've made the right choice." Chaos went to a filing cabinet at the back of the room and opened it. He fished out a red folder and handed it to Duncan, who begrudgingly took it, putting it under his arm to read later. "You fly out on Sunday evening. Be sure to read the brief. The admin girls will book your hotel and tickets. Thanks."
Duncan left the room feeling dejected. His bid for freedom postponed for the moment. Never mind, he thought to himself. Soon he would have the reference he needed to get a good security position somewhere else, and hopefully he would be able to spend more time with his family. He just had to get through the pain of telling them first.

Tears welled up in Tom's eyes as Duncan informed his small boy that he would not be able to attend the play. "There will be other plays Tom, and after Daddy does this one last job, I'll be able to spend much more time with you, I promise." Tom sniffed as Duncan cleared the tears from his cheeks. "You promised you would come to the play, but now you're not coming. It's bad not to keep promises; it just makes people sad." Duncan hung his head. "I know, but I really promise this time. After my trip next week we'll see each other lots and lots." Tom tried to smile, slightly happier by the prospect of seeing his dad more." Andrea was less pleased, but decided to say nothing for the moment. She knew deep down that Duncan hated hurting his family, but couldn't understand why he couldn't just fix the work issues, and get on with life.

A few more hugs from his dad and Tom had calmed down sufficiently enough to get ready for bed. "I'll read you a story in a minute," shouted Duncan as Tom climbed to the top of the stairs. Once out of earshot Andrea vented her anger. "I knew this was going to happen. If you can't do something, and you know you won't be able to, then for God's sake don't make promises to Tom. I'm an adult, and I can cope with these things, but Tom just can't." She shook here head in despair.
"So when are you going out?"
Duncan replied, "Sunday night."
"For how long?"
"A week."
Andrea was incredulous, "A week? What on earth takes a week in Moscow? Can't someone else go?"
Duncan shook his head. "No, I need to go on this one. We're bringing a specialist on, and I need to interview him as the most senior technical team member."
"Right, well, you'll have to live with the consequences if this carries on. I didn't marry you, and have your child, just for us to be stuck here all the time, watching my son being let down again and again. You better hope it gets sorted when you get back. I'm really fed up with this."

Andrea stopped as Tom popped his head round the banister. "Are you going to read me a story dad?" He held up a copy of The Lion, the Witch, and the Wardrobe.
Duncan turned to his son and smiled, "Of course I will. Come on, let's get you upstairs."

The temperature was near freezing as Duncan stood outside the plush exterior of Moscow's Metropol hotel. The old building was a beautiful piece of Russian architecture, close to the centre of Moscow, with its many historic buildings and squares. Looking around, he wished he could just be a tourist, and enjoy the city he was visiting. His work schedule was however, very carefully designed not to give him too much free time; minimizing any waste of tax payers money. It was nearing 8p.m, and had been dark now for a couple of hours. Red Square and its surrounding area was a beautiful site, lit up like a Christmas tree on this cold winters evening. Duncan exhaled, watching his warm breath freeze as it touched the Moscow air. He shuffled his feet to try to keep warm. After a few more minutes of waiting, he took a final glance at his silver watch, and made a move towards the agreed meeting place.

Just two hundred yards diagonally across from him on Teatralnaya Square was the famous Bolshoi ballet; the unlikely meeting place requested by Vasily. Duncan had never been to the ballet, and was more nervous about this, than meeting a potential colleague. His Russian was not particularly good, with his inability to read its alphabet hampering him still further. The street signs meant nothing to him, and deciphering them seemed more difficult than some of the codes he had cracked in the past few years. On an initial short walk around some of the city, the only thing he had recognised straight off was the Macdonald's logo.

The dossier Chaos had provided Duncan with had very little information on the man or his deeds. There was no indication of the targets real name, any of his habits, or even what he looked like. This lack of knowledge impressed Duncan. If someone could avoid the eyes and ears of the Echelon network to such an extent, then he could most probably do anything, or go anywhere, almost undetected. Alongside psychological profiling, and confirming his skills, finding out why he wished to join Echelon was one of the most important pieces of information Duncan was too obtain. It would be difficult for him to be objective, as trusting an individual was not one of his strong points. Up till now Ares had been the one who had met potential team members, but his retirement had left that space vacant. Even if Duncan had been the one tasked with meeting potential members, his experience would have still been sparse, as only three had been taken on in the time since he had joined CyberSecure. This was to be their first Russian, officially at least. Double agents had worked for Echelon during the cold war years. The fact that they were now officially seeking a Russian proved that the focus had shifted on to new enemies, primarily terrorist groups, such as Al Qaeda.

Duncan strode across Teatralnaya Square, passing by some of the trees growing across the square, to the entrance of the Bolshoi building itself. The building's white stone walls were lit up by the lights surrounding it. Its design was breathtaking, with huge columns at the entrance holding up the triangular stonework on top. Initially built in 1776, its name Bolshoi literally meant Big. Big it was. It held two thousand people during a performance, making it extremely difficult to watch for suspicious activity. People milled around the front of the steps, waiting to be admitted to the latest showing of Swan Lake. As Duncan joined the queue, he looked around for any indication of who Vasily may be. Almost every unaccompanied male under the age of forty could have been him. He decided not to give it any more thought; he would meet him soon enough, as he would be seated to his right during the show. All he could hope for now was no mix up in the seating allocation, which could, at best, be embarrassing, and at worst, blow his cover. He finally walked through the large oak and glass doors, and on into the foyer. An usher who spoke to him in Russian inspected his ticket. Duncan's confused look was a clear signal that he was not dealing with a Russian national, and he promptly asked Duncan if he spoke English. Duncan smiled, and nodded, before allowing the usher to show him to his seat.

Duncan scanned the area nervously, waiting for the seat to his right to be filled. The seat to his left was already taken by a large middle aged woman, who nodded to him as he looked at her. He nodded back, and smiled, before focusing on the stage ahead. As time wore on, almost all of the seats around him were taken, with the exception of the one to his right. He looked anxiously at his watch, pressing the small switch on the side of it to light up its face. It had gone 8:30pm, as the chatter of expectation waned, and a hush, prior to the beginning of the ballet, fell upon the audience. Still no-one had taken the seat next to him as the doors were closed and the ballet began. Was this a no-show on the part of Vasily? Had something scared him off, or worse still got to him first? He looked around impatiently, drawing some looks from nearby members of the audience. He decided to simply watch the ballet. If his contact did not appear, he thought to himself, he would at least enjoy the show. It wasn't everyday an agent had the chance to watch such a famous production.

Duncan began to believe that Vasily wouldn't show up as the interval drew near. He could not believe he had travelled all of this distance to simply find that his contact would not appear as arranged. Perhaps he had got cold feet at the last minute? One thing was certain; he would have to report this to his superiors, and it would not look good for Vasily, as reliability was always important in these situations. If he could not be relied upon to meet up now, it wasn't something they could have faith in for the future.

As the curtains closed on the first half of the performance, and people began to leave their seats, Duncan took another look round to find he was being watched by a small thin man, in his late twenties. He was dressed in what could only be described as a lumberjack styled shirt. He rubbed his black scraggy beard, which covered half of his face, and smiled at Duncan before getting up from his seat to join the throng of people heading for refreshments. Duncan thought this was strange, and began to feel rather uneasy. His mind raced; his heart-rate increasing slightly as he began to calculate his options. Should he stay here, or leave now and call in? After a minute or two of intense decision making, he chose to stay, and at least watch the end of the show. He would, however, be more aware of anything else suspicious.

Towards the end of the fifteen minute interval, as the quiet began to descend, Duncan became aware of someone seated in the chair to his right. He looked round, about to mention that the seat was taken, when he realised it was the young bearded man from the seat behind. He was casually slurping an ice-cream. He winked at Duncan. It was obvious now that this was Vasily. He had been extremely careful in ensuring Duncan was the man he was supposed to meet, having bought two tickets for nearby seats, affording him the opportunity to watch and wait.

He leaned over, and spoke in English, his accent slightly tinged by his Russian. "Excuse me, could you tell me who created this ballet please?" Duncan had been expecting this question. "Wagner, of course!" was his incorrect reply. The reply may have been incorrect in terms of who wrote the ballet, but in terms of password exchange it was exactly what Vasily was looking for. "I see, I always thought it was Tchaikovsky. We must discuss this later." Duncan agreed, "Of course. I would like that." Both men settled back into their seats to enjoy the rest of the show, safe in the knowledge that they had both made it this far.

The following forty five minutes passed swiftly. Although Duncan was not really a fan of ballet, he had enjoyed the experience, having decided at the age of 44, that life was too short not to savour anything different life presented him with.

Rapturous applause burst out from the audience, echoing around the grand old hall as the dancers took their final bows, and the curtains closed for the final time that evening. Calmly, Vasily leaned over, "Come, it is time for us to leave here. The more crowded it is whilst we depart, the better. We can go undetected that way." Duncan realised that despite Vasily's calm exterior, something or someone, was making him nervous; not surprising, considering this small, reasonably frail looking individual, had single-handedly wiped out the most violent mafia families in the Moscow.

Duncan decided he would have to deal very carefully with him to gain his trust. His file had mentioned that he had no known contacts, and Duncan was beginning to believe that he had indeed worked alone for some time, if not always.

They exited the building as quickly as possible; the bottleneck created by the mass of people intent on leaving at the same time, slowing their progress to a mere shuffle. Finally, after the passing of several minutes, they were outside the front doors, standing on the steps leading to Teatralnaya Square.

It was now bitterly cold, and a wet slushy snow had begun to descend, swirling erratically in the light winds which circulated around the square.

"You are hungry, yes?" asked Vasily. Before Duncan could answer, his contact had started moving away from the Bolshoi building in the direction of Red Square. Duncan decided it would be best to follow. "Do you know somewhere good to eat?" Duncan, aware that Vasily's English was not perfect, spoke as plainly, and as clearly as possible. Vasily nodded, and carried on at a pace which Duncan was finding difficult to keep up with. A lack of exercise and a reduction in the training regimes once required at CyberSecure had meant that Duncan's fitness levels were poor.

It was not far before the men had reached their chosen eating place. Godunov was a reasonably sized restaurant not four hundred yards from the Bolshoi ballet. Vasily led the way, shaking hands enthusiastically with a large man who showed them to one of the more secluded tables. They sat beneath an alcove at the back of the restaurant in the VIP hall. Duncan marvelled at the restaurants typically Russian interior. The wall lamps shaped as burning candles complimented its brightly coloured walls, decorated with ornaments and frescoes. Vasily and the large man conversed in Russian for a short while, whilst a waiter handed Duncan and Vasily a menu. The large man patted Vasily on the back before leaving. "This is the best restaurant in Moscow! Good Russian food." He indicated that the amount of food was also plentiful - something which pleased Duncan, who was now becoming hungry. In only a couple of minutes the large man returned, followed by the waiter, who carried two small pitchers, some bread, and three large plates of various foods. They were laid down in front of the diners, whereupon the large man once more shook hands with Vasily, and promptly left them to eat their meal.

"Eat and drink." Vasily pointed to the two pitchers in turn, "This is water," he paused, smiling; "this is Vodka!"
"Do you know the owner well?" asked Duncan.
"Once, let me just say, that I made his money troubles go away." He winked. "Now let us eat, we will talk later."

The men finished their meals, filling up on mushrooms, meat, bread and potatoes, with a small, or in Vasily's case, large glass of vodka. The conversation was not at this time allowed to turn to business, with Vasily interested in chatting about Russia, his mother country, and finding out more about the Metropol hotel, somewhere he had never stayed. It soon became obvious to Duncan that Vasily was extremely patriotic. This seemed confusing. Why would this man, so enthusiastic about his own nation, want to leave the country forever to work for a foreign power?

At close to 11:30pm, Vasily handed Duncan a scribbled piece of paper with instructions on how to get to his apartment. "Come at 10:00am. I will show you what I can do. I am trusting you. Please do not let me down!" He quickly got up from the table and strode out, waving to the man who Duncan now understood to be the owner of the restaurant. Duncan took a final sip of water, before pushing out his heavy oak chair, and walking over to the owner. He indicated that he would like to pay the bill, producing his wallet. The owner laughed and shook his head, making it obvious there was no bill to be paid. Duncan thanked him, before walking out into the cold Moscow night. He took a few seconds to find his bearings, and headed back to his room at the Metropol.

Chapter 7

Vasily settles in

Duncan walked towards the polished oak reception in the lobby of the Metropol. The surroundings were the most opulent he had ever been in. The brightly lit area was quiet at this time of the evening, its cream and black marble floor echoed to his footsteps as he made his way past the stone columns and up to the reception desk. He calmly asked for his key, "Room 104 please." The receptionist smiled, and reached under the counter to retrieve the key card. Duncan took it from her, saying his thanks, before heading around the reception desk, and into the lift.

Just outside room 104, Duncan afforded himself a quick glance down the corridor to ensure no one had followed him. No one had. He slid the key into the reader and entered. Switching on the lights, he removed the latest version of the Zaurus PDA from his pocket, before unceremoniously throwing his coat on the bed. He pulled up the dressing table chair and switched on the kettle, before pouring coffee granules and some milk from a small plastic container into a china cup. The Zaurus was then placed on the table before he removed his tie and shoes, which were then thrown across to a chair in the corner. He wiped his eyes, tired from the day's stresses and strains, wishing he could just get some sleep. It was important to make contact before he could sit back and relax with his coffee. Getting some rest was necessary, but the time shift from the UK to Russia had played havoc with his body clock, making sleep more difficult than usual.

He lifted the Titanium Zaurus, pushing a small blue button on the back of the device. The upper half, a thin sliver of lid, slowly swung open to reveal a secret compartment, just big enough to receive a fingerprint. He pushed his forefinger onto the space, which glowed red temporarily as it received the data from the scan. The light finally turned green, whereupon Duncan removed his digit. The upper part of the lid then closed, clamping itself to the lower half of the lid again. Finally the whole lid unlocked, its springs pushing it open, allowing the latest in small scale, crystal clear screen technologies to be used by the rightful owner.

Wireless connections were common place in hotels, the Metropol was no exception. Instantly the Zaurus obtained a high-speed network connection. Duncan tapped on the work profile icon, starting the Virtual Private Network client. Every piece of data he sent from here to Echelon was encrypted at the highest levels. He logged in to the remote access system and typed 'The Metropol is lovely, had dinner this evening with our dear friend, and will be given a guided tour tomorrow.

Duncan finished his sentence and logged out. Again, he pushed the blue button on the back of the Zaurus, which clamped it shut. There was no other way to open or close it.

The kettle had boiled, the steam clouding a nearby mirror. He carefully poured some boiling water into the cup, and stirred it methodically. He took a sip, before leaning back and putting his feet up on the table. He began to drift, nodding off temporarily, until a drop of burning coffee woke him with a start. It had stained his white shirt. Duncan cursed. Getting undressed, he crept into bed; his jet lagged state making it difficult for him to co-ordinate. Duncan put the cup on the bedside table, eventually finishing the remaining contents once it had cooled. A few minutes later he switched off the light. He was tired but unable to sleep - his brain buzzed. He wondered what Vasily would demonstrate tomorrow, and whether coming here was worth it. He also reminded himself that tomorrow he should phone home, to find out how Tom's play went. He missed his family. His surroundings may have been luxurious, but this was no longer the way he wished to live.

He closed his eyes and began to breathe steadily, rhythmically, trying to close his mind to all thoughts. Soon enough, he had.

A remarkably bright but cold day dawned as Duncan, still groggy from an uneasy sleep, attempted to haul himself out of his comfortable bed. He took his watch from the bedside cabinet - 8:04a.m. He sat up and rubbed his eyes, before heading for the shower, hoping this would bring him to his senses.

A short while later, sitting in the splendid surroundings of one of the Metropols many restaurants reading his complimentary copy of the Times, Duncan sipped his coffee and made important decisions such as which condiment to spread on his toast. After a few minutes of reading, he put down his paper and took a quick look around the room, whereupon he spotted a smartly dressed man, not five yards away. The man raised his cup to him. Duncan did not recognise him, but politely raised his cup in response, before returning to his breakfast. Who was he? Duncan tried to act casually, feigning continued interest in his newspaper, and finishing off the rest of his toast, whilst desperately thinking where he may have seen the man before.

A few minutes later Duncan finished his breakfast. Folding the newspaper and placing it under his arm, he got up from the table, before glancing across to where the stranger had sat. The space was now being cleaned by one of the waiters, ready for the next set of diners. Thinking nothing more of the incident, he headed back to his room, to prepare himself for the meeting with Vasily.

On reaching his room, he took his usual cursory glance down the corridor, before unlocking the door and entering. He walked in, carefully closing it behind him, and wandering into the toilet to relieve himself. He whistled calmly as he washed his hands, before drying them on the soft white towel that hung on the radiator. When he finally re-entered the bedroom, he was stopped instantly in his tracks; shocked to see the same stranger sitting in the chair in the corner smiling at him. Duncan was not armed, and began to panic. "Who are you? How did you get in here?" The stranger raised his hands, "Do you not recognise me? It is quite amazing what a clean set of clothes and a shave can do, is it not?"

Duncan was furious, "Vasily...what do think you are doing? If I had a gun, I might have shot you!" Vasily adjusted his seating position, but was still quite calm. "I trusted that you would ask questions before shooting. Is that not the correct way?" Duncan could do nothing but nod in agreement. Vasily got up from his chair, "So, have I impressed you? Would you like to see some more of the things I can do?" Duncan replied, "So far I am impressed, but why are we not meeting at your flat as arranged?"
Vasily became more serious, "My flat has become too dangerous for me to return to. I am aware that I have been watched over the last couple of days. I need to leave Russia now!" Duncan was unsure of this, "There are just a couple of problems. You don't have any plane tickets, and my tickets are for Friday. Also, there is no guarantee you can stay permanently in the UK!"
"That is not a problem. I used some SQL Injection to update the British Airways database. We are both booked in first class seats to Edinburgh." He looked at his watch, "We will be in the air in three hours. As for staying in the UK, I must trust you to fix the problem."

Duncan was surprised, "I didn't think BA would still be vulnerable to such attacks!" Vasily laughed, "My friend, everyone is vulnerable…you should know that!" Duncan nodded in agreement. "Now please," continued Vasily, "pack your bags and let us leave here." Duncan began packing, and within fifteen minutes was ready to go. They left the room and descended in the lift. "I'll need to settle up my bill; hold on a second." Duncan walked to the reception and began the process of checking out, whilst Vasily stood nervously in the background, scanning the lobby and main entrance. The smartly dressed blonde receptionist handed the receipt to Duncan, "Thank you very much Mr. Steele." Duncan was somewhat surprised, "Don't I need to pay for the room?" The receptionist checked the computer system again, tapping a couple of times on the keyboard. "Your bill has already been settled." She smiled, before continuing, "Have a safe journey, and thank you."

Duncan picked up his bag and walked away - stunned. "Did you pay for my room?" he asked Vasily. Vasily did not answer until the two men were outside. "I did not exactly pay, let's just say I adjusted some hotel records…they can afford it!"

Vasily and Duncan headed to the Taxi rank and waited for the next car to arrive. In less than a minute, a yellow Lada bearing a number on the door had pulled up. The driver was a large, bald man, who threw the cigarette he had been smoking onto the pavement, before picking up what little luggage his passengers had, and placing it into the boot. He opened the rear door, before getting back into the car, and sitting down without even a look at the two men about to get in.

Vasily leaned across, and in Russian instructed the driver to take them to the Airport. He then sat back in the chair, where he and Duncan engaged in light conversation, whilst making their way through the mid morning Moscow traffic.

Almost ten minutes had passed when Vasily began to get agitated. Duncan studied the driver sat directly in front of him, and then looked behind, attempting to catch his bearings. There was nothing obvious trailing them, and he began to wonder why Vasily was becoming so flustered. He wasn't sure who he should be more concerned about, the driver or Vasily.

"What is the matter?" Duncan whispered. "The taxi driver is going the wrong way!" Vasily shouted at the driver in Russian, "Hey, you are going the wrong way; this will cost us more money! Get back on the normal route!" Duncan took another quick look around and spotted a black car tailing them, only two cars back. Suddenly, as he turned to face ahead, the driver leaned across and pulled a gun from the glove compartment. In an instant Duncan had reacted. Shoving Vasily against the window, he grabbed the drivers seatbelt, loosened it slightly, before wrapping the remaining length round the drivers neck. As the driver's hand swung round to aim, Duncan punched him sharply in the back of the neck. The driver dropped the gun, which fired, blowing a hole in the front passenger door, before falling to the floor.

Duncan tightened the grip on the seatbelt and pushed his knees against the back of the driver's seat. He shouted at Vasily, "Get in the front and steer the car!" The car had swerved violently out of control for a few seconds, but now began to slow as the driver's foot was lifted from the peddle by the force of the strangulation. Vasily clambered into the front and threw a well aimed punch to the drivers face, making his nose bleed.

He quickly took control of the steering as the assassin began the last desperate throws of life. His face had gone from a bright red to a deep blue; his eyes bulged, and his tongue protruded, swelling as he died. As his struggle ended, the assassin soiled himself, before slumping in a heap. Vasily, tried not to vomit, concentrating on the road ahead. Duncan hauled with all of his might, pulling the driver by the neck, up and out of the driver's seat, leaving enough space to allow Vasily to sit down and control the car. Duncan released his grip and looked behind him, his hands raw from tightening the seatbelt. The trailing car had disappeared. He shouted to Vasily, "C'mon, the airport, as fast as you can, we need to get out of this damn country." Vasily did not hesitate, increasing his speed as he neared the outskirts of Moscow.

Duncan leaned across and positioned the assassin into as much of a sitting position as he could. The man's dead weight made it especially difficult to manoeuvre him, the smell of faeces hung in the air. Vasily was still panicking. "What will we do when we reach the airport? We can't leave him like this!" Duncan was calm, the possibilities playing out in his head. He worried about how calm he actually felt, considering he had just killed a fellow human. "We'll put the front seat down and cover him up to the neck in a coat. It'll look like he's sleeping. It should give us enough time to get out of the country." On reaching the airport they found an empty space in the car park as far from the terminal as they could. Vasily and Duncan exited the car, ensuring their victim looked comfortable. Then they locked the doors and collected their luggage, before walking off without a look back. "We should be okay as long as no-one spots the hole in the door." Duncan stated.

The men attempted to calm down, and checked in. They spent a nervous couple of hours in one of the small airport café's, praying their victim would not be found, before finally making it on to the plane. Somehow, they had made it.

The plane landed at a shade after 2:30pm Greenwich mean time. Duncan and Vasily had hardly said a word to each other on the way home. They had eaten their first class meals and watched the in-flight entertainment. Duncan wondered whether a reception party would be waiting for them in the form of the police; he hoped not. Now all they had to do was get through customs. A Russian passport in Vasily's case would make it more difficult, but the really difficult bit was over. All he now needed to do was tell them he was spending two weeks on holiday, and take it from there.

It took another twenty minutes to collect what luggage they had and pass all of the checks at Edinburgh airport. It wasn't on the same scale as the London airports, such as Heathrow and Gatwick, but it served its purpose. Duncan knew it well, having been a frequent flyer over the past decade.

Grabbing a taxi, Duncan checked in with a surprised Chaos over a secure channel. "The target is acquired; I have Vasily here."
"What, so soon? You're ETA was the end of the week!"
"Let's just say events overtook us." Duncan replied.
Chaos was quiet for a moment. "Take the rest of the day off, and present yourself to me tomorrow. Make your contact comfortable in a hotel...and ensure he stays firmly on your radar. Remove any computer hardware he may have."
Duncan nodded, "Will do."
Duncan closed off the secure voice over IP software that was built into the Zaurus, switched his Zaurus to standby, and

smiled at Vasily. "So, which hotel do you fancy?"
Vasily was quick to reply, "I hear your Queen lives in the Balmoral Hotel when in Edinburgh. I wish to stay there!"
"I don't think our budget stretches that far I'm afraid."
Vasily smiled, "It is okay, when in Moscow, I took the chance to book it."
Duncan started, "You didn't…"
"I have some money you know; I do not break into everything," Vasily interrupted.

Within thirty minutes the taxi was pulling up in Princes Street, just outside the famous old hotel. The weather was reasonably warm for a February day in Scotland, and at just a shade before three o'clock in the afternoon it was as busy as usual. Cars and buses roared past, as people, always in a hurry, desperately tried to cross the road. Vasily and Duncan got out of the taxi, and walked a short distance along Princes Street to take in a view of the castle, the Scott monument, and the surrounding area. "It is a beautiful city," Vasily murmured. Duncan folded his arms and agreed, "Aye, I guess it is. I live here, so I don't really think about it much."

Duncan ensured that Vasily had checked in, and asked him to hand over the laptop he had taken with him. Vasily protested, but understood Duncan's point that this was not the place to go war-walking, or hacking any of the local networks. "Don't worry; you'll get it back soon enough. You should take a break from it anyway; see some sites. There is plenty round this area, but please don't stray far. I'll call you tomorrow afternoon at 3pm once things have been worked out. Please be here!" With that, Duncan bade Vasily farewell, and headed off to buy some flowers for Andrea and a small gift for Tom. They would be pleased to see him home so soon. They'd never know what had happened in Moscow, or how close he came to never returning.

Duncan sat in Chaos's office. Chaos was more chatty than usual, considering this was a debriefing. Duncan had already explained what had happened in Moscow, and had given his opinions on Vasily, pertaining to his skills as a hacker.
"So, would you say he is a team player?" Duncan was less sure of this. "I don't believe so, but he is certainly very talented. It would be handy to obtain as much knowledge from him as possible." Chaos agreed, "Yes, that's an A1 idea. I'll get Riddles plugged into this one; assign him the task of gleaning the info we need."
Duncan queried this, "Do you think Riddles is the best man for the job, considering?"
Chaos looked at him blankly, "Can you explain your meaning?"

Duncan hesitated, unsure as to why he was being asked such an obvious question. "Well, he's socially inept! He may not get on so well with Vasily. I think it would be better if I spent a short time with him." Chaos laughed, "Nonsense man; besides, I have other things for you over the coming months." Duncan shook his head, "Err, no Sir. Remember, before I went to Moscow, you were going to sort out my reference on return." Chaos sighed, "Sorry -- went as high as I could. Negatives all the way I'm afraid. If you want to stay, I'll do my best to ensure you won't be spending too much time out in the field. How does that sound?" Duncan felt demoralised and somewhat used. "I'll hold you to that one Sir." Chaos smiled, and the meeting ended. "Get Vasily in. Ensure he is blindfolded so he doesn't know where he is for the moment. We'll start debriefing him today."

Duncan met up with an excited Vasily. "This is a wonderful place. I should have taken a holiday many years ago. I was, however, otherwise occupied at the time."

He prepared to launch into a list of where he had been, and what he had seen, until Duncan stopped him in his tracks.
"Sorry Vasily, but I'm going to have to stop you there. It's time to meet the team. I'll explain what is going to happen to you on the way. Come, let's get your bag packed and get out of here." Vasily settled his bill, and made the short walk down to one of the car parks near the centre of town. They got into Duncan's Mercedes, the tinted windows providing a modicum of privacy for its occupants. "Sorry, but you'll need to wear this." Duncan handed Vasily a blindfold. "If you could just put it on, that would be helpful.

The journey took almost an hour in the mid-day traffic, with Vasily talking constantly about his visit to Edinburgh's tourist attractions. Finally they drew into the gravel car park of the old house that provided a semi-covert base for CyberSecure. Vasily removed his blindfold, and along with Duncan, walked down the worn stairway to the basement. Vasily looked bemused, something which Duncan noticed. "Don't worry; it's not all so run down as this. Just a couple more doors and you'll see what I mean! You're lucky, one day I'll tell you of my first day!"

Sure enough, they walked through a large, heavy wooden door. Much of its red paint had flaked off and fallen onto the concrete floor. There was no door handle; no obvious way through it, until Duncan took a step to one side. With his right hand, he pushed one of the stones in the whitewashed wall. The door began to swing inward, providing access to a brilliantly lit corridor, which both men walked down. On reaching the end of the corridor, Duncan stopped in front of a solid steel door. An Iris scanner was mounted just above shoulder height; a DNA reader almost a foot below it. Duncan stood in front of the scanner, and simultaneously placed his hand on the DNA reader. After a few seconds, the security system asked him to state his codename. "Thor."

The doors slowly swung open, allowing him and Vasily access to the inner sanctum. "We take security pretty seriously here. Just try getting out again!" laughed Duncan, as the doors quickly sealed behind them. Vasily gave out a nervous laugh. A new stage in his life was just beginning, and he wondered, just for a moment, what he had let himself in for.

A few hours later, following an initial debrief, it was time for Vasily to meet the other agents. No access was to be given to the systems for a couple of days, until Riddles had witnessed and assessed the capabilities of the newcomer. Duncan had no doubt in his mind that Vasily was capable; he had already proved it in Russia. They walked down the familiar steel corridors to the meeting room where, just ten years before, Duncan had been briefed on the fated mission to Brussels. Even ten years on, there were still loose ends to be tied up from the mission. Hercule had disappeared, and had never yet been found, or confirmed dead; though many believed he probably was.

Vasily was introduced to the usual mix of agents. Loki, now nearing fifty, had not lost any of his natural ability to annoy, and even frighten new recruits. He had kept himself fit, even though he had been mostly stuck behind a computer workstation since Brussels. He shook hands with Vasily, "So, Vaseline...how's it feel to get out of a third world country at last? I didn't think you had computers in Russia!" Although Vasily's English was quite good, he did not understand why a small minority of people were laughing. "No, we have had computers for many years. I think you are mistaken as well - my name is Vasily. Loki replied, tightening his grip on Vasily's hand slightly, "Well, Vaseline, just don't get in my way and we'll be just fine; I'm not so keen on Russkies." Duncan decided it was time to move on, and escorted a confused Vasily away from Loki.

There was a more pleasant greeting from Terminus and several other agents, before it was time to meet up with Riddles. He had not ventured out to the canteen, almost never leaving his lab. His food was usually brought to him. The doors to the lab were sealed, with the same level of access required to enter it, as the outside doors. Vasily and Duncan entered, spotting Riddles in one corner, still working on his latest development, which would of course, according to Riddles, change the world. The room had changed little since Riddles had claimed it as his own many years before. It had been extended to include a bed, a shower, and an eating area to the far left. Many new books had been purchased and version four of the Sony Playstation, called the Power Station, sat in place of the old Dreamcast. The walls were a sterile white, although they had become dulled slightly. S.A.D lighting had been installed on the request of Riddles.

After a short while Riddles noticed the men, and lifted his head in a vague attempt of acknowledgement. Duncan walked over to him and introduced Vasily. "This is Vasily. He will be spending the next wee while with you. Have you set up the tests?"

Riddles looked at Duncan quite condescendingly. "My response is a positive one. If it is a requirement for myself to do something, it is always correct, and to deadline; unlike others within the organisation I could mention." He extended his hand towards Vasily, "My presumption is that you are the new Russian." Vasily shook Riddles hand and indicated that he was." After the shortest of handshakes, Riddles withdrew his hand and rushed over to the sink, washing it vigorously. This embarrassed Duncan, who apologised to Vasily, explaining that Riddles was slightly cuckoo. The Russian laughed and shook his head, still smiling on Riddles return. "I'm sure you are in agreement that we must take positive precautions when coming into

contact with foreign beings. MRSA is a danger to us all. Catching it would be extraordinarily negative for ones wellbeing. Now, let's get on. I don't wish to waste any more of my time than is necessary. Come with me." Duncan began to walk with Vasily and Riddles to a bench full of computer systems, but was stopped in his tracks.
"That will be all; you're not required. I'll call for you anon." Duncan was slightly annoyed at Riddles rudeness, even though he was used to it. He understood, however, that there was no point in arguing, so patted Vasily on the back and wished him luck before leaving the lab.

"Over the previous days I have implemented a target infrastructure," Riddles began, "affording myself the opportunity to obtain computational analysis regarding the timescales in which you require to compromise it." There is a laptop at the end of the bench. Your task is to map the network and retrieve the data mentioned on the white sheet of paper." He looked at Vasily. "Do you understand?"

They walked over to the laptop and Riddles booted up the Debian Linux operating system. The system prompted for input. Vasily sat down, and typed Nmap. The command was not found. He typed in several other commands, obtaining the same response. Vasily then typed ifconfig to obtain the laptop's network address. He looked up at Riddles, who was standing very close by. "I can download the tools I require to complete the task?" Riddles laughed, "You have complete access to the resources of the Internet. I will leave you to your task. I expect it will take a while," he scoffed.

This attitude annoyed Vasily, who began to enter commands at speed. Linux was his operating system of choice, and he had no problem finding his way around. The first task was to get to the server on which his security tools were deposited.

Entering the command sftp V451ly@195.107.42.12, he waited less than a second for a password prompt, before providing it and gaining access to the system. He changed to the appropriate directory, and listed the file contents. Everything he required was in there, and he duly began the task of downloading them. File followed file, Nmap, Nessus, nikto, hydra, netcat, hping2, john. An endless string of files, scripts, and exploits flowed to the laptop as Vasily rubbed his hands, and put his coat on the back of his chair. Situated close to the laptop, a mere two feet away, sat a wireless network card. Seeing that Riddles was engrossed elsewhere he grabbed it, and stuck it into the spare slot in the laptop. He quickly configured it, a huge smile crossing his face. The test network would only be the beginning; there were other things of more interest to him now.

Vasily began the process of scanning the systems. Initially, they did not respond to his network mapping tool. He changed the command, scanning the subnet which his laptop sat on, typing

./nmap –sP -v 192.168.1.0/24.

He waited for a few seconds. Several machines responded. He then entered more specific commands against the systems that had responded.

./nmap –O –T5 –v 192.168.1.5-10

Now Vasily began to concentrate hard. He started Nessus, entering the network addresses and port numbers Nmap had provided him. He sat back in his chair and folded his arms. All he could do was wait. This was easy for him; run of the mill stuff. He could do it in his sleep. Nessus finally returned its results. Nothing was vulnerable. This meant nothing to Vasily. He had noted that one of the servers was running Microsoft Internet Information Server. The web server was little used these days, apache and Linux having all but gained market control. He quickly typed another command, never missing a key –

./nikto –h 192.168.1.7 –p 80

More web server information was returned, including the version number, the web server response, and some other associated plugins. He laughed, drawing the attention of Riddles. "Is there a problem?" asked Riddles. "Vasily turned in his chair, "No problem - all is well my friend."

Vasily loaded some of his ASN.1 exploit code into the Linux file editor and made some small changes before recompiling it as kill-bill2. Next, he started a listener on his machine using netcat. He typed

./nc –vv –l –p 53

A successful attack would spawn a command shell, which would be sent to his laptop, which sat listening for an incoming connection on port 53. Finally, he was ready to attack. His fingers flowed over the keyboard as he typed

./kill-bill2 192.168.1.7 80 192.168.1.1 53

The cursor flashed at the bottom of the screen, followed by a raft of seemingly random ASCII characters before the line "code execution complete, shell granted, enjoy the view," appeared. There was, however, no command prompt at the bottom of the screen. He could not believe his exploit had failed. He hit return a couple of times and a terminal session opened on his screen. At the bottom of it, a prompt

c:\windows\system32\

He breathed a sigh of relief; then chuckled to himself, once more disturbing Riddles. "Whatever is the matter?" Vasily quipped, "Can you smell the burning my friend...your network, it is toasted!" He had full access to the system.

Having obtained a foothold on the target network, he began the task of compromising each of the individual systems. System after system fell as he funnelled multiple exploits through the compromised server. Once compromised, Vasily installed netcat or psexec onto each one of the systems, providing command line access to the entire target network. It had taken him less than an hour. Finally, he obtained the target credit card file and was about to call Riddles over to him, when he remembered the wireless card.

Riddles own laptop sat on an untidy desk, cluttered with books, networking equipment, and sweet wrappers. It seemed he had a penchant for Mars bars; probably one of the few vices he had Vasily thought to himself. Whilst on his short tour of the lab, Vasily had noticed the wireless access point. The lab was heavily shielded to ensure that no wireless signal could leak from it. He needed to attach himself to the network, so loaded an adapted version of Wellenreiter, which he had tweaked to crack the new, supposedly unbreakable, World Wireless Encryption Standard. He didn't hold out much hope of getting in, as a substantial amount of data would be required to obtain the encryption keys. He leaned over the laptop, shielding his actions.

He couldn't believe his luck; Riddles was downloading large amounts of information, providing an excellent chance of gaining access.

Another fifteen minutes had passed before the key sat before him. Using the latest version of the perl script 'chop-chop' the key was cracked - "ones-key" It was so simple. With this information he accessed the network. He stood up, "Do you mind if I rest for a second, this is a difficult test?" Riddles was pleased with this question, making him feel slightly superior. "Of course!"

Vasily walked towards Riddles desk in an anti-clockwise direction, taking the long route around some lab-benches so as not to raise any suspicion as to what he was doing. Riddles barely noticed what he was doing, his ability to concentrate on his own tasks legendary. As Vasily neared the desk, he spotted an ornately printed sheet of paper with the sentence 'Quiet...genius at work!" This was typical of Riddles's sense of humour. Riddles, however, also believed it. Vasily walked back to the chair and started a secure session with the laptop. "Surely it cannot be that simple," he murmured.

He typed the necessary command. *ssh –l root riddles-laptop* and waited for the prompt to appear. He then typed the password 'genius'. This did not work. He then tried 'geniusatwork'. To his disbelief, it gave him root access to the system. The system was at his mercy; he could do anything!

It was obvious that security wasn't as tight here as everywhere else. He found it unbelievable that Riddles had used a guessable password for the root user. He quickly logged in and began the process of looking around the system. Vasily was amazed to see the large file that was being downloaded. Porn-Queens.mpeg. How Riddles got away with this he didn't know. It was becoming obvious that other people within the compound turned a blind eye to many of his eccentricities.

He pondered for a second on what he should do, before deciding that on this occasion, it would be best to subtly show Riddles that he had visited. He changed the system prompt to Vasily-says-enjoy-your-pornqueens>, and quickly logged out. Vasily got up from the chair and stretched. Riddles walked over to him, "How is it going?" Riddles was dismayed to read the credit card number from the screen. "I see, yes, well...very good. Obviously I made it reasonably simplistic for you, seeing as you are foreign." Vasily shook his head, unhappy that Riddles should make such a comment.

Riddles called Duncan back to the lab. Rushing through the door less than five minutes later, he queried, "Well, how did it go?" Vasily laughed, "It was an easy task, Riddles has told me so. I would like to leave now to get some food perhaps?" Duncan agreed, and both men walked out of the room, leaving a grumpy Riddles pacing about. He was perplexed and annoyed. "Must increase the test complexity," he muttered to himself.

He sat down at his laptop, deciding that he would check how his download was coming along. He spotted the command prompt and slowly stood up, surprised, and a bit embarrassed. How could Vasily have got in? The link was encrypted and he hadn't noticed him sitting at his machine. No one that he knew had cracked the latest wireless encryption code. He felt the urge to recall Vasily, but his temporary embarrassment stopped him as he reached for the phone.

Duncan congratulated Vasily further, whilst showing him to his temporary accommodation. He always enjoyed getting one over on Riddles, whose arrogant attitude needed to be tempered occasionally. He derived even more enjoyment from Vasily informing him of how he had broken into Riddles's laptop to change the login prompt. Overall it had been a good day. Riddles had been left embarrassed, Vasily seemed to be getting on well, and finally, he would be leaving for home at a decent hour for the first time in months, giving him the chance to see his family for a short while. As he walked through the door and across the courtyard to his car, he thought to himself that perhaps things were changing after all.

Timeline June 2015

For almost a year Duncan's life had been better. He was spending less time at work and abroad. The pressure he endured as a Team leader and a trainer were minimal in comparison to what they had been. He was feeling comfortable amongst his work colleagues. Much of the work monitoring and removing the constant threat of hackers, was being tackled by the new Russian, who had firmly established himself as the equal of any; gaining the respect of even hardcore cynics such as Loki. There was nothing he seemed unable to complete with the minimum of fuss. He had settled well into his new life, having purchased a large house in the middle of Scotland most with his gains from the Russian mafia. No one asked him to return the money. What had gone before - was left in the past.

Almost a year and a half on from his arrival Vasily prepared to embark on probably his most difficult and time consuming mission. Hercule had still not been tracked down, even after the passage of almost eleven years. This had not caused an issue in the past, but his name had begun to crop up from time to time in communications across the Internet. Echelon was beginning to obtain an increasing amount of information mentioning the former Fourth Reich. Virus releases were increasing, and it seemed apparent that a Cyber army was being re-assembled. The patterns of destruction, and the targets, mirrored those seen during the time of the Fourth Reich. As far as anyone was concerned, Hercule was the highest-ranking member left. Suddenly he, or his ghost, was once more a potential threat.

Vasily's confidence had grown, having removed problem after problem. Now armed with all the knowledge and technology any former hacker could dream of, he relished each new challenge he was set. He knew what he would do on this occasion. He had already tracked most of the communication back to Berlin, having stolen lower ranking, Fourth Reich members' cyber-identities, to listen on specific Internet Relay Chat channels.

It was with this confidence that he met with Riddles, who had grown to dislike him and his abilities. He stood, arms folded, patiently waiting for Riddles to acknowledge him. He had been standing for a good couple of minutes, when finally his patience ran out, and he coughed deliberately to attract attention. Riddles slowly got up from his laptop.
"Ah, I see you are punctual for a change."
"I am always on time. I have been standing for a while, and have a plane to catch. Please, I would like you to give me my new field equipment. If I can get this I can continue with my work." Vasily's tone was cold and distant. At first he had laughed at the insecurities and jealousy Riddles had displayed. But after a year, it had become too much, and he now avoided the hermit as much as possible.

Riddles walked over to a grey bench at the far end of the lab and picked up a small metal box. "Your equipment is here." He handed the box to Vasily, who laid it down, before opening the lid.

In it sat a Titanium Zaurus SLC-4000, heavily converted for the field. It had been designed with security in mind. Biometrics built into the lid, an encrypted file system, and the latest iteration of Z4CK. It doubled up as a mobile communication device, configured for Secure Skype, and every form of wireless comms possible. Finally, if all else failed, it would self-destruct, sending an EMP through its internals. Riddles had always been proud of the conversion, and looked for a reaction from Vasily. Vasily was pleased, "Finally, I have been trusted enough to receive my own Zaurus," he mumbled. "Do be careful with it. It is the property of the British government, not your toy to play with! Your one is unique, one of a kind, as it is the first to have a built in Ion Cannon!"

Vasily's eyes lit up. "An Ion Cannon; how is it that you have created this? They require huge amounts of power, and it is impossible to direct the energy pulse." Riddles became noticeably excited. "This...sniff...is an incorrect assumption. My ten years of research has allowed me to develop an alloy strong enough to shield and direct the pulse. Whilst I am in agreement that it draws large amounts of energy, I have converted some of the power circuitry to allow a small pulse from an indirectly proportional power facility."
"How do I use the Ion Cannon?"
Riddles leaned across. "This small green button, which resembles the power switch, activates the cannon."
"So what is the range of the device?"
"At the moment, it is one metre."

Vasily pointed the Zaurus at a PC sat on the test bench in front of him. It had not been used for a while, the menu system having burned its image into the monitor. Before Riddles could protest, Vasily fired the device. Instantly the system switched off, dead to the world. "You have impressed me my friend," Vasily remarked, looking intently at the Zaurus.

"You also mentioned Z4CK? This is a new tool?" Riddles was bemused, "Has no-one demonstrated Z4CK? It was initially created by Thor, but I have improved it beyond recognition!" He pointed at the Zaurus, "Lay it on the table and log in." Vasily logged in using the biometrics software and started a small console in which Z4CK sat, waiting for a command switch." Riddles smiled. "Seeing as you have already destroyed one system, I will demonstrate this software on another of our old systems." Riddles typed at the tiny keyboard.

Z4CK -v --target --listen 1234 192.168.0.10 --overflow --wipe --lock

The cursor at the bottom of the command console began to flash. Within seconds, more text had appeared

....target acquired 192.168.0.10
...checking database for overflow vulnerabilities
...vulnerability confirmed
...exploit sent
...binding command shell
...sending reverse to port 1234 as requested
...system access acquired
wait
hit key for system wipe
...system wipe commence..............

A horrendous screeching noise began to emanate from the old computer system, forcing Vasily and Riddles to shield their ears. They continued to watch as Z4CK completed the task of locking the system.

...data removal complete
...bios lock complete
...system reboot commencing

The screeching stopped and the system rebooted itself, only to stop with the prompt

Hacked by Z4CK – Enter password for system restore.

Riddles turned to Vasily. "Impressive, is it not?" Vasily said nothing; he simply stood, staring at the prompt at the bottom of the screen. The screeching had sounded familiar. The prompt, sitting silently on the screen, brought back the painful memories of his brother's death. He had some suspicions as to who had stopped him and his brother all those years ago, and now, finally, his theory had been proven.

Riddles stood, waiting for an answer from Vasily. He mumbled in a subdued tone, "Yes, impressive." He brought himself back from the daze he had entered, an anger beginning to well up inside. "I must go. My plane leaves in a few hours. Thank you for the Zaurus; it will be very useful!" He chose not to look at Riddles, instead turning directly towards the door and leaving the lab. He had his proof, and finding it had been more painful than he thought it would be.

Chapter 8

Death of a network

Vasily went through the motions of packing his bag. He held the Zaurus in his hand, weighing up its huge potential. He had now obtained all of the information and hardware he had originally set out to. It had taken just over a year. In terms of hacking, it had been the finest and longest running social engineering attack ever undertaken. He now had a complete understanding of how CyberSecure and the Echelon network functioned, and the technologies they employed. Armed with the latest modified Zaurus and a binary copy of Z4CK, he began to realise that he would be unstoppable. He was trusted, and for a short while would be able to get away with anything. He placed the Zaurus in his pocket, and finished his packing. His immediate task of catching his plane to Berlin drew closer with every tick of the large white clock that hung on the wall behind him.

Duncan, being Vasily's boss, had gone to wish him luck, as he did before any assignment, but had found that he had already left. "When did Vasily leave?" Duncan asked Riddles, as he rushed in through the lab door.
"One hour - fifty-seven minutes ago, to be precise! Did he not report for a final briefing?" Duncan shook his head, "No he didn't. Did anything happen before he left?"
"I am unaware of anything unusual. I demonstrated the modified Zaurus to him."
"How did he seem?" Duncan asked.
Riddles scowled, "I do not like the word 'seem'. It is imprecise. I am unaware of anything unusual in his mannerisms!" He sniffed and returned to tinkering around with some components.

Duncan stopped for a minute to take stock of the situation. It was unusual for Vasily to just clear off like that without a final short briefing.
"Is there anything further I can do?" asked Riddles, obviously annoyed by Duncan's presence.
"No, nothing at at all. Thanks."

Duncan wandered out through the lab doors, checking his watch as he went. He decided to call Vasily, but realised he did not have the number for Vasily's new Zaurus. He quickly returned to the lab, where Riddles indicated that he had not provided a new SIMM card for the Zaurus. "It will be the usual number." Duncan picked up a stylised black metallic phone sitting on one of the benches and dialled the number.

A vibration made Riddles jump as a handset in his pocket began to ring. He then remembered. "Of course! Vasily gave me his obsolete phone when I provided him with the Zaurus. He let out a sneeze as he put the phone down, and immediately headed towards the sink to wash his hands. "I am sure he will call soon. Where would we all be without my mobile technology?" Riddles exclaimed.

Vasily sat on the plane, sipping a glass of water he had been provided by the stewardess. In an attempt to forget about the cramped seating and annoying kids sat behind him, kicking his chair, he switched on his Zaurus to use the planes complimentary Internet connection to take in some of the latest news on Slashdot. Attacks from hackers were on the increase again. He shook his head as he read over a story about a thirteen year old who had accidentally hacked into the DOD. How you can accidentally hack into something supposedly so secure, he thought to himself? He hopped swiftly from one website to another, not exactly sure what he was looking for, when he decided to start doing some research into the Fourth Reich. He searched Google for Hercule, adapting his queries to be as specific as possible. There was little there, but through the information obtained at CyberSecure, he was aware of what Hercule looked like. He had a fair idea of where he may be hiding, hence the reason for his current trip to Berlin.

He had been given the task of verifying his where-abouts before the armed forces were brought in to remove him once and for all. He did not relish the task, disagreeing with the methods implemented by the UK and US governments. As far as he was concerned, they were not much better than the government of the USSR before it split. Vasily had formulated alternative plans. These plans meant he would not be able to return to the west, but this did not bother him too much. He knew how CyberSecure and Echelon worked, and felt he could stay one step ahead.

He closed the Zaurus and leaned back into the blue leather seat, waiting to receive the usual British Airways Prawn or Chicken salad on a tiny plate. In his mind he began to put together the finer details of his plan. He would bide his time, removing everyone and everything he felt was a threat. He now had the best tools for the job, compliments of the British government.

Back at CyberSecure, Duncan and the rest of the team were blissfully unaware of the situation that would befall them over the next while. Duncan felt slightly annoyed and somewhat bemused that Vasily had not appeared for his final briefing prior to leaving for Berlin, especially as Duncan felt he could furnish him with more information regarding Hercule and the Fourth Reich.

The men bantered at the lunch table, laughing about some of the things that were going on in the world at large, or moaning about the usual management situation.

Home life for Duncan had improved. With Vasily keen to do so much of the work that Duncan had once upon a time undertaken, he could spend more time with Tom and Andrea. Chaos had, quite to Duncan's surprise, kept his promise on reducing the amount of visits abroad he now had to make. Duncan felt comfortable. The team had pretty much remained the same since he had joined eleven years before. He had become used to Loki and his ways. Terminus had become easier going since losing his Team leader role years before. Duncan was surprised that he had been so happy that Duncan had been promoted into that role. He still kept in touch with Ares, who had left just over a year before.

He also had a lot of respect for Vasily, who had been an excellent agent. He was glad that he had chosen to join them, as he would have made a formidable adversary if that had been his decision. Riddles annoyed him slightly, but there wasn't much anyone could do about that. Riddles would never change his ways, and had little opportunity to, considering he spent almost all of his time alone in his lab.

Duncan was now undertaking more security design work than hacking, which suited him. He had grown tired of chasing hackers round the Internet, and in some cases, round the world.

The men finished their lunch and put their trays back on the racks provided, before dispersing to their relevant areas. Riddles never ate with the rest of the men, always having his food delivered to him in the lab. He didn't even need to talk to the canteen staff. He simply entered his requirements into an on-line form, and took delivery at the specified time. His meals were different every day, but the same every week.

He ate fish on Tuesday, beef on Wednesday, and vegetarian on Friday. He was careful with his diet as his allergies extended to food as well.

Two weeks had passed and no one had heard anything from Vasily. Although his project could stretch for several months, he was to report back at least once a week. Duncan was becoming concerned for his safety. He wondered what could have happened, not believing for a second that he may have deserted. Several other agents had mentioned the possibility to him, but he had dismissed them out of hand. Loki was the latest in line to question Vasily's loyalty.
"The Russky bastard has pissed off, hasn't he?"
This annoyed Duncan. "I can't believe that? Why would he just disappear? Maybe someone has abducted him? Remember the Mafia had been looking for him. Let's not hope that that's the case."

Loki sat down at one of the consoles in the control room and stared into the Retina scanner. The system recognised him and provided access to the computer. He began to tap at the keyboard, bringing up a command shell. "Maybe he just got bored? Fuck me - I get bored every day. I should've left to do bodyguard work after that mess in Belgium; instead I'm stuck here doing this mamby pamby shite! Nah, he's away, one way or the other, he's fucked off!"
"Well, thanks for that Loki, cheery as always!" Duncan replied.

Duncan began to walk away from the control room but was stopped in his tracks. Just as he reached the door Loki shouted to him. "You do realise that whether he's been abducted or scarpered, that you'll have to find him! The British government can't have someone that knowledgeable about our internal networks running loose!" Duncan began

to walk toward Loki when the phone in the control room began ringing. Loki picked it up, "Control room, bored bastard speaking!" Duncan cringed; there was no easy way to control Loki, and as he neared retirement, there was no chance of him changing now.
"Okay, I'll tell him." Loki looked at Duncan, "The boss would like a word about Vasily. I'm impressed, he remembered his name!" Duncan shook his head as he walked through the door to make the journey to Chaos's office.

Following a short walk down the metallic corridors, Duncan found himself standing before Chaos. "Any word from our Russian?"
"No word I'm afraid, nothing at all. I can't understand it Sir, I thought everything was going well!" The main light bulb in Chaos's office had just blown five minutes before, leaving the desk lamp as the main source of lighting within the room. The lamp cast its light across the desk, providing only enough power to illuminate some papers, the laptop, and half of Chaos's face. It was in this atmosphere that Chaos informed Duncan that if nothing changed in the next week or so that he would have to go to Berlin to find his wayward agent.
"Would it not be better if someone else went? As team leader I feel I would be more valuable here!" Chaos gave an instant reply, "According to Terminus, you are the only one he seems to trust! Terminus will take your duties for the period you are abroad." Duncan lowered his head. "I see. Sorry, but my family is more important than being shunted abroad for God knows how long, so unless we can come to a compromise I quit!"
Chaos seemed astonished, "You'll quit? Why?" Duncan sat down on one of the chairs placed in front of Chaos's heavy oak desk. "If I start going abroad for unrestricted periods again, it will be the end of my marriage.

I do not really wish to talk about it. It is for the best that I hand over my access cards and leave."

Chaos was disappointed. "Okay. As you seem unable to see sense, and if that is your wish, I accept your resignation."

Chaos called Terminus to the room and informed him that Thor (as he called him) was leaving, and could he be escorted from the building. Duncan got up from his chair. "Would it be possible to say goodbye to the staff?" Chaos was unsympathetic, "They will be informed of your resignation in due course. Thank you for your time." Both Duncan and Terminus shook their heads, Terminus apologizing as the men reached the front door. "It has been a pleasure. Perhaps something will give us the opportunity to work again one day?" Duncan was not so sure. He said his goodbye, before walking to his car and sitting there for a short while. He could not believe that his time at CyberSecure had ended so suddenly, without so much as the chance to say goodbye to the people he had spent a quarter of his life with. His thoughts turned to home, and the future. What would he say to Andrea? He took comfort from the fact that he felt she would be okay about him leaving. Perhaps now he would be able to tell her everything. He decided that he would anyway, in case it took some time to get a new position.

A multitude of thoughts and scenarios ran through his head as he made the journey back to his house. He took a deep breath before entering, to find Andrea looking at him in astonishment. "What are you doing home so early? Is everything alright?"
"I quit my job!" Duncan replied.
"Why on earth did you do that?"
"Well, they were about to start sending me abroad again, and I really don't want to leave you guys all the time."
Andrea smiled, "Well, you'll get something I'm sure, what

with your experience. It's just a matter of time – maybe you can contract!"

Duncan was cheered up by her attitude. He would miss the variety of work at CyberSecure, but somehow he felt relieved that he had made the choice to leave."

Andrea fixed him a cup of tea. "Here ye go. Sit down and have this. I think you should take a few days to rest. You look shattered." Duncan sipped his tea, "I am a bit. Yeah a couple of days will do me good."

With the passing of just over six months nothing much had changed at CyberSecure. Even without Duncan they continued to stop the bad guys breaking into the government's most important systems. Hactivism undertaken by the Fourth Reich had, however, increased substantially, and they had now seemingly set their sites on gaining access to the Echelon network itself. No new agents had been recruited owing to the difficulty of finding, training, and in the end trusting new blood. CyberSecure had learned a hefty lesson from Vasily, an agent who had simply disappeared. Nobody had been able to confirm whether he had defected, been kidnapped, or even if he was still alive. The man who may have been able to find him had left around the same time, not keen on being forced into long absences from his family, something that a search for Vasily would no doubt entail.

Vasily was very much alive. Six months after leaving CyberSecure to find Hercule and halt the remaining threat from the Fourth Reich, he sat sipping a cool drink on a beach near Cancun. He had very quickly found Hercule in

Berlin, and after a few fraught hours had convinced him of his abilities and dislike for CyberSecure, Echelon, and the entire allied network. Both men had a common goal: To bring down Echelon. Only their reasons were different.

The two men had got on well from the beginning, but with the prospect of CyberSecure sending out a search party, they had decided it would be best if Vasily took a trip to Mexico, under a false passport of course. In the past six months Vasily had provided Hercule and his group with the information needed to give them a foothold into various government networks, but never once did he undertake any of the intrusions himself. He had bigger fish to fry. His first target was CyberSecure themselves. Ultimately he would ensure that if anything major on the Internet was to happen, that they would be the first to go; the blame for any ensuing damage would be attributed to their network. He was not interested in Hercule's goals for the Fourth Reich itself, but felt the manpower, and the ability to shift blame would be extremely handy when undertaking his own incursions.

He had spent the past couple of months attempting to reverse engineer Z4CK. Once he figured out how to decompile it, he would create the ultimate worm, using all of its learning and stealth capabilities. He decided to name this worm 'Tsunami'. It would destroy everything in its path, starting with Echelon. For the moment however, he had been unable to disassemble it. To get to it, and its source code, he would have to circumvent the security of the modified Zaurus. At all times he would be extremely careful, one mistake and an electromagnetic pulse could shoot through the powerful PDA, destroying its contents for all time. He had managed to disable the homing beacon, allowing him to quickly disappear from the CyberSecure radar.

Vasily had become impatient. He felt safe enough where he was, but knew that even though no extradition treaties existed between Mexico and the allied nations, this would not necessarily be a stumbling block to him being captured and brought back to the UK, or worse still, the United States.

He decided that now was the time to start his own campaign against CyberSecure, and duly got up from his seaside table, leaving a small tip and half of his drink, before moving inside to plan his attack. First he would remove one of his greatest annoyances...Riddles. He felt that Riddles was the reason for his brother's death, not fully appreciating the fact that he had been stopped by one of the few people he trusted, Duncan.

Like all competent computer hackers, Vasily had left a back door to the CyberSecure network in the form of a rootkit. It had been well hidden, having not yet been discovered by the best at CyberSecure. He was sure that his access would have been removed almost immediately he had disappeared, but his rootkit would give him super user access to one of the main entry points. The system was, like all of the other systems, completely firewalled off from the Internet.

He could have used Z4CK, but that would be too easy, and the Echelon network was geared up to dealing with attacks initiated from this piece of software; besides, he didn't really need it anyway.

The rootkit was extraordinarily clever, having been hidden within the Linux kernel, the core of the computer system. As the system started up, it automatically loaded the hidden software. If any administrator got suspicious, and studied the system, he would find nothing, as all of the software, its directories, and its processes were invisible. The network card had been set to listen for a specific string, whereupon it would allow complete access to the system, and provide the attacker with a command prompt. Vasily ensured he didn't have to bother with user ids and passwords. However, this was just the beginning. Once he had entered the gateway systems, he would make his way into the internal network, and from there, he would complete his initial goal.

Vasily not only knew the workings of CyberSecure's internal firewalls and computer systems, he was also aware of ways to circumvent the Intrusion Detection Systems. Powerful as the Open Source Security Information Manager (OSSIM) was, it could be beaten. It had been tuned to look for specific attack types. Vasily would use one he knew it would not detect.

Vasily took his laptop down from the top shelf in his cupboard, carefully removing some of the books he had placed on top to hide it. Mexico was no place to leave expensive IBM ThinkPad's lying about. He laid it down on a scratched table, ensuring he did not sit too close to the window. He had two reasons for this; it was easier to see the screen when shaded from the sun, and he was never sure if he was ever being watched. His paranoia, or as he termed it 'his sixth sense' had served him well in the past.

He logged into his system and brought up a console. Next he plugged a wireless network card into the system. Attached to it, was an oversized antenna, which picked up several open wireless networks. If he was going to intrude on any system, he was going to ensure it was not easily traced back to him. His apartment was situated close to the beach-side bar. He noticed that one of the access points was named 'Beach-side'. This would do nicely as any number of people in this public place could have used the access point in the past, or would do in the future. Vasily had compromised and now owned several systems on the Internet. He would chain his attack through many of them, jumping from Mexico, to Australia, then China to Germany, before finally hitting the server located in Scotland. This would more than likely lead the CyberSecure team on a wild goose chase. Once he had finished with the systems, he would securely wipe them to hide any trace of his identity. The owners would not be particularly happy about it, but they weren't important anyway.

Vasily connected to the wireless access point and quickly moved between the servers he needed to gain access to. It had been several weeks since he had used them, so it was possible the intrusions had been noticed and the systems hardened or rebuilt. He carefully logged in - each of them in turn giving him the access he needed. Soon he found himself sitting at the prompt of a small business system, which, according to Virtual Route, was located in Cologne.

Vasily sent the specially crafted string using the Netcat utility. He waited a matter of milliseconds before being greeted with a command prompt. He was in. Vasily smiled, letting out a sigh of relief. He now had very little time to complete the rest of his task. This part would not be difficult. He quickly started 'Elinks' - a console based browser, and browsed to the local intranet site. His browser downloaded a cookie, part of which was used for basic authentication and tracking purposes. Vasily edited this cookie data with information he had stolen from Riddles laptop a long time ago. He now clicked on the link for the restaurant, the website recognising him as Riddles. He quickly perused the dinner menu for that evening. Riddles had already made an order, but Vasily added a request for some extra ingredients to be added. He knew the canteen staff would not argue or even consult Riddles about the change. They did not like his condescending manner. He felt they were beneath him. If he didn't get what he wanted he often threw tantrums. This request would certainly be fulfilled, no questions asked.

Finally Vasily deleted a couple of log entries that had been created on the compromised server before logging off. He smiled at the thought of successfully completing his first goal. He was only sorry he would not be there to witness the outcome of his attack. He ran the commands to securely delete all of the data on each of the remote machines in turn, before finally closing his laptop, and putting it back on the top shelf. He then calmly walked to the kitchen to fix himself a drink and a quick snack, his work complete for the day.

Riddles busied himself with some research work. He was nearing the completion of a design for the usb3 device that would do almost everything. It would interface with the Echelon network for everything from logging in, to ordering food. He found ordering food on-line a chore and a waste of his valuable resource. He looked at the device, thinking that one day it could be used everywhere; it had endless potential. The finger print recognition was programmed to work only with the primary user. If you weren't the owner, you couldn't buy a thing. He decided he would call his prototype a life-unit.

He looked up as one of the canteen staff barged in through the door with a tray of food. This annoyed Riddles. "Are you incapable of knocking young man?" he said, frowning. The canteen staff member rolled his eyes, before putting the tray down on the table at the end of the lab. He watched Riddles for a second, waiting for a thanks of some kind. It never came. He shook his head before walking out of the lab. He was used to Riddles, but like the other staff, didn't like him much.

Some five minutes later Riddles decided it was time to eat. He blew his nose and stuffed his handkerchief back into his pocket. His hay fever had not been good this week, and it was really beginning to annoy him. He drew a magazine from the shelf, and sat down to eat. The first course of Spaghetti Bolognese was wolfed down, leaving the lapels of his white lab coat tinged with tomato sauce. Never mind, he thought to himself, some underling will wash it! He turned the pages of his New Scientist magazine, engrossed in an article about the latest scram jet propulsion technologies. He lifted the dessert spoon to his mouth and took a large mouthful of custard and crumble, savouring the taste of the rhubarb.

Riddles took another large spoonful, concentrating completely on his magazine. After a couple more mouthfuls of crumble he began to notice a taste he did not recognise. It was only then that he put the magazine down, and began to examine the contents of the bowl. He was starting to feel a strange swelling sensation in his mouth. Scrutinising the contents, he spotted the culprit. Mixed among the rhubarb, were stewed apples. Riddles began to panic; he knew he was allergic to apples. It had only been a couple of minutes since the first spoonful, but already he was going in to anaphylactic shock. His tongue, throat and other mucus membranes began to swell. His breathing became laboured as his respiratory system began to fail. Gasping for breath, he struggled to reach the lab door, only to fall short, knocking over some electronic equipment in the process. Trembling on the floor, he attempted to call out, his eyes reddening, beginning to water. His last moments were spent in a coma. Finally his body gave out. It had taken all of twelve minutes. Riddles body shook for a few seconds before a final quiet stillness came. He wasn't found for fifteen hours. His death had been as solitary as his life.

Almost everyone within CyberSecure was questioned following the discovery of Riddles lifeless body. The postmortem showed the cause of death as anaphylactic shock: A severe allergic reaction, due to ingestion of apple. Investigations began into how, what was initially believed to be an accident could have happened. A cursory glance over the food orders from the evening before showed that Riddles, or someone pretending to be Riddles, had changed the order to add in the stewed apples just before dinner was delivered. Intranet server logs were checked for corresponding IP addresses to make sure the order was made from Riddles's machine. The order had not. In fact, there were no corresponding log entries. Terminus, who had been heading the investigation, reported to Chaos. "We're sure it was no-one inside. We have our suspicions that it may have come from one of the gateway servers. NTOP noticed some HTTP traffic coming from the DMZ, which is really unusual."

Chaos was incredulous, "You mean that an external entity infiltrated one of the gateway servers, just to change a food order?" Terminus shifted his stance nervously. "Not just anyone. As far as I'm concerned this is murder. There are only two people I know with the skill, a dislike for Riddles, and the knowledge of his weaknesses to do this."
"Well, provide the answer." snapped Chaos.
"Duncan, sorry Thor, or Vasily."
"Right pull them in then."
Terminus hesitated, "We can bring Duncan in, but as you'll remember we have no idea where Vasily is; or even if he is alive!"
"I know; I know...I've been keeping my finger on the pulse. I'm aware that Vasily has been missing for several weeks," replied a frustrated Chaos.
"Several months Sir." replied Terminus.
Chaos scowled, "Don't get smart with me. Just get them in as quickly as you can."

Duncan had found it difficult to find another position that interested him. He had managed to get a few short-term support contracts since leaving CyberSecure, but today there was no work. The doorbell rang. "Who could this be?" he moaned. His motivation to do anything had been greatly reduced. The difficulty in obtaining a position he liked, or could feel secure in, had been tougher than he had estimated. He had begun to worry about his savings that were now starting to dwindle.

He opened the door and reeled with surprise at seeing Terminus's face. Duncan opened his mouth to enquire as to the meaning of the visit but was interrupted before he could speak.
"Come with me, there has been an incident." Duncan said nothing. He lifted his jacket from the coat hook, and grabbed his mobile phone from the kitchen table, before wandering outside. He locked the door behind him, and got into the backseat of the car, slightly bemused to find Loki sitting at the steering wheel, smiling. The two men shook hands, "How's it goin' Doughnut?" Duncan smiled, "I'm fine...I think. See you're still the same." Loki laughed, "Why change perfection?" Terminus seemed harassed, "Please, less of the idle banter. The sooner we get this sorted out the better." Loki threw a mischievous glance, "Fine, you said it!" With that Loki revved the engine, and put his foot flat to the floor. The tires screeched as he turned a near ninety degree corner. "Sorry, slight misjudgement," he laughed, as both of his passengers were thrown across their seats to the other side of the car.

Duncan sat in the interview room, still wondering what on earth was going on. He had been there for at least fifteen minutes, drinking a strong black coffee, whilst trying to get over Loki's mad driving. He was glad to have survived again. Finally, Terminus entered with Chaos and Loki. Chaos sat down on a grey plastic chair. Terminus stood near the two-way mirror on the left hand side, and Loki leaned against the wall behind Chaos.

Chaos began, "Coffee alright?" Duncan looked at everyone in turn, "Err, yep. Same as it ever was?" He replied, confused. "What's this all about?" He squinted slightly as the light directly above him began to project heat into his forehead. "Chaos leaned forward, talking slowly, and deliberately.
"We'd like you to inform us how you did it?"
"How I did what?"
"How you broke in."
"Broke into what?"
Loki began to get annoyed, "You fuckin' know what we're talking about...where do you think?"

Terminus held up his hand to calm Loki down. Chaos continued, "Did you leave a back door in one of the DMZ servers?"
Duncan took a deep breath, "Look, this is a bit ridiculous. I have no idea what the hell you're talking about. Why on earth would I want to break into here, when I spent most of my life defending the bloody place?"
Loki jumped towards the table, "Because you wanted to kill Riddles. He was a prick, but he didn't deserve that!" Duncan dropped the coffee cup he had been holding. "What, how did that happen?" The shock in his voice was apparent." Terminus now butted in, "We hoped you would tell us." Suddenly it clicked, "So you think I killed Riddles? No way! You guys have worked with me for years; you should know me better."
Duncan shook his head, "I didn't do it. I don't know anything about it, and I've got to say I'm sickened by this whole thing." He paused before pushing the chair out from behind him and getting up, "If you wouldn't mind, I'd like to

get the fuck out of here. I'll make my own way home." Chaos also stood up, "Please, not so fast. We do believe you. The shocked reaction alone confirmed what we were quite sure of, however we had to follow procedure on this one. We'll fill you in on the details of what we think happened."

For a further fifteen minutes the situation was explained; the cause of death, the changes made, and the implications for the future. Terminus finished demonstrating how the unknown hacker had got in. He put his pen down on the whiteboard ledge. Chaos turned to Duncan, "We think this was Vasily's work. He had the insider knowledge to do this. We'd like you back on board. We need someone to fill a multi-functional role, designer and agent.

Duncan thought for a few seconds, "We can talk terms. Lay them on the table and I'll see." Chaos agreed.

"In the meantime, do you have any further information on Vasily?" asked Duncan. Terminus shook his head, "Nothing. He obviously used multiple hops before attacking here. The last hop was traced back to Cologne, so maybe he is still in Germany." Duncan thought for a second. I doubt very much if he is still in Europe. Were we able to get the logs back from that server?" Terminus was quick to reply, "Nope, completely wiped."
Duncan looked worried, "Vasily is a powerful enemy. He knows us inside and out. Add that to the knowledge, experience and willingness to cause damage, and we have a dangerous opponent. We haven't seen the last of him. What of the Fourth Reich, any more from them?"
Terminus replied, "It's been surprisingly quiet, too quiet in fact. We're attempting to monitor them as well, but certainly nothing of any significance this week."
"Is the hole in the network secured?" asked Duncan.
Chaos replied, "It is. We must ensure this never happens

again. We haven't had an opportunity to wrap some process round it yet, and that's the next step."
Duncan sighed, "Action - not process, is more important. Let's get to work and see what else we can find."

All of the men agreed, ending the meeting abruptly. Duncan was the last to leave the room, switching the light off behind the group. He made his way with the others towards the communications centre. Terminus turned to him, "Welcome back. Maybe now we'll be able to run these hackers to ground."
Duncan seemed slightly concerned, almost distant, "I hope so; I hope so."

Late December 2017

Two years had passed since the death of Riddles. No more attacks had come from the Fourth Reich. If Vasily was active he still hadn't been detected. Small successes had been had by CyberSecure, but in general it had been a remarkably quiet two years. CyberSecure seemed no closer to finding Vasily than they had been two years prior.
In that time Vasily had kept up to speed with the goings on of the various government agencies and security authorities. He had not ventured a probe or a browser near their computer systems, much as he was tempted too. One thing he had learned from his time spent removing the core of the Russian mafia was patience. He and the Fourth Reich had been busying themselves for the big one; A full-scale cyber attack.

Vasily whooped for joy as he finally completed his modification of Z4CK. The once powerful security tool had now become a more powerful self replicating stealth worm. Its controller mechanism had been changed, allowing it to be unleashed on unsuspecting government agencies. It would be bought by certain foreign powers, which would provide large quantities of cash and a safe haven in return. Vasily didn't need the cash, but he would need a safe haven. He didn't wish to spend any time in prison, never mind the amount he would be sent down for if caught. He had tested his new worm named 'Tsunami' on a small test network. Utter devastation had been swift. He had reported this to Hercule.

"That is excellent news. Do you have an initial target?"

Vasily did not hesitate. "Oh yes my friend. We must strike first at the only people who may be able to stop us. We must strike the big 'E'." Hercule knew very well that this was Echelon.

Hercule's response was short. "Of course, our mutual enemy; enjoy."

Within a couple of days Tsunami had been placed in a latent state on thousands of systems world-wide. It sat, silently waiting for the final command string, the trigger. Vasily mopped the sweat from his brow, and took a nervous sip of some steaming hot black coffee. He sat in a down market Internet cafe, situated in one of the back streets of Prague. No one would check what he was doing, or care. It was perfect. He connected to one of the zombie systems and fed in the final command.

Tsunami -scan -link -all -start echelon -mailword regards

Instantly the software sprang to life. Its first task was to look for anything with the target name of 'echelon'. It began making DNS requests, search engine requests, whois requests, finding anything linked to its target. Phase 2 began within a couple of minutes with a vulnerability scan of some of the targets found. As it began the second of these tasks it sent information through the 'link' switch waking the next zombie, and the process began again.

Chapter 9

Zero day destruction

As each of the 1,000 zombies began their individual processes in turn, the affects on a generally stable core Internet infrastructure were as yet unapparent. However, no more than fifteen minutes later, almost 100,000 systems had been infected. Domain name servers everywhere began to slow down with the overwhelming 'DNS' and 'whois' requests fired at them in quick succession from each and every one of the compromised systems. The Internet's powerful search engines began to slow with the extra queries. Anything linked to the echelon network found as part of any of the two requests began to find themselves in a distributed denial of service situation. It would only be a matter of time before some way was found of breaking into Echelon. Every scan produced a result, every result produced a search, and so the cycle continued.

The combined parallel processing power was sure to succeed, battering down the defences of the most securely configured systems. Even sites dedicated to exposing Echelon were attacked. Within minutes, these less secure systems had fallen to the exploits thrown at them. Once attached, the worm copied itself onto the compromised system, reporting back to the primary zombie, before attacking further into the network.

At CyberSecure the attacks had been noticed almost the instant they had begun. Loki sat at the command console watching in astonishment at the increases in Internet activity. He had not seen anything quite so dramatic before. He quickly tapped at the keyboard, checking the requests and the searches being made. "Shit," he mumbled to himself as he realized they related to Echelon. Immediately he picked up the phone, calling first Terminus, and then

Duncan. "Hi, ye better get here quickly, all hell has just kicked off across the net, and it's aimed at us. I think Vasily has just surfaced!"

Within a couple of minutes both men were pushing their palms against the biometrics reader on the outside of the sealed control room door. It swung open, the noise from the doors vacuum seal attracting Loki's attention away from his console. Duncan immediately ran to the Intrusion Detection Systems. Bringing up the Open Source Security Information Manager web page, it quickly became obvious to him what was happening. "It's Vasily alright. We're being pounded, and he's using Z4CK. I recognise the signature!"

"That wee Russky bastard, I thought it would be him!" exclaimed Loki.

Terminus was as calm as ever. Duncan had never known him to be anything but calm. His efficiency should have meant he went far, but he had also been tainted by the Brussels failure years before. This was one of the reasons Terminus was keen to get hold of Vasily, Hercule, and the Fourth Reich. Revenge for a lost career was at the forefront of his mind.

Alerts continued to fire off as OSSIM reported scans, probes, exploits, and denial of service attacks.

"The volume of attacks is increasing by the second." Duncan stated, the concern apparent in his voice.

"We had better inform Chaos." Terminus reached for the phone. None of the men were sure what calling Chaos would achieve, but they knew that only he would be able to back up any decisions they made.

Chaos sat behind the large oak desk in his office blissfully unaware of the on going crisis. He tapped impatiently on his laptop, waiting for a reply to an email he had sent earlier that afternoon. His main priority was staffing issues. He had complained on several occasions that he could not provide 'follow the sun' cover, but the bureaucracy was grinding too slowly even for him. He held out little hope of obtaining a swift reply.

He sighed, and swivelled in his chair, glancing at the picture of his family he saw only intermittently. His long working schedules self-induced. His attention was drawn back to his laptop by a sudden beep.
"My God! They've replied!" Chaos couldn't believe it. For once, head office had actually had the decency to reply in a timely manner.

He opened the email to find the word 'regards' at the top of the message. This didn't make any sense to him. Perhaps they've added an attachment, he thought to himself. He looked around, and sure enough, there was an attachment. As he opened it, he was again bemused to find it empty. He quickly closed the email and deleted it. "Stupid idiots," he whispered under his breath.

Picking up a cup of coffee, which had cooled to a level he liked, he took a sip, almost spilling it as the phone rang. Chaos leaned across the table and picked it up.
"Yes…what is it…we're under attack? From where?"
As he finished his somewhat stuttered sentence, the network light on his laptop began to flash erratically. It wasn't until the hard disk began to grind, however, that he noticed a problem. "Hold on a second," he shouted at Terminus, "there's something up with this blasted laptop." He winced as the dull screeching grew louder.

Chaos's laptop had been compromised. Tsunami had finally found its way in via the head office mail system, and had in turn infected the mail boxes of several of the managers. The worm's clever design had allowed it to search for emails to reply to, making it more likely that the attachment would be opened. From there it had sent out a reply to each and every individual who had not yet received one, adding the text 'regards' at the start of the message. Mail began to flood the system. Once this had been exhausted it began the process of owning, and locking down the system, before beginning more scans, probes and searches. Internal networks were now beginning to fall to the power of this unstoppable, multifaceted worm.

Chaos's machine screeched, before suddenly stopping. The laptop then rebooted itself. "I think I've suffered a virus infection." Chaos stated, picking up the phone again.
"I'll be right there!" Duncan shook his head, a worried look crossing his face. His look was mirrored by Terminus.
"Better go and check the boss." He flew out of the control room and down the corridor to Chaos's room.

Chaos's laptop had rebooted by the time Duncan reached it. At the top of the screen sat the words:

Tsunami owns this computer. Any attempt to disconnect it from the network, or switch it off, will results in the destruction of all data.

"Switch it off." Duncan quickly flicked the power switch on the system, which fell silent. "What have you done? All of my data will be lost!" Chaos gasped.
"Hopefully saved some of the network," came the swift reply. For a short while everything fell silent. Duncan breathed a sigh of relief; sure he had limited the damage. Both men sat down. Chaos seemed in shock - Duncan was merely exhausted. "I suggest we switch all of our systems off, at least temporarily. You should probably advise head office to do the same." For once Chaos agreed. "I'll give the order. If you could touch base with the control room, we can initiate the damage limitation."

Duncan got up to leave the room when Chaos's phone rang once more. "He's on his way." Chaos put the phone down and held his head in his hands. Duncan didn't need to ask, but simply closed the door and sprinted towards the control room. As he passed each of the offices and living quarters, he could just make out a low-level grinding coming from most of the rooms he passed. He knew it was too late. "Switch all of the systems off!" he shouted to anyone he saw.

Finally reaching the door of the control room, he placed his palm over the biometrics reader. It flashed, before denying him access. Duncan had not noticed this, walking straight into the locked door. He tried again. Access denied. Through the glass of the control room door Duncan could see Terminus and Loki running around. The efficient sound proofing allowed no sound to enter or escape. Duncan banged his fist on the door, and waved his arms in the air in the hope of attracting someone's attention. Glancing at the computer systems located in the racks across the back of the room, Duncan could see network and hard disk lights locked. Text scrolled endlessly on some of the large alert monitors. The IDS, one of the most secure systems, had been completely compromised, sitting with the same message that had previously been seen on Chaos's laptop. Still no-one allowed Duncan in.

Another five minutes passed when suddenly, without any warning, the control room door opened of its own accord. All of the other doors also unlocked themselves. The physical security systems had now been breached. The worm would not stop; ever changing, learning, and compromising anything that stood in its way, before finally exiting the network, to find another target somewhere else on the Internet.

Duncan walked into the control room to join Loki and

Terminus in switching off all of the systems. With the exception of humming power supplies, all was quiet. The Tsunami worm had wreaked digital devastation on one of the worlds most secure networks.
"If it can do this here, what will it be like everywhere else?" Terminus asked Duncan. Duncan sat down in one of the control room chairs, shaking. "God knows, God only knows."

At the headquarters of the Royal Scottish Banking Group several security technicians sat monitoring the computer gateways in between obtaining coffee and throwing the occasional jibe at a colleague. They had just been audited, having been given a clean bill of health. Their Internet facing Web and Mail servers were fully patched against all vulnerabilities. They had not yet witnessed anything that would alarm them. Sure they were scanned, probed, and even attacked hundreds of times in a day, but security was tight enough to combat most things out there. Unlike Echelon and CyberSecure they did not have access to the same early warning systems. The first knowledge they had of any problem was when one of the email team ran over to their section.

"Are you aware of any problems? Virus attacks or new spam outbreaks?" A tall dark haired bespectacled man leaned over the desk, waiting for a quick answer to his direct question. The Security team were a surprisingly laid back bunch. Instant answers weren't their strong point.
"Why do you ask?"
The tall man grabbed a seat and sat down, adjusting his gold wire-frame spectacles. "Take a look at this." He pushed a sheet of paper with the statistics from the mail-scanner system in front of the security administrator.

"Our mail flow is going through the roof, and the CPU on the primary mail system is maxed out."

"Ian," the administrator called to the platform performance guru, "have you seen any problems?"
Ian flicked to one of the performance web pages. "Err, yes, you better come and take a look at this. All the DMZ network and CPU stats are going mad!"
The rest of the team crowded round the performance monitoring system as the first emails started popping into each of the individual's mail boxes. "Don't open anything right now!"

It was then that another member of the security team saw the first worrying alert. "This is saying we've been compromised. Something has written to one of the DMZ web server file systems!" Everyone turned to the security manager sitting in the corner near the window. He dithered for a second, unsure of the best approach, always wary of making controversial decisions. "What do you suggest?" He aimed the question at the whole team.
Jim piped up, "We need to get this machine off the network, and disconnect the Internet connection – at least temporarily."

The security manager swallowed uneasily as he took in what seemed to be the only option. In his head he hoped it was the right thing to do. He knew the company could potentially lose millions, and a wrong decision meant his job was on the line.
"Right guys, let's talk to networks and get the Internet pipe disconnected. Kev, Drew – run down to the data centre and switch off the rest of the Internet facing servers. I'll inform the business, they won't be happy, but it is for the best!"

The two technicians sprinted down to the Data Centre which was located in a bomb proof bunker over two hundred yards from the main building. It was a beautiful sunny day, and people ambled to their destinations, or sat on benches taking in the unusual warmth. The men had no time to take it easy as they rushed up the stairs to the main doorway. They flashed their ID cards at the security guard on the way, who took no real notice. He knew them anyway. After swiping through layers of security doors they finally reached the core of the network. Hundreds of servers sat in racks positioned in rows along the grey carpeted floor. The large, air-conditioned room was noisy but cool, something welcomed by the technicians, who were now rushing from system to system, unlocking each of the individual racks to get to the powerful servers within. Cabling ran vertically from the connecting switches straight into the systems. Drew and Kev found it incredible that they should be switching these systems off. The systems had never been down. Even during upgrades the systems had been failed over to a backup system, and now they were on the brink of switching all of them off. The consequences – almost a third of UK Internet VISA and SWITCH transactions would be halted, costing companies millions, and causing turmoil in a country that ran on virtual cash.

They had begun by powering down each of the systems in the correct manner, initiating the standard shutdown sequences. Their uncertainty soon grew to panic as the inexorable screeching of grinding hard disks began to overcome the systems they had not yet reached. Seconds later they were running around in a panic, unceremoniously unplugging any system they could reach in time. Sweat poured from the men's brows as they opened each door in turn, located the correct cables, and removed them from the sockets.

"How's it going Drew?" Kev shouted above the sound of the cooling systems and grinding machines."

Drew responded, slight panic in his voice, "I'm not getting round them quick enough – is there a way to switch each of the racks off?"

As Kevin and Drew reached the last row of racks it was obvious they had done too little too late. The worm had spread from the well-secured Internet facing systems to the internal systems. Security was seen as less important on these, with accessibility being paramount. The spread across these systems had been like lightning. The last of the systems to be reached were already either rebooting, or sitting with the message stating Tsunami's ownership of the system.

The senior network technician struggled to let himself into the server room. There was an air of exasperation in his voice. "We tried to shut down the network switches, but the worm used up all the available bandwidth on the network. We couldn't connect to them to shut them down...it was hopeless...how about you?" Kevin and Drew sat on a large wooden test bench. Kevin threw his set of cabinet keys to the floor - frustrated they had not been able to save many of the systems. "The damage is phenomenal. We didn't get to them in time." He pointed at some of the screens. All had the same, now familiar message. "Even if we manage to get all this back from tape, it's going to take us a while to get the transaction processing going again. I've never seen anything like this...it's worse than Code Red, Melissa, and Slammer put together!"

The network technician stopped for a brief moment to take in the enormity of the damage, before he ran over to the networking racks, and switched off the remainder of the switches. Tsunami had already found a way out of the network, and began the cycle of devastation once more.

"The business is keen to know how this happened." The network technician finally came and sat down next to the other men. "There will definitely be a review!"

"A witch-hunt you mean!" Drew remarked.
"Yep, this is where all the big bosses finally come out of their offices – to point the finger!" Kev shook his head.
"With this amount of money lost heads will probably roll!"
"It's typical. They pay no attention to what we tell them, and refuse to spend the money on internal security, and now the hypocrites will come out and ask why we didn't secure everything!"
Drew nodded in agreement, "You can't win. It takes destruction on this scale to make them sit up and take notice."
"I've no idea how long it will take to get everything back up and running, this bloody worm is still going to be bouncing round on the network, waiting to infect anything we fix."

All three men agreed that the situation was dire, but also knew they had done all that they could for the moment. There wasn't much the team could do against a zero-day exploit. Dejected, they headed back to their respective departments, knowing they had a lot of work, and a lot of awkward questions ahead.

Over the next couple of days, anything that had been connected to the Internet had been switched off, defaced, taken over, or destroyed. Havoc had not only ensued on the Internet, where the replicating worm had sucked up all of the bandwidth. The damage had been farther reaching than even CyberSecure or Vasily could have imagined.

Tsunami's ability to learn had enabled it to penetrate security, life support, power, electricity, telephony and early warning systems. Motor accidents due to traffic light failure had crippled both the emergency services and transport systems. Malfunctioning air traffic control and flight booking systems had meant almost all flights had been cancelled, mainly due to safety concerns. ATMs had randomly spat out money in some areas, and retained bank cards in others. Until the Tsunami worm, the world had not realised just how reliant on computer systems it had become. Everything was in some way connected, and reachable from anywhere else. Only the poorest regions in the world, where computer penetration was lower, or technologies were old, suffered less.

The Tsunami worm's devastation was complete. Almost every site on the Internet had been affected. Only those who had been forewarned, and had managed to cut themselves off in time had been saved. Some, who had decided to reconnect their systems prematurely, had been infected almost instantly by the worm, which still jumped from system to system at lightning speed. It would be difficult to find an antidote for such a complex piece of software, finding its way in through any means possible. It was unlike anything that had gone before it. Most had targeted a single, patchable vulnerability.

Following on from the computer chaos, came the physical chaos. Happenings in Cyberspace had for many years directly affected economies. The stock markets had crashed, literally, the worm suspending all trading. The human cost was beginning to mount as emergency services and hospital computer systems went into melt down. Transport and power failures meant essential supplies such as food and electricity were not delivered. Looting was widespread as gangs took advantage of the situation to steal the latest goods. Parents desperate to get food for their families walked into shops and simply took what they needed. With communication systems mostly inoperable, no-one was truly aware of how widespread the problem had become.

Broadcasting of any sort had also been badly affected. For one day, the networks fell silent. The worried cries of bemused people, left in the dark, desperate for information, reprised the world over.

At CyberSecure only the most secure, stand-alone communications and computer systems had survived. It was across one of these channels that Hades called in. The video conferencing system usually displayed a clear, crisp picture. Today, Hades thin face could barely be seen across the 12,000 miles separating him from the rest of the team. The world had seemed an extraordinarily small place, where communication was as easy with someone in the next country, as with someone next door prior to the Tsunami worm.

"How's it goin' Dunc?" His once straggly shock of blond hair had receded to the sides of his head during the years spent in Australia. He, like Duncan, had grown older, but had not lost any of his cheeky side.
"Pretty crap here Cam," Duncan responded, using his friend's real name. "How's it down in Oz?"
Hades smiled, "I would say same shit different day…but that's definitely not the case!" He rubbed the sleep out of one of his eyes.
"I just got up to find most of my kit gubbed. This bloody Tsunami worm caused total meltdown down here, and to think I slept through it!" The screen crackled and faded for a second, the volume decreasing temporarily. When the sound and pictures returned it was to Hades swearing at his console. "Bloody cheap shite! I told the arseholes not to buy this crap!"
Duncan laughed at Cam's exasperation. He always found his tantrums entertaining.

"Ah, there you are…couldn't see you for a minute. So where do we go from here?" Cam asked.
"Well, we'll have to discuss it, but we'll need to take a proper look at the damage, before we assess our next move. One thing's for sure, we're going to be doing a lot of overtime in the next while!" Duncan replied.
Cam agreed, "If only we got paid for it eh?"

Duncan nodded, the video connection beginning to fade again. A few seconds later it stabilised.
"The thing I worry about is how many hours I will be working. Yet again I'm seeing less and less of Andrea and Tom. Too many late nights - might be the thing that breaks it...it's already pretty stressed." Duncan sighed.
"Well luckily for me, I don't have that problem...me and the misses can't stand the sight of each other anyway. The more I'm out the better." The faint words "I heard that!" came from somewhere behind Cam.
He smiled, "I better get off of this...got the wee Sheila to attend to...if you know what I mean!"
Duncan saluted and shook his head, "Oh to be so upbeat all the time. See you, signing off."

An irate Hercule decided to pick up the phone and call Vasily. He was pretty sure that the damage done by the Tsunami worm would ensure that Echelon would not be able to track the call. He was also unsure if he would be able to get through. After several attempts, and some swearing later, a connection was made. The phone at the other end rang. Impatiently Hercule growled into the hand-set. "Pick the phone up you fool!"

A click was followed by a quick 'hello'. Hercule instantly recognised it as Vasily's voice. "Have you seen what your stupid worm has done?" Vasily was slow to respond. "If you are going to talk to me in this way, then I will hang up!" Hercule attempted to calm himself down.
"You were only supposed to destroy the Echelon network and a few government agencies! You're worm has gone too far!" He stuttered, attempting to not lose his temper further. "We have been infected. We are unable to do anything short of phone people you idiot!" The phone went dead and Hercule swore once more. Several more attempts saw

Hercule finally obtain a connection again.

"I lost my connection there."

"No you didn't," replied Vasily, "I cut you off. Do not ever call me an idiot. I warned you I would cut you off. Remember my friend, you need me more than I need you!"

Hercule took a deep breath, "Very well. How can we fix our systems? Do you have a fix?"

"No."

"No?" Hercule was astonished. "You can't easily reverse this damage? Then how are we to repair our systems?"

"In the same way everyone else will. You have technical people – they must advise you. In an insurgency such as this, there will always be collateral damage." His voice was calm, almost monotone.

"What?" Hercule was furious. "I demand that we meet up. We need to discuss this!"

"No my friend. That will never happen. The Fourth Reich had resources I needed. In return I have used my skills to destroy various government networks. It is up to you to further your cause. I obviously do not believe in something that looks to promote the Nazi cause, or help a group of people who perpetrated unspeakable cruelties against my mother country."

Hercule shouted down his mobile phone, "We will hunt you down for this. From here you are an enemy!"

Vasily laughed, "Your group is a joke. I have had more dangerous enemies in the past. Echelon and the mafia were the reasons my brother died. It has taken me years, but I finally have my revenge. You will not hear from me again."

The phone went dead. Hercule closed it, and sat down. He uttered quietly to himself, "Merde." All around him systems had been infected. Tsunami owned them all. They had attempted to recover one of the test systems, only to find their data corrupted. Like the rest of the Internet, they too were crippled.

Vasily quickly packed his bag. His small dingy flat near a brothel on the outskirts of Prague had served him well for the short time he had been there, but now it was very much time to move on.

Before leaving, he wiped the laptop hard disk of all data. He removed it, before wiping the system of all finger prints. Finally he dumped the chassis in the bin. No doubt it would be picked up, perhaps even sold on in a pub somewhere, becoming nothing more than a low end games system, or word-processor. Vasily stuffed the hard drive into his pocket, grabbed his bag from the bed, and took one last look at the damp flat that had been his home for the last few months. He knew he wouldn't be leaving the country for at least a while.

With transport links chaotic, worldwide travel had been stifled for the first time since September 11th 2001. Vasily had prepared for this eventuality; having withdrawn enough cash to allow him to survive for a couple of months. Most people had not been so fortunate, and now, with ATMs out of order, and banking systems reeling from the Tsunami worm, ordinary people found themselves unable to obtain currency, or use their credit cards.

As he walked down one of the back alleys, he slipped on one of the cobbles, twisting his ankle. "Damn, this place!" He threw the hard drive into a small skip, and continued to hobble down the road. He muttered to himself, "I will not keep living like this." In his mind he thought about the money located in a Swiss bank account he owned, and how he would spend it somewhere far from this wretched place.

It had just gone 11pm when Duncan finally pulled into his driveway. Andrea had waited up for him.

"It's started again hasn't it?"
"Sorry?" Duncan laid down his briefcase and walked over to give his wife a hug. She gently pushed him away.
"Tom and I have hardly seen you. Your hours are increasing again!"
Duncan was in no mood for an argument. "Yeah, that's the way it is I'm afraid. This Tsunami worm has had a major impact on all of the computer systems around the globe."
"I don't really care, all I want to know is whether or not you'll have time to see your family again. I understand, but Tom doesn't!" Andrea stood, arms folded, waiting for an answer.
"Look, it'll get sorted, and then we'll be back on an even keel...okay? Now I'm tired. I'm going to get something to eat and get to bed."
Andrea shook her head, "And then it's straight back to work in the morning...some life!"

Duncan was becoming annoyed, "You saw how it was out there. In several months I barely managed to get another job. It's what happens in this field of work at my age. You're right, it's going to be a busy time, and I can't guarantee how much I'll be here. I think the Tsunami worm was based on a piece of software I wrote years ago. We were the main targets for it. I have to do something about this!"
Andrea began to climb the stairs, "Okay, but whilst you're off saving the world, remember to give a thought for your son. His world is in a state of limbo!"

Duncan walked into the kitchen and opened the fridge. He picked up some sausages and eggs, and fried them up in a pan. Some fifteen minutes later he sat munching a sausage and egg sandwich, whilst sipping a piping hot cup of coffee. It wasn't the best recipe for health, or helping him get to sleep. On finishing he dumped the plate into the sink, before quietly walking upstairs with the remainder of his coffee.

The lights were off. His heart sank. It saddened him that he had ended the day on such a sour note - one that wouldn't get fixed for at least another twenty-four hours. He knew he would be awake before anyone else next morning, and yet again, he would be away before he could see his son. More than likely another day in his life lost.

Chapter 10

The rise of Sec-Net

An emergency meeting of the highest managers of the Echelon network had been called for the next morning. Duncan had been invited for reasons unknown to himself. Although one of the more experienced team leaders, it was unusual for him to be called into the presence of what was termed within the team as the 'High heid yins'. His invite made him nervous.

Terminus met him as he swiped in through the newly repaired security door. Nothing much else had been fixed, and many systems still sat in a state of limbo.
"Have you any idea why I'm required in there?" Duncan asked Terminus.
"I've no idea, but you better be careful what you say. I get the feeling they're not here to promote anyone!"
"I thought as much."
A steely look made its way across Duncan's face, "Well, they may look for a scapegoat, but it's not going to be me."
Loki walked down to the door, "If they give you any shit, just tell them to shove it up they're arse. They're a useless bunch of dumb fucks anyway...always looking to blame someone for the slightest thing.

A look of disapproval crossed Terminus's face. "We're all one team. You should have some respect for your superiors!
"People earn my respect, and these twats haven't." Loki quipped.
He walked up to Duncan. "Don't take any crap from them...it was the russky that did this, not you. Don't lose sight of that fact! It's not your fault you took the fucker on!"
"Cheers...I think." Duncan replied, as he began to head to

the designated meeting room.

A few hundred yards further down the shiny metal corridors, Duncan found himself standing before the doors to the executive meeting room. He drew a deep breath and paused for a second, looking at his reflection in the polished brass number on the door. It was as if he was looking at the entrance to a first class compartment on the Orient Express. He hadn't worn a suit that day; perhaps he should have, he thought. Maybe it would make a slight difference, adding a dusting of professionalism. After a short period he knocked, opening the door, after being asked to enter.

Duncan walked into the room with as much confidence as he could muster. He could sense a bead of sweat forming on his forehead, his hands becoming clammy, yet cold. Five men and a single woman sat round the table. Some looked up, staring directly at him; others scribbled notes on their black leather bound notepads, intent on completing their writings, or ignoring the minion who had entered their presence. Duncan had seen most of their pictures before, but had never met them. It was not common practise for these people to visit the outer lying, less glamorous communications centres.

Duncan was asked to take a seat by one of the men who he recognised as the head of counter intelligence. A paper was pushed in front of him. He glanced at it, half turning one of the pages to squint at the text on the second page. It read Sec-Net and the need for increased security. Duncan had never heard of Sec-Net.

Duncan wondered if any more important people would be joining them. The room had full video-conferencing facilities. A large screen hung on the beige tinted walls. Video cameras had been built into several nooks and crannies, allowing the focus to be changed depending on who was speaking. Then he remembered, much of the communication systems were still down, which explained why this small band of important directors and generals had actually travelled to Scotland. Duncan's mind began to drift. He thought to himself that had this been Paris, or Rome, there would have been more of them.

Chaos, the least senior of the group, introduced each one in turn. Again, some of them acknowledged Duncan, others merely grunted, or nodded their heads. Duncan received the best response from the lady sitting to his left. She had been introduced as the Director of security research, Anne Lawrie. Riddles had met her a couple of times to show her some of his inventions, and was of course enthusiastic of her, primarily due to the fact that she was someone who was actually interested in listening to him. Realising that he was in her presence eased his anxiety somewhat. He began to hope that this was slightly more than just a witch-hunt.

Following the introductions, Chaos handed Duncan an agenda for the meeting, and asked him to quickly read over it. Duncan read the text from the gleaming white sheet of paper, beginning to realise just how difficult this session may become for him. He would have to concentrate hard, and hope for the best Chaos would be there to help. That would be a first.

Colonel James White, a grey haired, clean-shaven man, started the questioning. His questions were, as expected, direct and to the point. He had a neutral accent. Duncan was unable to determine where in the UK he had hailed from.
"What can you tell us about this Tsunami worm that struck yesterday?"
Duncan's glance drifted around the table to each of the expectant faces in turn. "It seems to be a derivative of a piece of security software I wrote almost 15 years ago...adapted of course. We use Z4CK on our standard

issue Zaurus SLC-4000's along with some of the laptops. It's an extremely handy tool in the fight against cyber criminals." Duncan stopped, waiting to find out if this was enough information for the bosses.

"So," Colonel White continued, "can you tell me how this software...which I'm assuming is still top secret, got into the wild?"

Duncan paused for a second, throwing a rather confused look to Chaos. "I thought you would have already known that? A couple of years ago, an agent...Vasily, a Russian we recruited," Chaos butted in, "You recruited." Duncan was annoyed at the interruption, and the attempt to apportion blame.

"No Sir, if you remember, I was sent to Moscow. I seem to remember in fact, that it was you who sent me. I was about to leave at the time, but you would not provide a reference unless I completed the highly important mission first!" A few murmurs were raised around the table; a few looks of disdain were sent Chaos's way.

Chaos attempted to reply, but was stopped by Colonel White. "I couldn't give a monkey who did what. Do we know where this Vasily is?" He waited for Chaos to answer. "We're not sure," was the stuttered reply.

A look of surprise took the aggression out of the Colonels face. He looked to Duncan for further information. Duncan answered the query. "No, we don't know."

Colonel White shook his head in disbelief, but chose not to make any more of the situation. "Right then, as you can see from the agenda, there are several things that we need to do here, and pronto! If you wouldn't mind dimming the lights, and readying my slides." Chaos scurried off to perform the task he had been provided. A few minutes later the civilians and military personnel were staring up at a rather basic slide projected onto the wall.

"First, clean up this bloody mess. I want all hands on deck to get Echelon and CyberSecure functional as quickly as possible. It is a matter of national security." He again turned to Duncan, "Have you any idea how to stop this Tsunami worm?"

Duncan shook his head. "We're about to assess the damage, and then study any instances of the worm we can get. Our honeypot system was infected. It's a virtual machine, so we can take a snapshot of the damage done, and look to reverse it."

"Well you better do it fast. We can't afford to be down any longer than necessary. God only knows what's going on out there...something we need to know. Don't forget we are the eyes and ears of civilised society!"

"Second, we need to hunt down this Vasily chap, and put him out of action for good. "Chaos, seeing as he was your rogue, you organise it. I'll be expecting frequent updates!"

"Yes Sir." Chaos bowed his head, unhappy at being associated with Vasily.

Finally, we have been talking to several governments about securing the Internet for commerce in some way. We can't allow devastation on this scale to happen again. We're going to move from an unregulated system, to something we can control...it's how it should have been in the first place. Anne Lawrie will fill us in on what is going to happen here."

Mrs. Lawrie glided elegantly to the front of the room. She seemed confident, but unlike the others. Duncan did not get a sense of tension or aggression from her. She stood behind a stylised podium to the right of the large, crystal clear projection area, and put a small set of papers down in front of her. "As most of us in the room have been involved in Sec-Net to a lesser or greater extent at some stage during this year, this is mostly for Duncan's benefit."

She looked over at Duncan, "We can talk more about this

off-line later, if you need any further information." Duncan nodded.

Over the next twenty minutes Anne Lawrie laid out the basic plans for Sec-Net. A highly secured network, operated by a conglomerate of US and Europeans governments, funded partially by business. The network would be secured against all external threats, with rigorous access and process control set in place. The idea would be for most commerce to be conducted on this secure network. Any monetary transactions would also be carried out through the Sec-Net network.

The basic plans were simple. Everyone would have an identity on Sec-Net, and would be traceable. A high level design had been completed in secret, but the detail, including the security mechanisms and procedures, were still vague.

"This is where you come in Duncan," stated Anne, looking directly at him. Duncan was not a little surprised to be involved at any level in the project. "Me? What can I bring to this?"
"We'd like you to work closely with a few others on the design of the network; primarily the security mechanisms. You created Z4CK, and I believe that you are one of the best security technicians we have."

Duncan smiled. It was the opportunity of a lifetime. He then pondered for a second before giving his answer.
"But what about Vasily - we haven't found out how to stop the Tsunami worm yet?"
Colonel White piped up, "Don't worry about Vasily, we will put a team together to capture him; he can't hide forever! It won't be too long before he makes a mistake. Sec-Net will force the criminals out. There will be no other way to survive in our new connected world!"

"Finding the antidote to Tsunami is your priority. We need you to work to solve this problem. It'll mean long hours, but we know you're up to the task!"
Alarm bells began to ring in Duncan's head at the thought of long hours. "I would love to do this, but I'll have to back out. I can't spend too much time away from my family right now." Colonel White stood up. "Young man, you may be a civilian, but for you, this is not optional. If you don't do this, you won't work in security again, or anywhere else for that matter. Remember, when this is complete, it will be our connected world. Is that understood?"
Duncan was incensed, "You can't do that!" Colonel White smiled, "Of course we can; we're the government. Just explain it to your wife, she'll understand."

Soon after, the meeting was adjourned. The bosses were escorted to their waiting transport. Anne Lawrie bade farewell to Duncan, saying she would be in touch very soon. She handed him a sealed dossier with the basic design and proposal before leaving. Duncan looked down at the plain brown paper envelope, aware that the contents not only held the biggest project he would ever work on, but something which was a potentially life changing experience. He hoped it would be for the better, but somehow, he doubted it very much. He wasn't even sure if he liked the idea of controlling e-commerce or the Internet. The Internet was never designed to be controlled. Association with the project may even make him unpopular.

Shortly after returning to his desk Chaos appeared, unhappy that Duncan had disagreed with him during the meeting. "I'm sorry Sir. But as far as I was concerned, you were pointing the finger of blame at me regarding Vasily. I'm not willing to accept blame for this. Granted, perhaps my judgement in deciding to take him on was perhaps off, but you have to admit, he fooled us, and keeps fooling us all."
Chaos was still unhappy, but agreed. "Well, the sooner we

catch him, the sooner we can forget him."

Chaos began to walk toward the door, before turning back. "What are you waiting for? We've got to hit the ground running on this one. A paradigm shift like this does not happen every day; we've got to grasp the moment. It is imperative we provide options for an antidote to this Tsunami worm. Forget the process, just fix it!"
Duncan was surprised by his manager's attitude. He nodded, but said nothing.

Duncan pulled out the dossier, and laid it on the table in front of him. The font was small, making him squint in an attempt to read it. He reached into his jacket pocket and produced a pair of reading glasses. Years of staring into computer monitors had strained them, and he had finally, over the last year, resorted to these. Better than constantly wearing contact lenses, he thought. Besides, wearing them made him feel somehow more intellectual. He put them on and focussed on the dossier. Finally, over an hour later he put it down and pondered on what he had read. The idea of this super network, secure from attacks seemed in theory feasible.

The key would be to find a way to defend against Tsunami, which at that very moment was infecting anything reconnecting to the Internet.

------

1 Week later

The combined efforts of some of the greatest security experts and code writers had been less than successful in attempting to find a way of defending against Tsunami.

Duncan sat on a stool in the early hours of Saturday morning, sipping a coffee, and scratching his head. Terminus strolled back and forth across the lab floor. His black polished shoes squeaking rhythmically as he walked. Ten minutes of this was beginning to get on Duncan's nerves.

"This is hopeless." Duncan eventually piped up. He hit the keyboard in front of him with as much power as his finger could muster. "It's four o'clock in the bloody morning. What the fuck chance do we have of figuring out a fix at this time? What are we doing here? I should be in my bed, snuggled up next to Andrea!"
Terminus walked over to Duncan, rubbing his eyes. "Any more coffee in that pot?" Duncan reached over and poured the drink into a stained mug. Terminus was always efficient; usually everything was clean and in its place; it was unusual for even a coffee mug of his to be tarnished. He even washed his mugs and plates after each use. He was not keen on germs, but not to the same paranoid extent as Riddles had been. Duncan filled his own coffee stained mug as well, hoping that the extra caffeine would eventually kick in.

"I bet we're the only idiots up at this time!"
Terminus attempted to be upbeat, "That is unlikely. You can guarantee there will be others out there in the same situation as us. We've got to see this as a challenge. I have faith in your abilities; you just need to have a little faith in yourself."
Duncan sighed, "Yeah, I suppose so. The problem is that it seems like a no win situation for me. I should find an answer to it all; after all I did create the code it was taken from." He picked up his Zaurus and carefully wiped the screen, which had been smeared with sweaty fingerprints during an earlier brainstorming session.

Duncan suddenly perked up. "Wait a minute? What sort of state is your Zaurus in?"

"It seems fine," replied Terminus. "I was just using it half an hour ago to add something to the scheduler."

"Have you connected it to any of the networks lately?"

"Yes, my one is connected most of the time, whether wirelessly, or via the local area network. Why?"

Duncan stood up. "I can't believe we've been so stupid! The open-embedded operating system it uses seems to be untouched. The answer has been staring us in the face all this time!"

Terminus whooped, something that was unusual enough to startle Duncan. "You might just have something there! Let's test it for sure, we'll need an infected system...come on!"

Duncan had never seen Terminus so excited as the two men worked in a caffeine fuelled frenzy to put together a small test network. Again and again they released Tsunami in an attempt to get it to take hold on the test network. It failed to infect any of the handheld computers.

The hands on the large black and white analogue clock had just passed 5:30 in the morning by the time testing was complete.

"Success, I don't believe it!" Terminus stated, as the he left the workbench and collapsed into a comfortable seat in what Riddles had termed his relaxation zone. Duncan joined him, providing yet more coffee. They had broken the barrier of tiredness for the moment, the exhilaration of finding the answer providing the adrenalin rush they required.

"There are two things here," Duncan started. "Tsunami needs the search engines to continue to find vulnerabilities, and secondly, it seems Riddles has done an extremely good job of securing all of the open-embedded code on the Zaurus. All we need to do is replicate this OS."

"Congratulations Duncan. It seems we have the foundation for Sec-Net."

They chatted for some time, never thinking that perhaps they should depart and get some rest. When the remainder of the team began to arrive at 8am, they met them in the canteen for breakfast.

"Ya fucker!" Loki stated, as he heard the news. It's great that we found the answer before those blasted Americans. To Loki, everything was a competition. His ability to dislike extended to almost everyone except himself.

Chaos beamed, shaking Duncan's and Terminus's hands. "Excellent. Well done. This will provide the team with the kudos it deserves. I shall inform the board. I will need the detail of course. If you could provide this during the morning it would be greatly appreciated." Terminus and Duncan looked at each other. "We were thinking about going home for a rest, it's been 27 hours!" stated Terminus.

Chaos dismissed this idea. "Nonsense; call your families, and grab a few hours in the beds here. This is more important. World security is a dependency here. I'd like the report emailed to me by 12 noon."
The men turned to leave. "And thanks again. Good work." Chaos shouted after them.
"Prat!" Duncan murmured under his breath.

Terminus said that he would stay up and write the report, whilst Duncan got some sleep. Duncan returned to the room that had been his home just over 14 years before. Nothing much had changed. He grabbed a shower before calling his wife. "Hi, you'll never guess, we've found a way of stopping Tsunami!" Duncan was obviously excited. The excitement was not shared by Andrea. "Great. Now what? And why the hell did you not come home last night?

Isn't there anyone else who is capable of doing anything without having their hand held by you?"

Duncan was disappointed by Andrea's attitude. "I've been working all night. What do you think I've been doing? It's not a jolly you know! This is the most important project I've worked on…we're talking about the construction of a new Internet!" Andrea shouted down the phone, "Well, I'm glad to see you've got your priorities!" and slammed the phone down. Duncan put the phone down gently and collapsed back onto the bed feeling dejected. Terminus had walked in at the latter end of the call. "Trouble at home eh? I never got married myself. When I took this post on I knew it would be like this, so I avoided any complications."

Duncan closed his eyes, turning over. "Lucky you," he said sarcastically. Duncan lay quietly for a short while. His mind was in turmoil. This was not what he wanted. He knew his work-life balance was all wrong. It had been several days since he had seen his son, breaking countless promises in that time alone. He closed his eyes and buried his head in the pillow. The effects of the coffee was wearing off, exhaustion getting the better of him, slowly his body began the process of shutting down. A troubled sleep ensued.

Almost three more months had passed with rapid progress being made on the design for Sec-Net. Duncan had attempted to get home as often as possible with Andrea seemingly resigned to the fact she or Tom would not see Duncan very often for the time being. No longer did she seem angry, instead apathy had taken over - something that worried Duncan even more. A prototype for both client and server sides of Sec-Net had been completed, with Riddles's original life-unit being used to great effect. It allowed, through the use of fingerprint recognition, the chance to uniquely identify individuals across Sec-Net. As storage capacities had increased, it was possible to store a person's entire life history, including financial status on one chip. The life-unit would revolutionise commerce, being used for all monetary transactions in the future. As more companies joined Sec-Net, it would become impossible to buy even a coffee without a life-unit. Already the tender for mass production was out. Companies clamoured for the opportunity to be the first manufacturer of this new and crucial technology.

The life-unit's security was excellent. To make a transaction, the user would place a thumb on the back of the device, before inserting it into a special reader connected to the terminal and Sec-Net. On insertion, a digital photograph and signature would be displayed on the terminal screen, allowing the vendor to check the identity. It would be used everywhere from Airports to sports ground turn-styles. A life-unit would be programmed to only recognize the fingerprints of the original owner. The rugged Titanium design would make it almost unbreakable. Once all security had been checked, the funds for the transaction would be taken directly from the owners account. There would no longer be a need to carry multiple credit and debit cards, as banks were the first groups to join the Sec-Net project. They were extremely willing to spend funds on the project, so much had they lost through the Tsunami worm.

Many others however, reeled against the idea of Sec-Net. They saw it as a government attempt to increase control of the population. The life-unit was seen in many parts as an ID card that reported back every transaction that anyone made. It did indeed allow the government to track anyone, anywhere. Sec-Net had its enemies, primarily based in the anarchist and anti-technology groups. For obvious reasons, criminals and hackers did not like Sec-Net, although some saw its breach as a challenge. It's hardened, process driven design and architecture had made it, thus far, impervious to attack. Many tried, especially in the early months, but the hardened, open-embedded operating system, its web servers and mail relays held up to anything thrown at it. To use Sec-Net all users were forced to log in. All communications to and from the systems were encrypted, and any changes to company web servers were through designated staff only.

The Internet and much of infrastructure still existed. A digital landscape where Tsunami still roamed and a new generation of hackers and technicians learned their trade. Sec-Net became a living, breathing system only six months after work began. Quickly it grew, with companies clamouring to its guaranteed security. The fastest processors in the world and the best design could not make the system run quickly, especially in the early days. The strict, process driven, human interface to the system being the slowest and weakest link, with everything being checked and double checked before changes could be made. Sec-Net may have been secure, but in the eyes of many, the world of computer communications had taken a significant step backwards.

Chapter 11

Desperate times

Agent Shaw, codename - Athena, had spent much of her time located abroad. She was one of the few who had worked for Cyber-Secure prior to Duncan Steele, having progressed to head of Cyber-Secures small security team in the United States. On a monthly basis she would return to the UK to participate in important team meetings and the like. Now she had returned for good following her request to locate to Scotland in the wake of the Tsunami worm. To accommodate her status she had been installed as project manager for Sec-Net.

Duncan had always got on well with the woman who had initially interviewed and subsequently recruited him to Cyber-Secure. They were of a similar age, and she appreciated his skills, and manner. Duncan saw her as an extremely talented agent and technician, seemingly never putting a foot wrong.

Several things had changed since the Tsunami worm. No longer was there a requirement for codenames to be used, although Duncan had known many of his colleagues by their codenames for so long, that he still referred to them in this way; perhaps in the same way that a respected teacher who later in life becomes a friend may still be referred as Mr. So-and-so; perhaps because it's too strange to call them anything else.

Agent Shaw stood in the doorway to the room where Duncan and Terminus had been catching some sleep. Duncan had just woken up, and was attempting to focus, rubbing his weary eyes. His head thumped from the overdose of caffeine he had used to keep him awake on yet another late night. He stared across the room, finally making out the slender figure of Agent Shaw. Terminus turned over, interacting in a seemingly troubled dream.

Agent Shaw focused her attention on Duncan, walking up to the desk across from the beds. She sat down next to one of the laptops and swivelled the chair round to face Sec-Net's architect.
"Athena, how are you?" asked Duncan.
"I can't complain. Did you have another tough night?" She threw her long blonde hair back. Even in her early forties she was a stunning looking female. Her piercing blue eyes searched for every emotion in Duncan's face. As an agent in the field, it had been important for her to keep fit, both mentally and physically. She loved to play mind games - her degree in psychology a handy tool. Like Terminus, she had never been married, aware of the potential problems this could cause. "How is your wife coping with your extended absences?" Her question was filled with genuine concern. Duncan thought about it for a second. "Not too happy...I'm not too happy about it either, but what can I do? This won't be forever, right? I think she understands that. I hope she understands. She's been a bit distant lately too be honest."

Agent Shaw leaned forward in the chair, "Well, I think you're doing a great job; I'm sure she understands." Duncan wasn't so sure, "It's my son I worry about. I'll end up being a stranger to him." Agent Shaw got up and crossed the room, pulling the chair over to Duncan's bed. She laid her hand on his arm. "I don't have any kids myself, but I hear they are very adaptable. Take them both away on holiday when this is over. You'll see. It'll do you and them a power of good."

Duncan sighed, "I hope so. I get the feeling it may take more than that." Agent Shaw paused for the moment, "I'll see if I can get Chaos to give you today off.

You deserve a bit of a break. When was the last time you had the day off?"

"Oh, a few months ago I think. I don't keep tabs, time moves so quickly these days."

Duncan stood up and hobbled across to the sink to wash his face, stiff from not having moved for a few hours. The tap squealed as the water forced its way out. The noise woke Terminus who sat bolt upright. Without thinking he swivelled his legs out of the bed, before stopping instantly. Out of the corner of his eye he had spotted Agent Shaw and had decided that it would be better not to stand up, completely naked.

"May I ask what you're doing here?"

"Just checking in on the workers," was the matter of fact reply.

"Right, well, would you mind warning us in future?" Duncan had never seen Terminus embarrassed before, which made him laugh.

Terminus was not particularly impressed, "Look, it's a breach of protocol...that's all!"

"It's okay, I'm just leaving." Agent Shaw stated, shaking her head.

Duncan splashed his face with cold water. "It's been three days since I was home last. The desperation to set Sec-Net up is killing me. When are we going to get someone else in to help?"

"It's getting people we can trust that's the problem. We can't just hire anyone. I'm sure it is in hand," replied Agent Shaw.

Duncan shrugged his shoulders, not really impressed by the answer. "Whatever. Anyway, as I said, it's been three days, so even if Chaos says 'no' I'm still going."

Agent Shaw got up from the chair and headed to the door. She looked round as she left, "On you go. I'll sort it out. See you tomorrow, okay?"

Duncan finished washing his face, the cool water bringing him to his senses. "I'll get some breakfast, then go."
"Yes. Good idea. I'll get you along to the canteen if you just hold on a minute." Terminus tied his shoelaces before standing up to take one last look in the mirror. "Having no hair has its advantages sometimes; no mess to try and comb in the morning!"

Duncan laughed, "Fair point. I'm just going to phone Andrea, and I'll be right there." He picked up the phone, and waited for a few seconds. It rang out. "Strange, I would have thought she would have been in at this time in the morning…oh well, she will get a surprise when I get home."

The men sat down to a breakfast of scrambled eggs and bacon. Loki was already sitting at the table with a couple of the other technicians that had been drafted in from New Zealand. Duncan had not worked with them before. He was introduced to them by Loki, but didn't engage in too much small talk, his mind set on getting home to see Andrea and Tom. Loki was his usual grumpy self. He had aged over the fourteen years Duncan had known him, but was still slim and strong, despite being in his early fifties. He was still as vocal and opinionated as ever. "Aye, ye wouldnae catch me being forced tae work all the hours you've been here. Surely your wife is pissed off is she not?"
"She doesn't seem to be."
Loki laughed, "Well Doughnut, whether she is or isn't, just go hame and give her a good shaggin'. That'll sort her out."
Terminus winced, "You can't say that about a man's wife, it's off limits!"
"Terminus, lighten up, you could do with a good shag too."
At that moment Agent Shaw walked in.
"Here, Athena's fit for an old bird; just ask her, she'll help ye out!" Loki shouted out across the canteen.
"That's enough Loki." Terminus was already beginning to lose patience.

Agent Shaw walked across to Duncan, ignoring Loki's comments. "Chaos agreed that you should go home, take a break."
"Cheers, I'm just going."

Agent Shaw looked Loki up and down, and shook her head. "How's Pam?"
Loki was bemused, "Pam?"
Agent Shaw smiled, "Yes, Pam and her five sisters...you're only bedtime companion? It's not every man who can say he makes love to the one he loves most in the world three times a day!" The other men sniggered as she walked away.
Loki murmured, "Stupid old boot," and continued eating his breakfast.
"On that note, I'm off. I'll probably see you tomorrow!" said Duncan, getting up from the table.

Terminus thanked him for his help, whilst Loki simply made another crude remark. The New Zealander's laughed, stating they may have more time to chat when Duncan returned.

Duncan drove his silver Mercedes into the driveway of the house that had been his home for several years. The street was strangely quiet for this time in the morning. Andrea's small blue Vauxhall Corsa was not in the driveway, but Duncan was not particularly worried. It was, after all, Wednesday morning.

Wait a minute; Tom should be off school, Duncan thought to himself. I wonder where they have gone? At that moment, one of Duncan's neighbours flew out of their house and crossed the road. "Is everything alright?" Duncan gave her a confused look. "As far as I know; Why?"
"Don't you know Andrea moved out yesterday?"
Duncan began to panic, his stomach tightened and throat

dried, as his ability to speak disappeared. He jumped to the door, making a clumsy attempt to unlock it. "Yes, she took a load of things with her. I thought you knew!"

Duncan didn't hear his neighbour as he finally managed to unlock the door and open it. He walked into the hall, then through to the kitchen. "Andrea, Andrea? Tom? No, they can't have gone. They can't leave now, just as I'm getting things sorted out!"

Duncan's neighbour stood on the doorstep, unsure what she should do.

"Where did they go? Did she say?" asked Duncan in a panic.

The neighbour simply shrugged her shoulders.

Duncan thanked her for informing him before calmly closing the door. He did not wish to share his anguish with the rest of the street. He ran up the stairs, again calling out. There was no answer from anywhere in the house. It felt empty and hollow; a shell without life. Duncan had not spent much time there lately, but he felt the difference. He rushed back downstairs and into the living room, desperately hoping to find something that would give him an explanation. Perhaps Andrea just felt she needed a break. He scanned the room, looking for a note of some sort. "Surely, she wouldn't leave; not without phoning me first?" Duncan's eyes fixed on a small yellow piece of paper lying on the mahogany dining table. His heart began to beat faster and he attempted to catch his breath. "Calm down," he said to himself, breathing in slowly. He walked over and picked the paper up. Part of him didn't want to open it. After what seemed an agonising few seconds, he finally did.

Duncan,

I'm so sorry but we can't live like this anymore. I feel we have grown apart over the last few years and I can't actually remember the last time we spent any time together as a family. I know you love us, and we love you too, but I feel that the time has come for us to finally put an end to things. I can't recall how long I've been trying to get you to see the effect this whole work thing is having on the family. Too many times now I've seen Tom upset because his dad has broken yet another promise to be there. You don't see it, and I'm left to deal with the fallout every time.

As for me, I have spent quite a few nights on my own feeling sorry for myself, wondering when or if you will be coming home, or whether you're safe. It needs to stop now. It's obvious we have different priorities in life. It would've happened at some stage anyway. It's just no fun anymore. Sorry.

I hope you can understand my reasons, and let us all get on with our lives. I'll be staying with my parents for a short while. Please don't call or come round as this would just cause more distress for us all. I will of course arrange for you to see Tom through our solicitor, and I'm assuming you will not be seeking custody, you wouldn't know where to start anyway.

I'm sorry it's come to this. We did have some good times, but that was a long time ago.

Tom and I send our love, and wish things had been different. As Tom's father there will always be a special place for you in my heart. Bye.

Andrea.

Duncan folded the piece of paper and dropped it onto the table. He stared out of the window, numb. It was over. His marriage was over and he hadn't even given it a chance. As the thoughts of what had happened began to sink in, he buried his head in his hands. What now?

He decided to call Andrea's parents, something he had been asked not to do. Andrea's father answered the phone.

"She's not here right now, and even if she was, she wouldn't want to talk to you. Please don't call again." He paused for a minute to wait for a response, but none came.

"Look, Andrea and Tom are upset, something I don't like to see. You'll hear from us in due course."

"When?" asked Duncan. "Please, you don't understand, I'm going to change, if she is there let me speak to her."

"As I said, she'll be in touch. I understand you're upset, but you brought it on yourself."

Duncan heard the familiar click of the receiver being replaced before the phone went silent.

Duncan replaced his handset slowly. He felt weak. He was still finding it hard to believe he had lost his wife and son; everything seemed unreal. He sat for a few minutes in a daze, trying in vain to get things straight in his head. Right now he needed a shoulder to cry on, but there was no one there. His whole world, not just the house seemed empty. Duncan didn't know what to do. Years of under cover operations, and dealing with criminals had not prepared him for the loss of his family.

Any appetite he might have had was gone, a thousand memories running through his head as emotion welled up from the deepest pits of his stomach.

He picked up a picture of him and Tom on a summers day a few years earlier. The feeling of emptiness consumed him. He felt sick. Eventually he began to sob, clambering up the stairs to the bedroom, where he lay down on the neatly made bed. Duncan buried his face in the pillow and began to cry uncontrollably. He could still smell Andrea on the sheets. Irrational feelings of self-harm began to filter slowly into his head. He fought to ignore them. Finally, he curled up into a foetal position, and cried himself to sleep.

It was several days before anyone from Cyber-secure made the journey out to Duncan's house. Numerous calls and messages had remained unanswered. The mail lay on the floor just below the letterbox, untouched since its delivery. Duncan had made himself the odd cup of tea, but had not eaten except for a single bowl of cereal the day before. The bowl still sat on the table, the left over milk beginning to curdle and smell. The house was a mess; but why should he tidy it up? What was the point? What was the point in anything any more?

The doorbell rang several times before Duncan decided to answer it. Wearily he got up and ambled, half clothed, towards the front door. He unlocked it to find Agent Shaw standing there. "What the hell happened to you? We've been worried!"
"Andrea has left me and taken Tom with her. I could have prevented it happening, if I hadn't spent so much time at work." Duncan walked through to the living room followed by his colleague. "I'm really sorry, is there anything I can do?"
"Can you get her back?" asked Duncan, slumping back down against the wall dejected.
"Are you just going to sit there?" she asked. "Why don't you go and get a shower and change? You look a mess - you've not even shaved. Come on, we'll go out and grab some breakfast; well actually it's nearer to lunch time. We can talk about it."
Duncan pulled his legs up toward his chest, "I can't say I'm hungry."
"I know, but you need to get out of here. It'll help you think more clearly; it usually helps to talk. Come on, let's get going, I'll take you out for lunch. Surely you wouldn't turn down a lady's offer now would you?"
Duncan sighed, "Yeah, I suppose I better do something. There is no point in rotting here."
"Great, now come on, let's get going."

Duncan made his way up to the en-suite bathroom. He removed his stained T-Shirt and ill-fitting tracksuit trousers before stepping into the shower cubicle. The warm water was a welcome relief for his aching, tired limbs. Almost 10 minutes had passed, when Duncan, still in the shower, heard a knock on the en-suite door. Agent Shaw opened it.
"Do you mind?" Duncan asked, covering himself.
"Sorry. I'm not looking, don't worry," she said with a smile. "I was just making sure you were alright in there. Are you going to be long? I'll need to get back to Cybersecure at some stage, so if you want to do lunch, we'll need to get going now." Duncan hadn't realised the time. He had been lost in a day-dream, his mind churning over the possibilities of how, or if, he could fix things with his wife.

"Just hand me a towel and I'll get out now."
Duncan opened the cubicle door and grabbed the towel from Agent Shaw. "Right, hurry up and get dressed. Don't be shy; it's nothing I haven't seen before!" Agent Shaw laughed.

As Agent Shaw closed the en-suite door she became aware of another presence standing behind her. Andrea stood at the bedroom door, arms folded. Her anger at the intrusion was obvious. "Who the hell are you?" she scowled, becoming aggressive.
"I'm one of Duncan's work colleague's." Agent Shaw replied, holding out her hands in a gesture designed to calm Andrea down.
"Are you now? Well, I might have bloody known. It wasn't fucking work after all! I knew he was up to something, the bastard!" Duncan stepped out of the shower. "Andrea, you're back. We need to talk. Oh thank God!"
"Thank God? There's no point in hiding it. You couldn't wait to get this floozy into the house could you?"
Duncan and Agent Shaw protested, "It's not like that!"
"Right, so is this what you usually do with work colleagues?

No wonder you've been so secretive over the years. All the time I thought you were working, you were at it with her!"
"Now hang on a minute," Agent Shaw began.
Andrea screamed, "Keep out of this! I heard what you said, nothing you haven't seen before? You two make me sick."
Andrea stormed down the stairs, followed by Duncan in nothing more than a towel. Reaching the bottom of the stairs, Duncan, still wet from the shower, slipped on the laminate flooring. Andrea stopped and turned as she opened the door. "I ought to have been the one who put you on your back, you liar! I'm going to make sure Tom has nothing more to do with you." Andrea slammed the door, causing the rickety old letterbox to crash to the floor. Duncan decided it was best not to follow her into the street.

Any chance of reconciliation now seemed further away than the Sun. He watched out of the kitchen window as Andrea drove off at speed. There was no way of getting Andrea to listen to him. He knew it was over.
Agent Shaw appeared at the kitchen door. "I'm so sorry."
Duncan lowered his head and leaned back against the wall. "You didn't do anything. I won't be coming in today. I'll be back tomorrow...probably.

Vasily was finding life in Prague tough. He had expected to have left the country by now, but even he had been taken by surprise by the devastation caused by the Tsunami worm. He always thought he would have some access to the Internet, or some way of obtaining cash from his major accounts. This had not been the case. Several governments had swung into action to seize the assets they knew he owned. He was being hunted mercilessly. Vasily knew that if caught, it would be at least a hefty jail sentence, but probably worse. He had seen what governments were capable of, working outside the law.

Worse still, his 2000 euros were now worthless. A run on currency following the crash of the Internet had made cash world-wide valueless. Even though he had been extremely careful, he was becoming desperate. The world, for the moment at least, had returned to an age of bartering. Like many, Vasily had nothing much to barter. Electronics, especially computer systems held no value. What were you supposed to do with them now? Once upon a time it would have been easy to find currency, connecting to the Internet, and almost at will shifting funds around. Even weeks after the Tsunami worm, there was little Internet access with only critical services online. Paper, pens and pencils were now worth more. At least you could write on paper.

As Vasily watched desperate people swapping anything they could for food, the magnitude of what he had done hit home. If the very people he watched knew what he had done, he would have been lynched in that very place.

He had made many enemies in the underworld. He was convinced the Fourth Reich was also looking for him. They were the least of his worries. He feared the British government most of all. He had lost his advantage, and now wandered aimlessly through the back streets of Prague, always looking over his shoulder, suspicious of anyone. He wished he had not sought complete revenge - taking the chance to destroy Echelon and Cyber-secure. It was now impossible to manipulate and hide in the networks that were once his playground.

His Zaurus SLC-4000 was still functional, but useless with no networks to connect to. He pondered whether he should try to sell it. It would bring in enough for some vegetables or coffee. For the first time in many years he began to panic. What was he to do without the means to live? He began to devise a plan to get to Switzerland and the bulk of his money. He hoped that by the time he made it their, his millions would be worth something. For the moment a cup of coffee would have to do.

Unbeknown to Vasily, Hercule had disbanded the Fourth Reich. His will and determination to obtain rights for Belgian Nazi's pointless. The last one had died at the ripe old age of 102. Although they were still seeking to further the old Nazi ideologies, he no longer wished to be in any spotlight. He still resented Cyber-Secure for the death of his colleagues in Brussels many years before, but he no longer felt there was any point in attacking websites, especially as most of them were down. The still rampant Tsunami Worm was infecting almost every device they connected to the Internet. They, unlike Cyber-Secure, did not have the technical resource capable of repairing their connected systems.

The contacts still loyal to his cause had obtained a new identity for him along with 100,000 euros. With this, he sneaked across the border to Holland. He quickly bought a ticket with the intention of flying to one of the poorer South American countries where he hoped his 100,000 euros might be worth something.

Chapter 12

Better for some

Duncan returned to work a couple of days later. He didn't exactly cherish any of the challenges laid before him. The dollar and the Euro were only beginning to recover. Inflation, which had climbed to record heights, had begun to decrease. Only a few computer systems had a presence of any sort on the Internet. He spent most of his time in meetings, sitting across from Agent Shaw, who from time to time threw a reassuring smile. The main topic of conversation was ensuring the security of Sec-Net, and hunting down Vasily in an attempt to bring him to trial. At almost every meeting Duncan was asked the same question. Had there been any sightings? Had Vasily been up to his old tricks?

Duncan couldn't understand why his bosses didn't realise that Vasily, wherever he was, had nothing to connect to in order to make a nuisance of himself. Time and time again he explained that nothing for the moment remained of the Internet, and like most people Vasily had been returned to the dark ages, whilst plunging monetary values would provide a man like Vasily almost no ability to barter.

"He's probably scratching a living somewhere. For the first time in years, it's the farmers, manual labourers, and people who can actually make real things that are the winners."
"So, there have been no sightings then? That is what you are telling us?" asked Chaos. "Vasily is the only hacker to breach Echelon's defences…we must reduce this threat surface by capturing him. I'd like to see you step up to the plate and take the bull by the horns on this one!"
Duncan shook his head, "Threat surface! For God's sake, will you stop talking management bullshit all the time?

I think we would all appreciate it if you would speak English for once!"

Chaos was taken aback by this outburst, but said nothing.
Duncan inhaled, and spoke in an apologetic tone. "Look. If I know Vasily he will be trying to get to his money, which is probably tucked away in a bank somewhere in Switzerland. As we now have a link to many of the largest banks I suggest that we monitor any attempts to withdraw large amounts of money. The fact that it is worthless would mean most people won't bother."
Duncan paused for a second to take a gulp of water before continuing.

"But, I have a feeling that his mistrust of banks and inability to get to his funds by means of computer system will see him attempt to close his account and withdraw everything he has. We need to get these banks to monitor withdrawals of 10 million euros or more. Knowing how easily he removed and shifted money around in the past makes me think he has accumulated at least that!"

It was agreed that this would be the way forward. They would sit and wait. Bank security would pick up individuals attempting to withdraw large amounts of money, their photograph would be taken and processed through the Sec-Net central security network. Posters would also be sent out, something that would take time, as many of the continental distribution networks had been brought to their knees.

Duncan knew Vasily would have to eventually surface. His money meant too much to him. It was all he now had.

The meeting was adjourned and Duncan made the lonely walk down the long metallic corridor to his room. The fact that the corridors of Cyber-Secure now buzzed with energy and many more people, made no difference to him. He could see nothing. He had not seen his son in weeks and things between him and Andrea had become unpleasant. His coping technique involved shutting everything out and working tirelessly on his designs and improvements for Sec-Net. For the moment it wasn't working. In essence he was still empty, prone to outbursts; his patience levels low. He had gained weight, and his health had begun to suffer, bingeing one day and fasting the next. He drank copious amounts of strong black coffee laced with sugar; a stimulant that did not help his mood swings and made his sleep erratic.

The people around him in general understood. Ares and his wife had been mutual friends to both him and Andrea, and did the best to help him out, adding in the occasional phone call to ensure he wasn't thinking of doing anything stupid. Even Loki kept his distance and remarks to himself for the moment, something which Duncan appreciated.

Duncan buried his head in his work. The rapidly increasing size of Sec-net meant new technicians were being constantly hired. Agent Shaw undertook the task of interviewer, something Duncan would have done, but had been excused for the moment, following his harsh treatment of one poor candidate. His mind was not really set on being nice. He looked forward to the capture of Vasily, and worked tirelessly on finding someone he now considered his nemesis. He had become bitter towards him, blaming him in part for the break-up of his marriage.

Agent Shaw knocked on the door to Duncan's office.
"What now?" Duncan shouted at the top of his voice. Agent Shaw tentatively opened the door. "I beg your pardon? Is that any way to greet a potential customer?" Duncan glanced upward on hearing her voice, "Sorry. I'm just a bit stressed. I think the coffee is making me forget things. I've a lot on my mind. One minute I have an idea, the next it's

gone. Have you any idea of how frustrating that is?"
"No," was the simple reply.

Duncan put down his stylus and closed his Zaurus, exhaling deeply as he sat back in his chair. "I can't go on like this. I've got to try to get on with life; otherwise I'm going to stop functioning soon. At this rate I'll lose my job. If I do that it'll be the end of me...I know it.

"Don't be daft. You won't lose your job. You're fundamental to Cyber-Secure and the Sec-Net project." She paused for a second. "Look, I know you're not exactly in the best of moods, but how about we go out for a meal tonight? Perhaps it will cheer you up?"
Duncan wasn't so sure. "No, I'd just be miserable."
"Well, maybe we can talk some things through. I'll book something and if you're still not happy when we get there we can call it a day."
A faint glimmer of a smile crossed Duncan's face. "Fair enough, how can I refuse such an offer?"
"Great, I'll book it then...tonight at eight?"
"Fine, thanks...I appreciate it."

Agent Shaw left, leaving Duncan trying to remember what he had been thinking about. He could have done with a holiday to try to clear his mind, but he knew that wouldn't be possible for the moment. He picked up his latest cup of steaming hot coffee, and thought better of it. He put it back on the table and decided to work hard to get himself a little bit fitter. Getting the time to do this was going to be a problem, but at least he could cut out the caffeine.

The restaurant could be termed as rustic. Pierre Victoire, situated part way down Victoria Street in Edinburgh had once been a big brand name. Now it had gone back to its roots as a small family run restaurant. The flickering candles threw a display of shadows across the roughly finished cream walls. The diners sat at the scratched pine wood tables. The close proximity of the tables gave the restaurant a cosy feel. The unevenly tiled floor finished off the effect of a French country kitchen. It provided a comfortable atmosphere for single professionals or older couples with no kids.

The small white candle positioned in the centre of the table felt inappropriate to Duncan, but he said nothing as both he and Agent Shaw dipped their rolls into their French onion soup.
"It's ridiculous after all these years that you call me Athena or Agent Shaw. For goodness sake, will you start calling me Susan?"
"Sorry. Old habits die hard," replied Duncan.
He thought for a second how comfortable he felt in Susan's company. A feeling of guilt washed over him.
"So, was this an okay choice?" asked Susan, watching Duncan to figure out whether his response would be genuine.
"Yeah, it's great…thanks."
"But?" Susan enquired, picking up on a not entirely happy tone.
"Well, I feel sort of guilty for being able to relax with you, if you must know."
"Susan smiled and leaned across the table. Don't feel guilty. You're not doing anything wrong. Just having a meal with one of your long term colleagues…the only sane one you have!"
Both of them laughed, and for the first time in a long time, Duncan felt completely at ease. The conversation moved from topic to topic, some of it serious, but much of it was light hearted. Duncan felt like a teenager again, and it suddenly dawned on him how attracted to Susan he really was.

A few hours and couple of bottles of red wine later the couple sat outside Duncan's house. "Well, thanks so much. I haven't enjoyed myself like that for ages."
"Neither have I," replied Susan.
"Duncan began to feel awkward, unsure whether to invite his companion in for a coffee. He didn't want the evening to end just quite yet. He was feeling good, no doubt in part to the wine he had consumed over the previous couple of hours. Eventually, the silence was broken by Susan.
"Well I could really do with a coffee, if you have any?"
Duncan was relieved, "Of course, of course. Come on in. I'll put the kettle on."

Duncan switched on the kettle and waited patiently for the water to boil. His mind had wandered to earlier in the evening, when he was suddenly brought back to the present. He felt a pair of arms encircling him. He swivelled round slowly. Susan looked up at him, before leaning her head on his shoulder. He brought her closer to him, running his fingers through her hair. He closed his eyes. It felt good.
Susan whispered up to him, "You know, I don't feel like a coffee right now. Could I have a glass of water?"
They released their grip momentarily and Duncan filled a long glass with some ice cold water. He handed it to her. Her eyes sparkled - the air electric with anticipation.

She smiled, and spoke quietly. "Come on."
She laid her short pin striped suit jacket on the table, releasing her slender figure. Her cream blouse was no longer tucked into her knee length skirt. She kicked off her shoes and took Duncan's hand, leading him upstairs to the bedroom.

Vasily sat in a makeshift soup kitchen. He had decided not to sell his Zaurus even though it was of little use to him for the moment. He wasn't sure if it would ever be of use to him. The soup kitchen had been opened in an old church hall located at the centre of a small village near the Czech border. It was packed with many other people in the same predicament. It was a bizarre sight. People in suits sat side by side with the poor. The devastation caused by the Tsunami worm had caused stock market crashes and spiralling inflation. With money almost worthless in some of the Baltic nations, everyone shared the misery together.

Vasily had given up on the idea of trying to get his money back; there was no point. It was worth nothing. He would try to build his life once more; start again. The economy was nowhere near a state of recovery, unlike some of the western nations such as the UK and US.
He would bide his time for as long as it took. IT systems would come back on-line at some stage, and when they did he, would be ready and willing to offer his services to the highest bidder. He reminded himself he was one of the best. Already word of the Sec-Net network was spreading and he was keen to try his luck at an attack on it. He slurped his soup hungrily. It was hot, burning his lips, forcing him to slow down a little.

Vasily looked up from his bowl and scanned his surroundings. The hall was well lit, allowing him to watch the faces of the people as they tore chunks out of their bread. It was obvious that many were extremely uncomfortable, even embarrassed about being there. It was reasonably quiet, except for the clunking of spoons on bowls, or the occasional noise of a small child crying. There must have been over one hundred people in the place. Most paid no attention to anyone else. Some stared back as Vasily watched them, forcing him to withdraw his gaze. He did not wish to draw too much attention to himself. Most would have strangled him had they known who he was.

All too soon he had polished off his rather thin vegetable

soup. It had heated but not filled him. The bread he had been given was hard, but he had eaten it none the less. He was about to leave when he felt the sudden presence of a large man seating himself to his left. Vasily thought this strange as the man had no food. As Vasily got up he found the stranger was sitting on his coat tails.
"Excuse me," he said, giving his coat a tug.
The man grunted, and stood up. "Are you looking for an argument?" Vasily was dwarfed by the man, but kept his cool. "No. I merely wish to leave here."
"That's good." The man glanced over Vasily's shoulder. Something which Vasily spotted. He turned his head to see another man standing behind him. He recognised neither of them.
"The man leaned over and whispered in Vasily's ear. We know who you are. We know where your family are. Most importantly, we know what you have done. I think the people in this room would like to know as well, don't you?"
Vasily began to sweat. Who were these men? He delved deep into the darkest corners of his mind, but their images or names appeared nowhere. He felt it would be for the best if he went with them rather than be left to a mob.
"I will come with you. Where are we going?"
The large man laughed. "Now, that is a surprise!"

People were aware that something was going on, but none of them had the will or interest to stand up and ask any questions. As they witnessed Vasily being removed, many of them returned to eating their soups, or trying to control their children.

Once outside Vasily was bundled into a car and driven along a dark road. "So finally, we have the creator of the most devastating worm in history. How does it feel to have destroyed the Internet?" Vasily recognised the voice of Hercule instantly. He turned to face Vasily and smiled. "You lost me a lot of money, now I want it back!"

Vasily replied, "You do not scare me Hercule. The Fourth Reich is a joke!"
"Who said anything about The Fourth Reich?" He produced a low pitched guttural laugh. "If you are not afraid of me...wait until you meet the boss!" Vasily was knocked unconscious from a fearsome, well placed punch from his left side. As he slumped back into his seat Hercule smiled. "You deserved that." He turned round in his chair as the car sped onward to its destination.

Almost fifteen minutes later Vasily began to stir as the car drew up to what looked like a slightly run-down stately home. The rain had begun to crash down hard on the windscreen as they pulled up to the large, ominous front door. The car screeched to a halt, spraying gravel a few feet across the car park. His captors exited the car. Hercule walked through the doors, which had been opened by another large bearded man. The beard barely covered a scar that ran down from his eye to his chin. The others slapped Vasily across the face in an attempt to waken him. He was not fully awake as he felt himself being hauled by the shoulders out of the car and up the steps. He finally opened his eyes on hearing the large bang of the front doors closing.

A white haired man in his fifties stood over Vasily; staring down at the Russian attempting in vain to get up.
"You're not supposed to cause him any harm."
"We had to ensure he didn't know where he was going. Knocking him out was the only option!" Hercule replied.
"Hmm, I suppose that is a reasonable excuse for such an action." He began walking toward a grand stone staircase, which dominated the middle of the hall. "I wouldn't usually bother about injury, but in this case we need his brain, please ensure he can use it!"
"Of course," replied Hercule, as he ordered the men to remove Vasily to his room.

Vasily was lifted to his feet and dragged down what seemed to be a never ending stone walled corridor. It was dimly lit. The stone hallway floor had given way to polished wooden floorboards. Vasily was aware of the echoes of the men's boots as they pounded it. Within a few seconds Vasily was thrown on to a bed. He sighed with relief as the men left, and the door was slammed and locked from the outside. At least for the moment nothing would happen to him. He was in no state to think any further ahead. He turned over in the bed which was surprisingly comfortable and closed his eyes. He was sure that he would be forced to move from its soft mattress soon enough.

Sometime the following day Vasily was rudely awakened by one of the men who pulled back the thick heavy curtains covering a window that had not been cleaned for years. The dust from the curtains hung thick in the air, making the man sneeze. The bright light emanating from the tall window forced Vasily to cover his face. He sat up, slightly panicked, ready to defend himself if need be. The tall, heavy set man saw his panic and grinned to himself. He shook his head and beckoned Vasily off of the bed. Vasily was less than sure of what was about to happen. He hesitated, until the large man lurched forward and dragged him out of the room, and back down the corridor, stumbling as he went.

"Where are we going?" Vasily asked, knowing he would probably not get an answer. To his surprise he did. "Breakfast." He was bundled through the doors of yet another large room, and into the presence of Hercule and the grey haired man. They were eating breakfast. This was bizarre to Vasily. With so many people suffering, and with food shortages across the country, these people had obtained food aplenty. They ate hungrily, only looking up for a second to ask Vasily to join them at the table.

"What is going on?" Vasily asked, as he eyed the croissants, coffee and bacon spread across the heavy wooden table.
"We will explain later," replied the grey haired man. "Now eat. You cannot negotiate on an empty stomach."
"I cannot say I am hungry." Vasily folded his arms in defiance.
The grey haired man exhaled slowly: not happy that his patience was being tried in such a manner. "It is your choice. I warn you however, try my patience, and the food on this table may be the last that ever passes your lips." He paused, allowing Vasily time to think. "Starvation is a terrible way to die!"

Vasily decided it would be best to co-operate, at least for long enough to find a way of escaping. He ate the bacon and croissants hungrily. He sipped the black coffee, the caffeine and sugar giving him a high he had not felt for several days. Finally, when all of those present had finished, the grey haired man rang a bell that sat next to him on the table. The man who had bundled Vasily into the room returned and stood directly behind him.

"Now. I'm not going to give you the privilege of knowing exactly who I am. All you need to know was that your, shall we say hacking activities, destroyed our family. You somehow managed to set brother against brother back in our mother Russia. To add to that, you stole what little was left. It is now time for you to pay us back!" Vasily looked at all of the men in turn, unsure in what way he could pay his captor back. The grey haired man continued. "You created the Tsunami Worm. As far as we are concerned you are still the best hacker there is at the moment. Therefore, until we find someone better, we need you to get our money back through breaching some of the targets we designate for you."

Vasily protested, "Many of the large corporations are protected by Sec-Net; it is unbreakable." Hercule leaned over, "Nothing is unbreakable - you will find a way!"
"But it will take time, and I have no computer systems or access to any of the networks!"
The grey haired man smiled, his steel blue eyes glinting in the sunshine that beamed through the large window. "That has been taken care of. As for time, we have all the time in the world. I wish you to consider this to be your new permanent residence and place of work. You will be working for us for, shall we say, some time!"

He grinned at Hercule, who nodded his head. He then turned back to Vasily. "Of course, the fact that you cannot terminate our contract doesn't mean we cannot end yours. Toe the line, and one day you will have repaid us. Step over it," he paused for a second and reached into his pocket producing a gun that he laid carefully and deliberately on the table. "Well," he said slowly, "I think you can guess!"

Vasily leaned back in his comfortable chair. "Well, the sooner I get started the better I think."
"A wise choice. Hercule will brief you. We need all the information you can provide us on the people we are up against. Now I must leave here. I have other business to attend to."
The grey haired man left the table, and walked out through the door.
Hercule also stood up. "Come with me. I'll show you where you will work."
The men walked down several flights of stairs, where the stone walls changed to reinforced concrete. The floors were also concrete. The heavy doors situated at the end of each corridor were automatically closed and locked whenever the men passed through them. There was no escape from this place. At the end of each corridor, placed high up on the walls, were surveillance cameras.

Big brother was watching them.

On reaching the depths of the labyrinth Vasily came to the place he was to work from. It was surprisingly plush and well equipped, with racks full of networking and security equipment. Various workstations and servers sat on a large polished table that spanned the room. The walls had been whitewashed, and a large bookcase not unlike that used by Riddles sat against the wall on the left hand side of the room. A small toilet and washbasin was situated in a side room next door. A fridge, kettle, and to Vasily's delight, food, sat on a small kitchen unit. "Here, you will create for us whatever we require. We think we have provided you with everything you need. If there is anything else, ask; you might get it. You are free to do what you wish - within our limits. Everything you do will be logged, and we are always watching you!"
"How about a walk outside?" asked Vasily.
Hercule laughed, "You still have your sense of humour, which is good...as you are going to need it! Now let us get on."

Chapter 13

Closure

The year 2031 had dawned in much the same way as the previous twelve since the destruction of the old Internet and the conception of the two rival networks, Black-Net and Sec-Net. Black-Net had acted as a breeding ground for many of the best technicians. The unrestricted network, which held many of the same facilities as the old Internet was used for everything except big business. The best technicians learned their trade on it, their security skills honed by the constant attacks from hackers, spammers and viruses.

Sec-Net as yet had not been breached - an amazing achievement considering the volume of attempts that had been made to batter down its defences. Everyone from the world's most renowned hackers to script kiddies had, up until now, failed to get through its firewalls and closed source operating system. It was known to have been built on the open-embedded project, the operating system which had been the most popular on hand held systems such as the Sharp Zaurus. Now it had been strengthened and it's secrets guarded by a few programmers and technicians sworn to secrecy. It was in no way a forward step from the Internet of old. Security was paramount, meaning speed of website and application deployment was slow and expensive.

Sec-Net had become so successful that it had been separated out from the Echelon and Cyber-secure networks. The Sec-Net Corporation was a multi-trillion dollar concern, making its money not only from charging its clients, but also from advertising and searches. Its search engine had been built on Google technology, a company it had procured, or consumed, depending on which viewpoint one took.

Duncan Steele was still chief architect, but now, having reached sixty years was looking forward to his retirement. He had made plenty of money from Sec-Net and had not in fact needed to work for several years. He was now more settled with his life, his only nagging issue being the amount of time he could spend with his son, his son's wife, and their young family. He and Agent Shaw, whom he had had a short fling with several years ago, had been unable to commit to each other, being more dedicated to their work than anything else. They still had a great fondness for each other however, and often socialised.

The few years following the destruction of the Internet had been an exciting time for anyone interested in computer networking. It had also been lucrative, especially if you were lucky enough to work for Sec-Net.

Most of Duncan's old work colleagues had retired. Chaos had talked management speak to the very last day, his leaving speech typical of how he had conducted himself for the twenty years prior. Loki had left, remaining extraordinarily fit and defiant for a man of his age. He seemed to be determined to live forever, and had started his own security consultancy at the age of 65. It was more physical than technical, which didn't surprise Duncan, as he had always been the hard man of the team. Terminus and Agent Shaw remained, and Duncan had grown closer to both, allowing them all to talk about the good old days in the way older people do. Hades had also retired, determined that he was going to enjoy life in Australia to the best of his abilities.

The heavy workload and strains placed on all at Sec-Net was not exactly conducive to healthy living. Years before Duncan had been fit and healthy, having rivalled the best in the country at his favoured sport of fencing. Now, his age and way of life had caught up with him. He looked older than his sixty years and ached almost every day. He felt weak; his muscles seemed more of a strain to carry, than a benefit to him. His diet of fast food had left him tired and unhealthy. Over the last few years he had gained a considerable amount of weight, but had, for no real reason, begun to lose it again. He had become more concerned about the blood in his stool, dismissing it at first, not wanting to say anything about this embarrassing problem to anyone. But after some further research he realised that it was a problem, and he began to fear the worst. He sat with Ares, who he still met up with occasionally, drinking a latte in one of the many coffee shops in Edinburgh.

"Do you think I should see a doctor?" asked Duncan
Ares looked at him in disbelief. "Of course you should you idiot. It could be anything. My time in the army taught me very quickly that when it comes to personal health, there is no room for embarrassment. See a doctor and get it sorted!"
Duncan continued to sip his coffee and take a minute to look out of the window at the busy street. It was filled with young people walking by at a pace.
"Do you ever think life has passed you by?"
Ares smiled, "Christ, yer talking as if yer time's up! You're only 60 man! There's a good few years in you yet!"
"I know, I know. I just wonder where it's all gone. One minute you're a kid, the next you're in your thirties, and now...I mean I don't feel I've achieved that much!"

Ares put his coffee down, and took a large chunk out of a sandwich. "You've seen and been through more than most. Right at the forefront of technology and cyber-crime - remember all the things we did? The world of technology has changed and much of it is down to you."

"True, but I wish I could have spent more time with Tom and Andrea. I regret losing that."
Ares sighed, "You know it doesn't pay to wish your life

away. From the day their children are born people are wishing, and looking forward to the next thing they are going to do. Before you know it, the kids are married and gone, and the only thing you can't have are the years you wished away. I get the feeling that that's what has happened with you. It's important to enjoy what's happening at the time. It's time to start living now. Go mad. Do something for yourself. Christ, retire and enjoy your time…you've got the money!"

Duncan smiled, "You're right. Stuff it…I'm going to do that. There are a couple of months before I retire but I've had enough. I'm going now. It's time I had some fun. I only have one last thing to do!"

Half an hour later Duncan and Ares had finished their coffees and were saying their goodbyes. They stood outside the coffee shop in the February cold, wrapped up in their long coats. "And see a doctor about yer problem!" Ares said, patting Duncan on the back. Duncan promised he would, and hobbled off slowly down the street to his car. Little did he know that Ares had stopped to watch him straining to get into his vehicle. Ares shook his head and started off in the opposite direction, gravely concerned for his friend.

In more than ten years of captivity Vasily had achieved many things on behalf of his captors. He could have escaped, and indeed had the opportunity on several occasions, but he felt the consequences would have been too great, besides life was reasonably good. He simply played the game and hoped that at some stage, as promised, he would be released. He knew this would not be until he had broken into Sec-Net, something which, after all of these years he had only just achieved this morning. He could have instantly informed his masters, but he decided that he would rather have a sniff around first. Doing too much at once would surely raise the suspicions, if not the Intrusion Detection Systems of the giant Sec-Net network.

He had made it in through a little known back door that someone must have unwittingly added. Sec-Net had now become so large that it was becoming difficult for them to monitor all of the systems. They had become complacent, and not unlike the owners of the Titanic, had believed that this network was unsinkable. Vasily had found the chink in the armour, and true to form it was human.

He clenched his fist in jubilation as his latest exploit broke through the operating systems defences. He then set to work bedding his new listening software in before moving onward and upward through Sec-Nets critical systems. The electronic mail system would be a good start. He rubbed his hands and gulped down and mug of Arabic coffee. He had dined on the finest of foods in the last few years, the mafia wishing to keep him in good health, having found him extremely useful.

He made a few forays further into the network, scanning as tentatively as possible for traffic on port 25, the electronic mail port. After several hours, which passed in a flash, he had sniffed enough traffic to gain a lot of new information. Suddenly, something grabbed his attention, which made him sit up and smile. It was an electronic mail stating that Duncan Steele, the senior architect of the Sec-Net network would be retiring within the next couple of weeks and that he would be having a leaving celebration at the Indian Curry House at Edinburgh airport.

Many of Sec-Nets upper management were invited to join him on this occasion, and were reminded that, for a change, they should dip into their pockets and buy the drinks.

Vasily laughed. He had no hard feelings toward his old mentor, the man who had introduced him to Cyber-Secure, but he did harbour a grudge against Cyber-Secure and Sec-Net itself. He decided in an instant to inform his bosses, who would surely be watching anyway.

It was with a tinge of sadness that Duncan pushed his Zaurus across the table. "There. That's the email out; let's see who turns up! It's amazing how quickly life flies by. It's been almost thirty years and it's time to unplug the old Zaurus."
Terminus agreed, "I won't be far behind I don't think. I'm nearly sixty five now, and that's as far as I'm going. It's not the same job now anyway. When was the last time you went hunting, whether physically or electronically like we use too?"

Duncan smiled, "A long time. Leave that to the young guys...mind you it would have been nice to get hold of Vasily. He should have paid for his destruction of the Internet." Terminus agreed, "I wonder where the hell he disappeared to. I always get the funny feeling that he will one day miraculously appear."

Terminus stood up, "Are you remembering our lunch tomorrow?"
Duncan thought for a second, "Damn, I can't make it. Sorry, but I've got an appointment with the doctor."
"Nothing serious I hope?" Terminus asked sounding concerned.
"Nah, it'll be fine. He'll probably run a couple of tests, and give me some pills to be getting on with."
"Fair enough; tell me how it goes will you?" He headed towards the door, stopping just as he reached it. He turned to face Duncan. "Oh, and your leaving meal...count me in. I'm sure there will be a few more people who fancy it too.

It'll be a pleasure to see an old dog off!"

Vasily finally plucked up the courage to mention his exploits. He looked up at the camera with a solitary arm raised in the air. He knew he was being watched. His thick Russian accent was positively upbeat. "I'm in. Come and get me. And call the boss. I have some suggestions to make on how we can progress this!"

Less than an hour later Vasily sat in a meeting with Hercule, the grey haired man, who was now in his seventies, and a new young pretender to the throne. "You have been here for ten years, and your debt is almost paid." The old man spoke with as firm a tone as ever. "There are only a couple of things we need you to do." Vasily sat up, wondering if he should protest. He had provided excellent service over the past years and was keen to be given his freedom, especially before he reached fifty. He decided he would not, instead listening intently to what the grey haired man had to say.

"We appreciate the amount you have taught my young nephew here. He has learned many secrets from you. I can see you now trust us. Many men would have been worried about becoming of no use to us. You have been loyal, and as per my code I will release you, your debts paid in full.

"You have mentioned to us that there is to be a leaving celebration for the Sec-Net Architect. This means there will be many of the important Sec-Net people attending. All I need you to do is point out their table at that meal. We wish to, how should I say, take care of them!"

"Once this is done you can go. We will provide you with everything you need." Vasily agreed, only too happy to be given the chance of freedom. "The meal is next week.

Hercule will set everything up for you. We'll arrange papers, clothing and flights. We'll even provide you with a small amount of money to ensure you can go wherever you wish."

Vasily was surprised at being given such a good deal. He got up to shake the grey haired man's hand, but was told to stop. "We are not friends. I do not wish to shake your hand. You have paid your debt and that means you can go. I have kept my word. Now go!"

Vasily withdrew his hand and nodded his head. "I understand. You will never see or hear from me again." With that, Vasily left the room to make the journey back down to the depths of the building where he had spent most of his time."

The younger man turned to the two older men, "I cannot believe you will let him go!" The grey haired man laughed, "Oh we won't. We won't. It will not only be Sec-Net who feels our wrath next week. You will see!"

Czechoslovakian Airlines flight CK322 touched down at Edinburgh exactly on time. Two men, one of whom was Vasily, gathered their identical briefcases from the lockers above their seats. They were smartly dressed, wearing the finest business suits. All of their fake papers were deemed to be in order. They passed through customs without a problem. They carried no weapons, but the larger man had been informed of where to collect a gun from a locker within the airport grounds.

They stood in the airport foyer for a short while surveying the landscape. The airport was busy at this time of year; the vast amount of holiday makers added to the general business users passing through the airport terminals. The high-tech systems installed as part of the airport security would not pick the two men out as unusual. Matthias, Vasily's travelling companion on this occasion, had been chosen for his strength, patience and efficiency. The two men walked over to the designated locker where Matthias took out a black leather bag. Vasily had been briefed that it would contain a gun, but the speed with which it was deposited into the briefcase made it impossible for him to be sure. He had not been told how this attack would be carried out, but he knew where it would take place. His final task was to point out the Sec-Net team, allowing Matthias to do the rest.

At almost 2pm on the Friday afternoon, Vasily and Matthias entered the Indian Curry House just outside the terminal building at Edinburgh airport. All had originally agreed this was a strange location for such a restaurant, but the quality of the food meant that people from the surrounding areas made the effort to eat there. It was busy that afternoon, but the two men were lucky to obtain a table near the back of the restaurant. They were seated, Matthias acting as calmly as ever, whilst Vasily began to panic, sure he would be recognised. He managed to keep his cool long enough to get to his seat. The men had just sat down when a large group led by Duncan Steele entered the building. He shook hands with the waiter who seemed to know him. Terminus and Athena were others that Vasily instantly recognised.
"Is this them?" Matthias asked.
"No. I do not recognise anyone from that group," came Vasily's reply. The men sat for a few more minutes when Vasily, sweating profusely, leaned over. I need to excuse myself for one moment...I think I am going to be sick. It is my nerves. I will be as quick as I can."
Matthias took the gun from the briefcase, keeping it out of sight. He gave Vasily a warning tap on the knee with it. "You had better. Try to escape and you will not get far." His voice was extremely threatening.

Vasily smiled, "Of course," he said, and calmly walked off towards the toilets carrying his briefcase. Matthias grinned as he watched him walk off with the briefcase firmly gripped in his right hand.

"No matter what, you will not get far," he mumbled under his breath.

Vasily entered the toilets; feverishly searching for any possible escape route. He spotted a small window providing the only light into the room. Closing the toilet door behind him, he quickly clambered onto the sink nearest the window and attempted to open it. It would not open far enough. He didn't hesitate; smashing the glass with the briefcase. Luckily for him the noise from within the restaurant had been enough to shield the sound of the window breaking. The customers were completely unaware of anything untoward happening. He dropped the briefcase out of the window and followed quickly, twisting his ankle on completing the drop to the ground on the other side. He howled momentarily, before forcing himself to get up and hobble off towards the terminal building.

He would leave here soon. He had planned it meticulously, right down to the funds he had yet again stolen from his mafia controllers. He had one last thing to do before disappearing forever. He pulled a titanium life-unit from his pocket and dialled it. It made a connection at the communications hub of Sec-Net, who had also become the largest wireless telephony provider. Whilst waiting for it to be answered he walked to one of the coffee shops on the ground floor of the airport terminal. This would be a good vantage point, allowing him to see anyone entering or leaving the terminal building. He also had a good view of the entrance to the Indian Curry House outside.

By the time he had sat down the call had been answered.

Duncan Steele had looked at his life-unit in bewilderment as a call from a number he did not recognise had came in. He answered it none the less.

"Hello?"

"Duncan Steele. We speak again after many years."

Duncan instantly recognised Vasily's voice, but was silenced before he could alert anyone.

"Come and meet me. I am sitting in the terminal building across the road. Come alone. If you do not I will not be there by the time you reach the building."

"I'll come. I have a few questions to ask. Where shall I meet you?"

Before Duncan had finished his last question the call had been cut off.

Agent Shaw put her hand on Duncan's arm and asked him if everything was okay?

"No problem. I've just got to head over to the terminal for a few minutes, got something to sort out and need a bit of privacy. I'll be back in five minutes. When they take the orders I'll have the chicken Korma and a Cobra beer," replied Duncan.

With that, he got up and wandered out of the glass fronted building. He limped slowly, almost cautiously, across to the Terminal's main entrance. Walking as upright as possible through the door, he attempted to hide the breathlessness even this short walk had caused him. His focus dashed from check-in desk to passer-by, until the coffee shop finally grabbed his attention. A man he did not instantly recognise stood up. He had thinning hair, was clean-shaven, and wore a smart grey suit.

More than ten minutes had passed since Vasily had left the table. The Indian waiter walked towards Matthias. "Would you like to order now?"

Matthias hadn't even noticed, so intent was he on watching out for Vasily. He had put the gun in his pocket, still keeping it ready for use at some stage. The waiter attempted to attract Matthias's attention and asked the question again. "May I take your order Sir?"

Matthias finally had his concentration broken, and decided to order to move the waiter on. "Yes...okay," his tone was one of frustration. He glanced quickly at the menu. "I would like a glass of mineral water, and garlic naan bread. That is all...thank you."

The waiter took the order. He thought better of querying the small order, instead walking off through a door at the back to the kitchen. Matthias was becoming angry. It was obvious Vasily was not returning. He had been listening to the large group of people that had entered not long before, and noticed Duncan Steele leave. He was now pretty sure that these people were his targets. He too dialled a shiny life-unit and waited for an answer. A short wait followed, whereupon Hercule answered the call.

Matthias spoke quickly, "The target is acquired, and our bird has flown."

"I expected as much," replied Hercule. A remarkable calmness could be heard in his voice as he completed his final instruction.

"Hit the targets, and remove Vasily."

Matthias simply switched off the life-unit, disconnecting the call. He grabbed his briefcase, stood up, and began walking towards the large group. He took a wireless device from his inside pocket, and placed his hand into the pocket containing the gun. He found a small button on the device and ran his finger over it.

"Goodbye Vasily, the pleasure was all yours."

As these words ended he pressed the button.

Duncan walked towards the man, finally recognising him as an older, well turned out Vasily. They both sat down at the same table.

"You have not worn well my friend," Vasily shook his head, looking Duncan up and down.

"You are no friend of mine Vasily. You lost that the day you left, committed murder, destroyed the Internet."

"But I have made you rich have I not? I mean - you are the architect of Sec-Net!"

Duncan had no answer for this. "I hope you have finally come to turn yourself in?"

Vasily laughed, "No my friend. You are one of the few people on this miserable planet I respect and feel anything toward. I have come to save your life!"

Duncan threw Vasily a confused look, "What do you mean?"

Vasily lifted the black briefcase, "I've spent ten years paying their money back in ways I know best. It's strange, but after all the things I have done for them, even they underestimated me. They were planning to kill you, and whomever else they found from Sec-Net. I've finally managed to break into your precious systems...it was tough however." He nodded his head in appreciation.

"And you've saved my life by warning me of this?"

Vasily shook his head and laughed, "No." He patted the briefcase, "You see, they planned to kill me too. They thought they could detonate a bomb and take us all out at once." He paused to watch Duncan's reaction. Duncan did not move.

"So where is this bomb - In the briefcase?"

"I switched briefcases. My foolish travelling companion is likely to detonate it soon, thinking that I have run away! My hacking skills have a use. I knew you would be here. I knew what they planned as my fate, and I've managed to obtain a considerable amount of money from under their noses...just like the good old days. Duncan was becoming

anxious, not listening to Vasily's boasts. "And where is this travelling companion?"
"Why, in the restaurant across the road – I expect it will go off any second!"

The enormity of what Vasily said struck him like a bullet. Duncan got up and lumbered as quickly as possible toward the terminal doors. Vasily shouted after him, "I would not recommend going back now!"
"Fuck you Vasily, I have friends to warn!" Duncan grasped for his life-unit in a vain attempt to call his friends.

Agent Shaw could barely hear the ringing tone of her life-unit above the noise of a busy lunchtime at the Indian Curry House. Orders had just been taken for the large group of Sec-Net professionals assembled to celebrate the retirement of Duncan Steele. Finally, after several rings she picked it up and placed it against her ear, shielding her other ear from the noise. The caller ID had told her it was Duncan. "Hi, what are…?"
Duncan screamed into the life-unit, "Shut up, someone in there has a bomb, it's in a briefcase, raise the alarm; get everyone out!" Agent Shaw looked around for anyone looking suspicious. A large, smartly dressed man was moving from the back of the restaurant, a black leather briefcase in one hand. Agent Shaw stood up almost in slow motion, as she watched the man put the other hand in his pocket.

A deafening roar shot through the restaurant as the blast from the briefcase instantly vaporised Matthias into miniscule pieces of blood flesh and bone. The power from the blast shook the building to its foundations, blowing out the windows and violently catapulting anyone in its way out through the glass frontage. Limbs were torn from bodies, as wood, glass and steel cut a swathe through the restaurant customers, shredding anything in the blast's path. The shock wave set off car alarms in the nearby car park. Only seconds later, as the dust began to settle, the restaurants roof caved in, its concrete blocks and steel girders dealing a crushing death blow to many of those who had not died instantly. Agent Shaw and Terminus had been caught in the full force of the blast, a shard of steel from a table leg embedding itself in the back of Terminus's head, killing him instantly. Agent Shaw had been blown backwards out through the shattered windows. The force of the shock wave had knocked out the windows of the main terminal building across the street. Duncan was thrown to the ground, his head hitting the polished marble floor.

He had no idea how long he had been unconscious for, when finally he stirred, dazed and bemused. Using all of his remaining strength to get up, he slowly turned towards the coffee shop, looking for his nemesis, his vision still blurred. Like a ghost, Vasily had gone.

Duncan dragged himself across the street to what remained of the restaurant. Sirens and alarms screamed as chaos and confusion reigned in the heat of the mid afternoon sun. Duncan looked down at the appalling sight. Torn limbs and melted skin lay everywhere, blood, sprayed as far as the eye could see, adorned the surrounding walls and pavements. People with shrapnel injuries writhed in agony, reaching out for help. Worse still was the smell of burnt flesh, and the sound of the wailing, moaning, dying injured.

Duncan found Agent Shaw and limped quickly to her, falling to his knees next to her broken body. Her hair and face were black and bloodied, her eyes closed. The clothes had been blown from her body, what remained of it. She was gone. Close by laid the severed hand and wrist of a small child, still clenching a teddy bear. Duncan broke down and wept -

huge waves of guilt washing over him as he digested the surrounding scene, the dead and injured. He looked up to the sky, following the smoke plume...wishing he could have stopped it all. He wailed, and began to rock back and forth, "I should have seen this...why didn't I see this?"

Finally, and before he could walk into the rubble of the building, he was taken away to an ambulance, where he sat...numb, unable to hear, or comprehend.

The month following the bombing had been the worst Duncan Steele had ever known. What should have been a celebratory and relaxing time had turned into a time of questions, mourning and sadness. At the best of times he hated funerals, but saying goodbye to close friends one after another had almost broken him. He was tired and weak from the stress.

At the end of the month Duncan was delivered a final blow. He had been diagnosed with bowel cancer, which had spread too far to deal with. His time was nearly up. For several days he sat, feeling sorry for himself, looking back on what he felt was a reasonably short but eventful life. He wished he could step back in time and change things. Perhaps going to the doctor earlier when he first discovered the bleeding would have been a good idea?

Eventually he stopped feeling sorry for himself, and sat staring at the details of his bank account. Slowly he began to calculate how he would separate out his funds, and went through the difficult but necessary process of creating a will. He did not have to think too hard as to where everything would go. He had few close friends, and little family to speak of. He decided he would spend most of it. Live life - what was left of it. He walked over to his computer system

and logged in to check if Hades was on-line. He hailed him, the traffic diverting from his computer to the life-unit. Hades answered. "Old man; how are you coping?"
"Well, you know things could be better. Just a quick question, what are you doing for the next 6 months? I was thinking of moving to warmer climes."
Hades smiled, "If you'd like to pay a visit, then I'd be delighted to see you, as long as you get rid of the sour puss!"
"I'll do my best...I've got a wad of cash to waste. Just got my results back from my tests and they're not good...gave me around 6 months. It was then I realised I haven't done enough mad things over the last few years...grew up too quick I think. Six months should be enough to fit some in."
Hades interrupted him, "So you thought you'd wander down and party hard...well as hard as you can! Of course, and you can stay with me, save some more of that cash for what it's really for. Anyway, I've got to go, send me the details; I'll look forward to drinking you under the table!"

Duncan's spirits lifted. Finally, at the age of sixty he had managed to map out some future for himself. Over the next few days he busied himself with the details, ordering his tickets, selling unwanted possessions and preparing for his trip. Australia was a destination he had seen little of.

The taxi driver helped the frail old man with his bags. He felt a modicum of sadness as the black cab drove away from the house that had been his home over the last twenty years. The 'For Sale' sign flapped in the wind as the Scottish skies opened. The sound of rain had always relaxed Duncan, just as well, considering where he lived. He sat back in the seat and took in the passing countryside as they sped their way to Edinburgh airport.

It was still drizzling as the taxi drew up outside the airport's main entrance. The Scottish weather provided a cold damp day, which was now growing dimmer by the minute. A smartly dressed Duncan stepped clumsily onto the pavement, he groaned slightly as he lifted the weight of his bags from the back of the car.

Hurriedly wrapping his long black woollen coat around him, he attempted to shield himself from the cold wind that blew a fine drizzle into his face. He finally managed to haul his bags on to the kerb and took time to look up and study his surroundings. The taxi pulled away, its tyres throwing up a watery spray from the road behind.

Duncan stretched as best he could; the pain from his uncomfortable taxi ride having taken its toll on his feeble frame. Old beyond its years, it had served him well, but continual punishment had now taken its toll. His muscles, not as strong or flexible as they once had been, at least gained some relief from the change to a standing position.

He took a single deep breath. Before him lay the concrete jungle of Edinburgh Airports Terminal 1, behind him the ongoing construction work - necessary since the bomb blast. He looked round, taking in more of his surroundings. Billboards advertising the latest in computer technologies advised that the biggest companies always got the job done, or that Microsoft Linux was the best. This made him smile. Taking in his surroundings was a natural instinct, something that he had nurtured over many years. The faint smile eventually faded from his gaunt features as he focused on the entrance: the way ahead - the start of something new.

Digital Force – www.z4ck.org

ABOUT THE AUTHOR

KEVIN Milne has over 15 years of experience in Information Technology, a third of this in the Information Security arena. He holds a wide range of qualifications including Cisco Security Specialist, Checkpoint CCSE, RHCT and Infosec Professional. He has also passed the ISS Ethical Hacking exam.

Kevin currently works as a security specialist for Europe's largest mutual assurance company, where his remit covers the provision of security consultancy and penetration testing. Kevin is also a director of Open-Solutions Consultancy ltd, where he provides open source and security services to customers in Scotland.

Kevin has been involved in fencing for over 20 years, having won Scottish titles at various levels, as well as finishing second at the Scottish championship in 1995, 96 and 97. He also represented Scotland at foil in 1991, and 93.

LaVergne, TN USA
16 February 2010
173232LV00001B/41/A